Heather Finch

Jenny Benjamin

Heather Finch
text copyright © Jenny Benjamin
Edited by Benjamin White

Published in North America and Europe by Running Wild Press. Visit
Running Wild Press at www.runningwildpress.com Educators, librarians,
book clubs (as well as the eternally curious), go to www.runningwildpress.com.

ISBN (pbk) 978-1-947041-94-3
ISBN (ebook) 978-1-947041-95-0

Remember
February, three years ago

Saturday's child works hard for a living. Heather Barrington recited this line from a children's poem. She was up before the sun on a womb-dark Saturday morning in February to write before her family got up. She reviewed her pages from the day before; her main character Millicent Monvail, so orderly and astute, solved mysteries. Heather loved the neat squares of lives in her made-up tourist town on Madeline Island.

Her thoughts flowed easily; her fingers flew over the keys. An hour passed without movement from the chair, and when she glanced out the window and saw the sun was up and filling the sky with a pink and blue haze, she stretched with satisfaction. She'd done it – she'd hit her daily writing goal, and Marc and the kids were still asleep.

This Saturday was hers for the taking. Of course, the day included household obligations, but maybe she would bring up a date to Marc. It had been ages since they had done anything remotely like a date. And sex, well, her body had gone into an almost celibate state lately because they both had been so busy in the last year or so. She had a new mystery out, plus multiple freelance projects, and more committees and task forces had come up for Marc at the station. Tonight, she would try – really try – to be interested in him, to want to go to bed with him.

Gym shoes squeaked across the kitchen floor. Heather sat up and ran her fingers through her hair, a nervous gesture. She sprang up to catch Marc before he went to the gym.

In the kitchen, Marc stood at the counter and bent over the paper. His fit physique sometimes made Heather feel too soft and curvaceous. Though she did yoga and tried to stay in shape, her taut dancer's body was a form of the past, like a celestial being somewhere in the night sky, a constellation she could hardly locate, even with a telescope.

"Good morning," she said to his back while getting more coffee.

Marc didn't look up, but said a quick, "Good morning, honey."

"Are you heading to the gym?" she asked, though she knew the answer. Marc went to the gym every day, even on weekends, even in the igloo cold of February, when all Heather longed for was to go back under the covers with a book. Should she ask him to go back to bed with her? What if he said no?

"Yeah," he said, finally looking up. His face, though slightly creased, was still handsome – handsome in an almost too-perfect way. She hated to admit it, but she'd kind of like something to be askew, something too large or too small, but instead, he was built, beautiful, and somehow, even after eighteen years of marriage, unattainable.

"Would you want to try for a date tonight?" Heather asked. She didn't recognize her own voice; instead of being heavy and sexy, it came off squeaky.

"Can't tonight, honey. I have the service gathering for the force. We're meeting socially, but we're really going to hammer out how to divide up service projects for this year. We'd meant to do it over the holidays, but you know how that is. It's too busy."

He approached her, and she hoped for a real kiss, but he pecked her forehead like he did Tessa. But with Tessa he had a proud gleam in his eye. With Heather, his mind seemed to be on to the next thing.

"Maybe I could come along?" A last-ditch effort, and part of her didn't want him to say yes. When she pictured another evening on her own, with wine and a book or a movie, she settled into liking that better.

"Oh, honey, you'd be bored out of your skull. How about a rain check?" Marc ran his palms over her arms. "You name the restaurant, and we'll go."

"Okay." She broke away from him, both relieved and annoyed.

The upstairs hallway creaked. Jackson was up early, as usual, even though it was Saturday.

Heather felt so much more comfortable and herself around her kids than around her husband. Especially with Jackson, she was always happy to see him; if she knew they would be spending time together, she looked forward to it like a kid waiting for a birthday.

"There's your boy," Marc said, an edge to his voice. He went to get more coffee and stopped at the counter, holding briefly to the edge.

"Are you okay?"

He shook his head. "Yeah, fine. Just got a sudden headache. Weird, but it passed." He reached for the coffee pot and had to steady himself on the counter again. "Whoa –"

"Here," Heather said and closed the distance between them. "Let me…" she didn't finish. Let her what? Absorb his head pain like she tried to absorb every ripple of discontent in their home life? Instinct set in, so she put her hand to his shoulder. The color had drained from his face, and he breathed in and out slowly. After a few long seconds while she waited for him to say or do something besides take deep breaths, Marc composed himself and put his mug in the sink. He broke away from her steadying hand and bent to gather his gym bag. He stood with deliberation.

"Maybe you should skip the gym, Marc," she said. "You could be coming down with something."

"It's nothing," he said, sharp as tacks.

Taking two steps forward, he turned to her and said, "I am not missing the gym or tonight, any of it. You can't stop me."

Heather stepped back. The biting tone was usually saved for more serious arguments, usually about the kids, for instance, how Heather was too harsh with Tessa and how she babied Jackson. In Heather's mind, the opposite was true, but she had learned to bite her tongue during these discussions, to keep the peace.

"I wasn't trying to keep you from going, Marc. It's just –"

He turned on her, his hands shaking, and said, "It's always just with you. You're always putting things off. Always, oh damn, damnit, Heather, I think I'm going to be sick."

Marc grabbed the counter with both hands, but his knees gave out. Heather braced herself and put her arms out to catch him. His six-foot, muscular frame crumpled. He fell backwards onto her lap and then they settled on the kitchen floor. She grappled for the garbage can as Marc moaned and cradled his head. He spewed vomit all over himself and writhed in her arms.

"It's okay, it's okay," she said in a shush-baby voice, one from the kids' infancies.

Jackson trotted down the stairs.

"Mom, oh, man – here, I'll get," Jackson said without finishing. He snatched the kitchen garbage and shoved it under Marc. The lengthy can stretched between Marc's and Heather's splayed legs.

"Something is not," Marc muttered. His speech slowed; his body felt like 200 pounds of wet sand in a nylon bag.

"Marc. Marc," she said, shaking his shoulders gently, "can you stand?"

He shook his head and wretched again – this time in the trash can.

"Mom, what's going on?" Jackson said. He hunched and grimaced at the smell. He was still in his flannel pajama bottoms and blue sweatshirt. Odd details ticked in front of Heather's vision: the kitchen floor had puffs of dust along the floorboards; Marc's back had larger muscles than she thought; it had been so long since she held him, especially like this.

This. This. What was this? What was happening?

Marc's legs twitched; his head rolled back in a flop. Heather cupped her hand and kept his head from hitting the cabinet.

"Mom, we better get Dad to a doctor," Jackson said and stood. He went to get car keys from the hook on the wall, but Heather waved her hand.

"No, call 911, this is something, something came on fast," she said; her throat felt tight and her stomach started doing flips.

"Okay," Jackson said.

Numbers were dialed, and Heather held Marc. She rocked back and forth, going numb on her backside and all down both arms because he was so big.

"I feel strange," Marc said suddenly.

Heather jerked forward, and Marc knocked his knees against the metal can. From the other room Jackson's voice was shaky, but Heather heard their address presented correctly, and she had an odd moment of remembering Jackson at five, saying his address back to Marc in this very kitchen. Marc was in uniform and Jackson looked terrified, as if his entire life depended on reciting, 12225 East Carlow Circle, Glenview, Wisconsin. What was their zip code? At the moment, Heather had no idea.

Marc's howl of pain broke her from her reverie.

"My fucking head, my fucking head is going to explode!"

"Okay," she said, panic rising in her like a tide set in fast forward.

Suddenly Tessa was there, too, in her pajamas and bare feet. Tears streamed from her eyes, and Heather started the *shush, shush* again. Minutes ticked by in a blur. Marc's body went from tense to slack and back to tense. This made Heather's body respond in kind, soaking up his reactions to whatever raged in his head.

"I hear sirens, Mom," Tessa said, squatting next to them like a much younger child. Tessa stayed a few feet away. When Marc yowled in pain, Tessa shrank back with an animal's flinch.

"Yes," Heather managed to say. "The sirens are coming here." – an inane statement.

The blaring howl from the approaching ambulance made Heather's heart pound faster, so much harder she felt sure a vein pulsated on the outside of her neck.

Within minutes, Jackson was answering the door, ushering in a herd of men in paramedic outfits.

What are his symptoms?

What time did this occur?

Does he take any medication?

Has he been conscious this whole time?

Can you see this light, Mr. Barrington?

Can you hear me, Mr. Barrington?

Can you smile for me, Mr. Barrington?

Can you move your left side, Mr. Barrington?

Is there a history of stroke in his family?

Marc on the stretcher.

Marc wrapped in blankets and harnessed.

Marc lifted.

Marc out the door.

Follow, Heather told herself.

"Do you want to ride in the ambulance, Mrs. Barrington?" the tallest paramedic said.

"Mom, I'll follow in the car with Tessa," Jackson said.

Heather nodded. She wanted to scratch her skin off; instead, she grabbed for her coat hanging on a hook near the back door.

Flashing lights outside.

The sun was hazy behind the February sky.

She stepped up the metal stair of the ambulance and hunched over.

The sirens blared, and they were off.

Live
Early June, present day

Heather Finch pulled the covers over her head, inhaling the scent of her own unwashed hair – something like oil mixed with the curry chicken she'd made the night before.

Get up, she told herself, just get up. Check email, refuse social media.

Sounds of shuffling feet came from the kitchen below her. A cabinet door opened and shut, and then the coffee grinder buzzed for longer than she would have had the patience for.

Must be Jackson, not Tessa, she thought, and popped up. She threw the covers up, smoothing the thick down comforter and longing for when she would be right back beneath it, sleeping, and made her way downstairs.

Once on the stairs, she took in the sunlight filtering through the windows and making streaks on the dusty kitchen floor.

Jackson, her boy, hunched over the counter, reading.

"Morning, Mom," he said without taking his eyes from the page.

The beauty of him – her perfect baby boy, now metamorphosed into a young man, twenty-one, tall, built like an Olympic swimmer, and though he could probably get any girl he set his lovely blue eyes on, he spent most of his free time with books, or pounding the asphalt in their Milwaukee suburb with his worn-down running shoes.

"Hey, sweetie, you're up early," she said and shoved her coffee mug under the spout while yanking the pot with the other hand. Once she filled her mug half way, the pot went back in its place with a hiss.

"One of those mornings, huh, Mom, when you can't wait for it to drip through," Jackson said, glancing up with a half smirk.

"Something like that," Heather said, wanting to hug the boy, but shuffling past him instead, to the refrigerator to get the cream. "What're you up to today?"

"Working, then home. No plans."

"It's Friday," she said casually, hoping he wouldn't take it as a judgment. She didn't want him to feel like he had to have weekend plans. Tessa always did.

"I'm working late. I told Fred I'd help him build two more vermicomposting houses. It'll go until dark." Jackson looked up at Heather and smiled. "I know, it doesn't sound exciting, but it is. Each will have a start bed of 1000 red worms, food waste, newspaper, so we'll be producing twice as many castings that can be used to fertilize the soil in our greenhouses, and they'll yield additional compost tea."

"Yum," Heather said and sipped her coffee. Bliss. Heavenly bliss, this thing called caffeine.

"Yeah, the 'tea' is packed with nutrients we use all over the farm," Jackson said, his eyes dancing. "You want to come to the city and see it when it's done?"

There he was, her little boy. He had always looked to Heather, and not his dad, Marc, for approval. Marc had always been doing something else, even after his stroke, when his brain was off in cotton candy land, in some residual memory, some vestigial nerve synapses kicked in, and he still drifted off topic whenever Jackson mentioned something he was interested in – be it his work at Green Life Urban Farm in Milwaukee, or a book he had read, or a poem he'd written, Marc brought up his own youth, his time in a rock band, his police training, or his workout routine.

"I'd love it!" Heather said and swooped in for a peck on the cheek.

"Want some eggs?" he asked, moving his body nimbly around her to get to the eggs and milk.

Scrambled. She'd take it, even though she preferred fried. It wasn't every day a man made her breakfast, even if the man was her firstborn. Yes, she'd take it.

"Yes, I'd love some." Heather got out of his way; she could tell he wanted full reign of the kitchen counters. She slipped over to the breakfast nook and sat. Soon there were soft sounds of Jackson cooking, and then, the bombast above them. Tessa was waking. She was all foot stomps and door slams while Jackson glided through his days, unnoticed by most.

"Queen Bee is up," Jackson said without looking up from the eggs.

"She certainly is," Heather said with a smile.

Heather knew she should go to her home office and work. That meant writing. She had two more chapters on her latest mystery, actually marketed as "cozy mysteries" because they were light and disposable and easily forgotten. She didn't mind the writing so much, but she dreaded the yearning to flip over to Facebook or Twitter or email – to connect with someone, anyone, who was outside her physical world. She craved it…and hated it.

"Here you go, Mom," he said. He sat next to her and scooped his eggs onto his toast like he used to as a kid.

Her mouth opened to thank him, but Tessa entered.

"I need my blue blouse, Mom." She paused and forced a smile. "Good morning." Her lithe body was wrapped in a towel, her long blonde hair stuck to her face and neck in wet streaks, and her gray-blue eyes flashed something: resentment, anger, or just pure demand.

Heather chewed her eggs and followed them with a swig of lukewarm coffee.

"Mom –" Tessa started and stopped.

"It's hanging in the laundry room."

"Thank you," Tessa said in a rush. Jackson caught Heather's eye and smiled.

Before Heather could take another bite, Tessa had run off toward the laundry room and Jackson had sprung up, plate in hand, and kissed the top of Heather's head.

"Bye, Mom," he said.

"Goodbye." Heather waved to his back.

Filled with sustenance, Heather headed to her office. Once inside, she pushed the door shut with a gentle click. Listening at the door, Heather heard Tessa walk across the kitchen, up the stairs, and into the bathroom. Even the hair dryer blared under Tessa's command. Heather sighed and slipped to her desk.

Four hundred words – that was all she committed to each day, knowing full well that if she wanted to finish in time for her editor's deadlines, eight hundred was more on track. It just felt insurmountable lately. Since Marc's stroke at age forty and his death just six months ago at age forty-three, she found she had something to say that went beyond Millicent Monvail, her detective heroine who always solved the safe mysteries surrounding her small tourist town on Madeline Island. Her mysteries used to flow from her, like hot streams of lava. Now, they tended toward what she called "bog writing," which felt exactly how it sounded: her mysteries were something to trudge through to pay some bills. The only recent good that had come from Millicent was that her entry had made her the finalist for a writer's retreat in Scotland. If she won, actually won, the grant, she would spend eight weeks of the summer in an isolated Scottish cottage in the Highlands. She could work some on the Millicent book and write whatever else she wanted while living in a completely new place.

Heather opened the Word document, then minimized it. She clicked on her email with a flutter in her chest. Would there be news from the Solace Art Fund? Connecting felt like an eternity. There was nothing exciting in Heather's inbox, only advertisements and a notice from Facebook that she had messages. Clicking over was far too tempting. She wouldn't spend much time there; she could even post something on Millicent Monvail's page for the new book. That way she was working.

The red icon indicating a Facebook message gave her a rush.

Once on Facebook, the heart flutter tickled her insides, down to her groin. Ridiculous, she thought, to have this reaction from a message. Absolutely ridiculous. But it was another message from a childhood friend and classmate who had lived down the street in the same subdivision. He had long moved away, while she had long moved to another house to prolong the same suburban existence.

The boy, now a man, of course, was named John Timmer. He had asked to be her friend on Facebook two years before, when she was at the peak of caring for Marc, and that's when her love/hate relationship with social media had started: she craved connection and hated herself for living through other people. John Timmer encompassed the epitome of this: his actual career was a professional skydiver for a team based in the United Kingdom. His face shots from the air while he clutched some first-time diver made Heather get a hitch in her throat, like she no longer knew how to breathe. She'd scroll through his posts, seeing wide sky and wind- blown smiles, alongside multiple shots of rolling countryside in the United Kingdom.

The images filled her with such longing, she thought she might collapse from the inertia of her own life – her own small, sad internal life where the only escape was to a small-town murder she made up in her own mind. But John became more than someone to envy on Facebook. At first, short, civil catch-up chats were exchanged, and then, over time, she grew excited to correspond with John about books, movies, and other day-to-day events. These chats often saved her from despair while caring for Marc.

When she recently realized that some of John Timmer's posts came from an organic farm not far from the residency she hoped she would win with her mystery pages, well, the obvious thing to do was send him a message about meeting in person. In the most recent one, Heather revealed she was a finalist for the grant competition, and if she won, she would be living near where he was stationed.

"Let's see what you have to say, John Timmer," Heather said to the book shelf, looking away from the wedding photo she only kept up because of her children.

Click.

Hey, Heather Finch,

Thought I'd shoot you a message before I head to England. Have you heard about that writing gig, yet? I have a good feeling you're going to get it, so if I remember right, that means you could be UK-side about mid-month, right? I'll be back in the Highlands in three weeks or so, so I'll see you on the other side – you won't be in Glenview anymore. –J

"Mom!" Tess burst in the room without a knock. Heather jumped and shut off Facebook with a jolt.

"What is it, Tessa? You scared the life out of me."

Tessa hung on the door handle and leaned in; the room filled with a fresh scent of strawberry shampoo and body lotion. Her long, blonde hair flowed over her slim arm in thick waves. She flicked her eyes to the bookshelf and back at Heather.

"Sorry, you working?" Tessa asked, but smirked, like she could see right through the back of the laptop to the phantom of scrolling social media waiting for Heather's login again.

"Ah, yeah, getting ready to."

"Anyway, I was going to go out with Ashley, Owen, and everyone after school. You remember it's my last day in that hellhole high school, right?"

"Of course." There was so much more Heather wanted to say, but she clamped her mother-mouth shut and waited for more.

"Of course to remembering, or of course to going out?" Tessa's phone tinged and her hand went to it instantly, but her eyes stayed on

Heather and glinted in the morning light.

"To both, but be home at midnight." An arbitrary time, but Heather liked to show some sort of authority. "And do you have a designated driver? Do not get in a car with –"

"Mom! I'm not a total idiot. To answer your question, Ashley is driving, and she doesn't drink."

"And Tessa, I know you and Owen are starting to date –"

"Mom, that's over. We're cool, though, just friends."

"Oh." Heather glanced at the wedding picture and her tall dancer's body with the miniscule bump of the first trimester of pregnancy. "Just be careful, you know, protected."

Tessa rolled her eyes. "Covered, Mom," she said and closed the door.

Heather waited to hear Tessa gather her things. The front door slammed, and the house seemed to sigh with relief. Heather touched the wedding picture with her fingernail, tracing an X over Marc's face. A childish action, but the cool glass under her fingertip approved, though his image kept smiling in his black tux. He was so fit, muscular and tall, with blond hair and blue eyes. And she? She was twenty-one at the time, 5'7" – her body slim and firm – with only the shades of her present curves. She ran her fingertip over her veil; it flowed with her long, brown hair, which was braided with flowers. Her face broke into a tentative smile, more out of obligation than joy; her dancing scholarship at Lumiere University would soon run out because Marc had gotten her pregnant; her youth was about to be snatched away by the yoke of motherhood; her education would be put on hold and cut in half from a Bachelor's to an Associate's, though it took her four years to finish a two year program at a community college while Marc went through police training and certification. No wonder her slate-colored eyes were stormy in the picture; no wonder her usually bronze-colored skin looked pale, a mix of ash and chalk. She was certainly not the glowing bride.

Heather let her hand fall and then snapped her laptop shut. Her desk chair creaked when she leaned back, letting her chestnut brown/hazelnut-now-dyed-shoulder-length hair hang over the back. She suspected she would be one-quarter-gray-streaked without the color. She ran her hand over her full breasts and to her stomach that still had a little bump from three pregnancies – two live births and one live death, a term she'd made up when her second child died in his seventh month. Her mind flashed to the delivery and then clicked off. She would not go there today.

There was too much to do, and the girl in the wedding photo was far away, like sea glass catching light on a long, sandy shore along a path that snaked ahead of her into a new world with rocky coasts. Could the Scottish seaside be before her? Could Heather Finch finally finish off her truncated youth? She laughed out loud, not recognizing the new bubble in her chuckle. She'd have to wait and see.

Live

Early June, present day

The day was cool for June, with a breeze coming off Lake Michigan, enough to make Heather wear a long-sleeved shirt (despite having on shorts) for her walk along the lake with her best friend, Leann. She sat on a bench near the McKinnel Marina and pointed and flexed her toes, a warm-up she used to do each day before deep stretches and then hours of dancing. Now her Achilles Tendon seemed to creak like unoiled hinges; her ankle bones popped, so she rolled them, hoping to loosen up before their speed walk. For the last ten years, she and Leann had a walking date and would meet twice a week for a fast-two-mile walk. They usually met at Deer Brook Park in their Glenview suburb, but once in a while, when the sky was clear and the air heavy with humidity, or when they simply needed a different view – one not mottled with strip malls and Starbucks – they would change their routine and walk on Milwaukee's lakeshore. Today was such a day; the air seemed to hold an expectant breath, exuding its inherent odor that, on a bad day, smelled like dead fish, but today, was crisp and new, like a field of blooming violets. Or maybe it was Heather's mood. She had received good news the day before and couldn't wait to tell her friend about it. Her skin tingled when the air moved over the hair on her arms. She inhaled and exhaled slowly, pretending she just stepped onto a stage to dance one of her favorite ballets, or a samba, anything, just to feel her body move again, like it used to.

Heather's body hunched in a parenthesis over her knees, and she felt a tap on her back.

15

"Hey, you," Leann said, "ready to hit it?"

"Absolutely," Heather said and hopped up. She took off on the paved path that ran along Bradley Beach.

"Whoa, you got get-up-and-go this morning," Leann said, trotting a little to catch up. Usually Leann led the way, her long legs at top speed. Leann stood taller than Heather, and as she said, she was "built like a linebacker," which wasn't true from Heather's perspective. Sure, Leann had grown fuller over the years, especially after having three children, but to Heather, Leann still had a youthful beauty. Her sandy blonde hair was cut in a stylish way; her brown eyes still sparkled like they used to when they were kids; her long body, though a little rounder, still had a spring that Heather lacked.

"Tell me, what's up?" Leann leaned over, waiting for the news.

Heather felt a tightening in her stomach. Once she mouthed the words, then it would become really real, not just a mirage in the distance. Real.

"I do have some news. Some good news," Heather said, taking in how the sun made the blue of the lake sparkle like an undulating floor of precious gems. No murky slug pond today, only sapphires, she smiled to herself.

"Tell me before you take off in your internal private land, where you get this faraway look, and I won't be able to reel you back until we get a cappuccino at Allison's Cafe."

"I won." Heather beamed at her best friend. "I actually won the writing retreat contest."

"No way!" Leann stopped and grabbed Heather in a bear hug. "Oh, Heath, I knew it! I am so happy for you!"

"Thanks, friend," Heather said and pulled free of the hug, "but let's keep walking. I feel like I want to get in better shape. You know, kind of like a fresh start."

"Sister, if there is anyone who needs a fresh start in this world, it's you." Leann squinted as they started up the incline on Lake Road; it curved away from the lakeshore, but brought them into the shade of the pine, maple, and dogwood trees that grew thick in Lake Mile Park.

"Remind me, Future Traveler to the British Isles, when you go," Leann started, but paused to wave to some walkers they often saw on their lake route.

"It's the Scottish Highlands, actually," Heather said and smiled. Leann had never been one for details; over the years she confused names, dates, or details from the minutiae of Heather's life, but, for the big things, she was one hundred percent present, and not once had Leann dropped the ball. Not once had she not shown up when Heather called crying because Tessa wouldn't nurse, or Jackson broke his hand, or when Marc had his stroke, and every small, torturous moment when Heather cared for Marc; it was Leann, her bulwark, who kept her going. Their walks propelled her to move forward, even when every inch of her being yearned to stay in pajamas all day and never crack open the door to the outside world. Leann kept pulling on her, saying, "Come on Finchy," like when they were six-year-olds and Heather wanted to stay in and play Barbies or read books, and Leann insisted they join the neighborhood kids for a pick-up game of kickball. Leann always jumped into the mix while Heather hung back, but Leann never let her stay on the fringe. Heather skated through her school years for the most part, even through high school, because Leann forged a path for both of them.

"Right, Scotland is even better. Oh, I can't wait for you to be somewhere else for once! But wait, that means you're not here for what – the whole summer? How the hell will I survive my kids and my marriage without you?" Leann paused, hands on hips, on the path for two seconds, but then broke into a wide grin. "Who the hell cares, right? We're going to be nothing but walking on air about this. Wow – you won with one of the mysteries, right?"

17

"Yep, good ol' Millicent Monvail prevailed, even if it felt like I bled them. I feel like I'm finally living again, not just surviving," Heather said between breaths. The hill got steeper through the park, but they would be rewarded with a long downhill slope, and then Allison's Café after they finished.

"Of course you feel that way, sweetie, it was so hard for you. How many late thirty/early forty people do you know has to take care of a husband who's a stroke victim? Right, *no one*. Do you think the retreat will help you, you know, process all the hard stuff about that time?"

Leann, the angel, never brought up things from Heather's past without an opening. That was one of the main reasons Heather loved her so much.

"I don't know. I want to focus on new writing, but I will be isolated, which breeds reflection. So being alone so much could make me relive it all and cry myself silly."

"True, who wouldn't weep like a baby over your shit the last three years, but let's say it's going to be cathartic, and don't the Scots make Guinness or one of those great heavy beers? You could bring your laptop to a pub and drink Guinness for strength." Leann giggled and blew out three long breaths once they reached the top of the hill.

"Guinness is made in Ireland, but there are a lot of whiskey distilleries in Scotland. You know, Scottish whiskey," Heather said.

"Oh, right, and kilts." Leann paused and bent over at the waist. "Give me a minute. All this excitement and that fucking hill are going to send me into cardiac arrest."

Heather stopped and tilted her head to the tree canopy. The word "resplendent" popped into mind. The way the sunlight filtered through the green leaves: *resplendent*.

Leann straightened. "Find yourself a strapping Scottish highlander who wears a kilt all the time – you know they are commando under those – and screw the daylights out of him."

"Hey!" Heather turned her head, making sure no one on the path heard Leann.

"What? You need to get laid. Enough of this holy retreat from all things sexual. You're gorgeous, and youngish, and come on, Heath, it's been forever. Use this as an opportunity."

"I'm going to an isolated Scottish cottage in the Highlands for the sole purpose of writing. That's why I submitted to the contest, and I need to produce a certain amount by the end of the eight weeks."

"Eight weeks! Shit, that is a long time. That's all right. I have my dear husband Brian, the love of my life, to watch baseball with and to talk to. Oh, wait. That's right, we don't speak to each other anymore."

Heather laughed. Leann talked about Brian like that, but in reality, they had been devoted since high school. Whenever Heather thought of the phrase soul mates, she pictured Leann and Brian.

"And my lovely teenagers, those smelly boys, and don't forget my tween girl, what a sweetheart. I will have so much quality time with them. Oh good, the downhill is up ahead. Let's celebrate with caramel mochas and muffins. Don't look at me like that. You can splurge more than I can."

"Okay, but let's add an extra walk this week," Heather added.

"Fine, fine, little miss dancer legs."

They walked in silence for a few minutes. Heather took in the sloping green hill and the panoramic view of the lake shore. Other walkers and runners dotted the path they had just traveled; bikers raced through the surges of wind off the lake; brave bathers threw out blankets on the sand, even if the chill of the breeze battled the rising sun in the sky.

"Wait a minute," Leann said in a rush. "I totally forgot. Have you been keeping in touch with John Timmer from grade school? He's there, right? So you can hook up with him."

"Not a hook-up, my friend, but yes, he'll be back in Scotland soon after I arrive. And he said he'll be there through the summer." Heather's insides did that social media twist again.

"Heather, if I recall, he's not so hard on the eyes. That's if he hasn't really tanked in the looks department, not that there is anything wrong with looking as positively middle-aged as Brian and I do."

Heather cracked up. "You two look great."

"Nice of you to say, but the question is how does John Timmer look? Can you tell from Facebook?"

"Yeah, he has a lot of pictures posted."

"And?"

"He's, he's — he looks very similar to what he did in grade school and middle school."

"Pretty fine. Not necessarily my type, but what about you?"

"He's …" Heather didn't know what to say. Of course, she could tell her best friend that she had studied his photos down to the exact detail, but Heather believed most of that had to do with the kind of life he led. What could be a freer occupation than being a professional skydiver?

"Okay, I'll fill in some blanks for you," Leann said. "He's tall, I'm sure, which is good for your stature. Sandy-colored hair, maybe some gray now, but that shows up less on honey hair. His skin is fairish, but not so fair he burns like hell. He probably gets some freckles in the summer. Cute. Wait, get out, isn't he some kind of extreme sports guide?"

"Skydiver."

"So he must be really fit, right? Like great arms and abs."

"Maybe," Heather lied. The man's physique seemed to be out of a catalog.

"Maybe means 'hell yes' in your understated way. What ever happened to him after middle school anyway?"

"He went to West High."

"That's right, the private-public divide that happened after middle

20

school. I wanted to go to public high school, but then I might have missed out on marrying Brian — what an absolute *loss* that would have been." Leann blew out a long breath behind her sarcasm.

Heather smiled and picked up the pace down the hill toward the café. Her mind wandered to memories of John Timmer from grade school and middle school. They were the kind of friends who did well on class projects together in grade school. She had a vague memory of working on a diorama of the planets with him and another girl. But her most distinct memory made her cheeks flush red; she was grateful for the exertion from the hill minutes before to hide her blush.

Leann said something about buying the mochas and then she started humming a tune Heather didn't recognize. Heather's mind reeled back to sitting at a round table in catechism class when she was in eighth grade. John Timmer came into the room, and though he could have sat at any number of tables, he chose the seat right next to Heather. If anyone else was at the table, Heather didn't remember; heat pulsed through her body, not from the exercise, but from the memory of John next to her. She had been so quiet, so quick to slide into the background, but her body had developed, and her hormones had started waves she couldn't control. She and John had worked on some workbook exercise, probably on the sacraments, and toward the end of the lesson, he took his hand and slid it between her thighs. He rested it there, not moving, and she froze but caught his eyes, which gleamed with a knowing she didn't understand, and then he whispered, "Is this okay, Heather?" Her throat had had cotton building up onto her tongue; her body had radiated a heat she had never felt before; his hand had felt like hot embers soaking through her jeans. She hadn't been able to speak then, but she'd nodded her head. *Yes, yes, yes.*

Remember
February, three years ago

The low thrum of the monitors, the click of the IV from which medicines foreign to Heather ran into Marc, the rhythmic whoosh of a breathing machine – all lulled her into a daze, a horror daze where she had to keep telling herself, *This is real.*

How could it be real? Her hands had shaken uncontrollably in the ambulance, so hard she'd had to stuff them into her pajama pockets. Then the questions, the rush to surgery, the waiting, and now, the new real that squashed her into a hospital sitter. She felt like a cracked cage – a locust shell like those that had scattered all over her lawn in high school during the summer of the cicadas. There was no summer here, no warmth.

Heather shivered and pulled her sweater tighter across her breasts. Who had brought her the fresh clothes? Leann? She had been in pajamas, and then, like a costume change behind the scenes of someone else's life, she materialized in jeans, a turtleneck, and a cardigan sweater, her favorite with the deep pockets.

A nurse entered, silent as snow, but wearing a smock with bright smiley faces on it that screamed her entrance. Heather tried to keep her eyes from ticking off the faces, counting each perfect sphere and imagining really bad things impaling their crescent smiles.

"He's stable," Shannon said; her name on the white board had a smiley face, too. The name next to CNA (certified nursing assistant, Heather had learned) read "Ingrid," and though Heather had imagined a robust, German woman with blonde hair and piercing blue eyes, Ingrid, a petite Black woman who looked Tessa's age, appeared out of nowhere throughout the night, changing the urine bag, checking the chuck pads for a bowel movement, adjusting the catheter. She did the dirty work and wore no smiley faces; Ingrid kept Marc's body in operation while Shannon monitored, injected, and called the doctors.

How quickly Heather had learned the routine; how suddenly this new life boiled down to hospital minutes.

"Dr. Ghani will be in shortly," Shannon said while adjusting the IV port on Marc's hand.

"Do you know what time?" Heather asked.

"Not exactly. He's started his rounds, so it shouldn't be too long."

"Do you think I have time to get a cup of coffee?" Heather stood and stretched, ignoring Marc's bundled skull that looked like a gauzy wasp's nest.

"Hard to say," Shannon said with a click of her tongue. She pulled her smiley smock over her belly and hips and smiled. "You know surgeons." Shannon nodded her bobbed, blonde-brown head.

"Actually, Dr. Ghani is the first neurosurgeon I've ever met," Heather put in, defending the man who had saved Marc's life, a tiger man from Egypt with intense brown eyes and an energy that broke open a room upon entry. Heather didn't want to come off as a smart mouth, so she curbed her tone, "I don't want to miss his evaluation. I'm grateful for all he's done – all of you have been wonderful." And she meant it; Smiley Shannon was obviously a good nurse. Wouldn't she have to be to watch one patient so intently in ICU?

Shannon's eyes softened. "We have your cell number. I'll call it if he shows while you're gone. Take a break."

"Thanks." Heather gathered her purse and phone, not knowing if she really should leave his side, but she had stayed with him all night. Leann had said she'd make sure the kids slept and were fed in the morning. They weren't even thinking about going to school any time soon. Who knew if Marc would survive the night, today, or any day after that?

As Dr. Ghani had said, "Marc is in the acute, post-surgery phase. Time will tell." Then he'd fixed his gold-brown eyes on Heather, connecting them in this life-saving union. Somehow Heather knew Marc's life from this point depended on each choice she made, and that first choice had come with saying yes to a surgery that drilled a hole in her husband's skull to relieve the pressure from a brain hemorrhage usually diagnosed in the elderly.

Heather's boots squeaked on the newly polished floor of the ICU. She hit the button to open the automatic door and turned to get one more glance at Marc's curtained room. If he died while she drank a vanilla cappuccino, she'd never forgive herself. But she left the wing anyway, her body drained and her joints achy. She needed something to give her a lift, even if it came in the form of a brief caffeine buzz.

Once safely deposited in the cafeteria, her hands warming on the paper cup while the sharp smell of coffee touched her nostrils, she opened her purse and pulled out her cell phone. Signs were posted all over ICU about how cell phones had to be turned off or they would interfere with the monitors and other life-saving equipment. She sat and scrolled through her messages. She had several from her parents and brother, Marc's family, his squad, and then Leann. She skipped them all and read Leann's text, which told her she'd bring the kids to the hospital around 9 a.m. It was 8:45. Heather typed a quick text, saying she was in the cafeteria. Her heart lifted a little with the prospect of having Leann with her when Dr. Ghani came to assess Marc.

Within a few blank minutes, when Heather stared at the fake potted ferns or beyond them to the vending machines, inanely counting how many varieties of chips they had, Leann, Jackson, and an ashen Tessa walked through the doors leading from the south parking lot. Leann wore a harried, worried expression that she instantly masked upon seeing Heather hunched at a Formica table. Jackson's normally tan-colored skin, even in February, appeared translucent, as if, even from a distance, Heather would soon be able to make out the bodily details beneath skin level.

My poor boy, and Tessa, what in the world would Tessa do without her daddy?

Heather put her hand up in the best cheerful wave she could muster and then stood. Standing seemed to command more authority, to project she had everything, even something as haphazard and monitored as Marc's gas output, under control. She held up her machine-made cappuccino and motioned to the coffee stand for Leann, who looked desperate for more caffeine.

Jackson and Tessa rushed to Heather, and all three embraced. *This is it, no more self-pity.* She had to get it together for her kids. She pulled back and smoothed Tessa's hair like she used to when Tessa was five, or eight, or even, if Heather could sneak it in, when she was eleven, when Tessa had become a touch-me-not.

"How is he?" Tessa croaked, tears pooling already.

Heather mimicked Shannon, the smile nurse, and said, "he's stable."

"So he'll be all right?" Tessa's voice was so eager, so child-like, Heather had to press her nail to her palm to cause pain. The shock of it snapped her to attention, so she could keep from sobbing in front of them.

"Well, he's still in what the surgeon calls the 'acute stage' post-surgery, but it's good news he came out of it and had a restful night," Heather said. Yes, if restful meant comatose, then Marc rested.

Jackson seemed to read her thoughts; his clear, blue eyes searching her mind for inconsistencies in her story. He opened his mouth to speak, but Leann arrived with a tray heaped with pastries, juice, and more coffee. Heather's stomach turned. How in the world would she ever eat again? Bile rose up her throat and slid down again. She sat, clutched her stomach, and pretended to be thrilled with the prospect of baked goods.

"Look at these croissants, kids," Heather said, dancing her fingers along the paper coverings. "Thank you, Leann, for everything." Stop, she told herself, digging the nail again, *don't cry*.

Leann caught her eye and patted her forearm. "Of course, you got me riding shotgun all day, and then some if you need. My sister is taking over for me on my home front, and Brian isn't completely useless." She smiled and popped a bite of muffin in her mouth. Heather's mind flashed to something Leann had said years before, when her sister Jessica was going through a divorce: "I've learned that when you go to support someone through a trauma, bring your own snacks. They may not want to eat, but you'll be starving, and a little bored. I found that out with Jessica, who dropped five pounds within two weeks. I put it on for her."

Heather grabbed Leann in a quick hug. Leann chewed and patted Heather's shoulder, "It'll be okay, Finchy. It really will."

"I don't think I can eat anything," Tessa said. "I want to see Dad, but I'm afraid to see him. How's he look?"

Heather swallowed her lukewarm coffee and paused with the paper cup on her lips. "He has a lot of bandages on his head. The breathing tube is still in because they need to be sure he's breathing on his own before they take it out. He has an IV." Heather's voice drifted off. She wanted to prepare them, but she also didn't want to freak them out so much they'd never set foot in the room.

"I don't think I can do it, go in and see him, I mean," Tessa said. She clenched the edge of the table. Her chewed fingernails whitened from the pressure.

Jackson swallowed a bite of bagel and nodded to Tessa. "Sure you can. Dad can probably hear what's going on. Having us there will help him get through this."

How'd my little boy, now seventeen, get so wise?

"Has he woken up at all, Mom?" His eyes flashed Heather a quick glance. Heather thought she may be able to snow Tessa, shield her from the worst of this, whatever this would be, but Jackson, on the other hand, would see the puppet strings behind her performance.

"No," Heather said. Leann started humming something, a church hymn? "He hasn't, but any time now Dr. Ghani will come in and evaluate him. We'll know more then."

They sat in silence for several long minutes until Tessa's quiet sobs mixed with the clanking of serving ware and metal containers being filled with scrambled eggs and sausage in the serving area of the cafeteria. The smells turned Heather's stomach. She reached for Tessa and rubbed her shoulder, saying, *shhh*, just as she had to Marc after he'd collapsed. Was that only a day ago? How could things change so fast?

Jackson bit his lip and shook his head. Tessa wiped her face with a paper napkin. Leann hummed. "Peace is flowing like a river" – that was the tune. Heather's phone buzzed, and she grabbed at it, pressing the screen to answer, "Hello?"

"Hello, Mrs. Barrington, this is Shannon."

"Hi, Shannon, is everything okay?" Heather's stomach seemed to have dropped to her feet.

"Yes, your husband remains stable. I wanted you to know Dr. Ghani is on the ICU floor. He's with one other patient, and then he'll be in to see your husband."

"Thank you, thank you so much for letting me know." Heather clicked off. "Dr. Ghani is coming, let's get back to the room."

Heather hurried to throw away the trash. Tessa grabbed her arm. "Mom, I don't know if I can go in there."

Heather didn't have the patience for this, but she looked in Tessa's blue eyes filled with total, unabashed fear, and paused. She cradled Tessa's cheek in her palm. "Yes, you can, sweetie, be strong for your

27

dad. You can do it." She took Tessa's hand and pulled her down the hallway. Jackson and Leann trailed.

When they entered Marc's cloaked room, Dr. Ghani was already bent over Marc, flashing lights in his eyes, and saying things to Shannon who dutifully listened, her hands on the laptop keys taking notes.

Heather yanked at Jackson and Tessa to stand in the corner of the room. Leann positioned herself the farthest from the activity, balancing her right hip on the radiator vent. Once Dr. Ghani's body no longer obscured Marc, Tessa gasped and cried silently into her hand. Jackson took her in his arms, his eyes wide, and turned away. Heather wanted to comfort them, but she also wanted to be ready for instructions. She pulled out the notepad Leann had brought and poised a pen, ready for anything. This, she could do; she took notes all the time when writing her mysteries.

"Hello, Mrs. Barrington," Dr. Ghani said, crossing the room in two long strides and gripping her hand in a firm clasp. The hold of his strong hand moored Heather, but just as easily as his strength had secured her in place, it propelled her forward because as Dr. Ghani moved back to Marc's bedside, so did Heather, even though each molecule making up her body wanted to break apart, drift from the hospital room, and resume another shape. Instead, her pen in hand, she waited for him to speak.

"It is very good that your husband made it through the first night after the surgery. He has not regained consciousness, but this is not unusual with the severe bleeding that occurred on his brain. I know I told you a skeletal version of what was happening with your husband last night after surgery, but I will go into more detail as we head into recovery. With his stroke, a hemorrhagic stroke, there is a weakened vessel that ruptures and bleeds into the surrounding area of the brain. The blood compresses the tissue, and as I said last night, we had to drill the hole into the skull to relieve this pressure."

Heather's pen scraped her notebook furiously. She knew about the drilled hole, and hearing about it again made her stomach do more flip flops.

"The drilling relieved the pressure. Your husband had a subarachnoid hemorrhage, and this kind occurs on the surface of the brain, so the bleeding was in the space between the skull and the brain. This positioning and your quick response are the two things that most likely saved his life."

The stomach flip flops blossomed to a feeling of pride. Dr. Ghani, this beautiful Tiger Man, had complimented her. Maybe everything would be okay.

Dr. Ghani snapped off his latex gloves, foisting an image in Heather's mind of him in bed with a woman, positioning his sleek brown body over her, saying, "Now for the examination" as he adjusted his gloves. Heather touched her forehead, afraid she was losing it completely. Who had sexual fantasies about a doctor while her husband lay inert and near death beside her?

Apparently, Heather Barrington did.

"So," he continued, "you are still listening, yes?" His brown eyes connected with hers. Heather felt the blush on her cheeks, but forced a smile, and nodded her head.

"I am," she said. "Please go on."

"Good," he said. "So with this kind of bleed, we had to re-route the blood flow, and since your husband is so young, I thought his body would respond well to a shunt."

"A shunt?" Heather said. "Aren't those put in hearts?"

"Yes, but it is the same concept. We put in the shunt wherever we need to direct blood flow. In this case, it is in his skull. During this acute stage, before he wakes up, I need his head to be at this angle. We do not want it to dip below or above because the brain is adjusting to the new mechanism. The nursing staff knows this, but once he wakes, it is helpful that a family member is with him, to be sure he stays at this angle. This is understood, yes?"

"Yes," Heather said. "I'll be here."

"I can help, too," Leann piped in from the back of the room.

Tess remained in Jackson's arms, but said, "I'll stay."

Jackson squeezed Tessa tighter, "Me too."

"Very good," Dr. Ghani said. "The family makes the most of recovery. It is good he has such support."

Heather wanted to ask so many questions:

What will he be like if he wakes up?

How long do I have to watch his head level?

What's going to happen to him?

What's going to happen to me?

How did this happen?

Her mind raced, and she could tell Dr. Ghani was getting ready to depart, so she blurted, "How did this happen? He's young to experience a stroke, and so healthy."

Dr. Ghani turned to her. "Yes, it is always a shock to see strokes in one his age, but it does happen. Hemorrhagic strokes account for around thirteen percent of stroke occurrences. Your husband, despite his excellent health, most likely had an arteriovenous malformation – a blood vessel that had been malformed all of his life. It is like living with a tiny time bomb on the brain. It sat inert, showing no symptoms until the very moment it was ready to burst, and that moment was yesterday morning. With one his age and his health, there would be no reason to scan the brain for such a malformation. This is my suspicion. I read his records and the intake information, and there is not a large history of strokes in his family. His condition is what you native English speakers call a fluke, yes?"

"Yes," Heather uttered. Fluke, fluke, fluke – her life now hinged on this fluke – what would happen next and next and next?

Dr. Ghani must have noticed her drifting into her own mental world because he took her hand in another firm clasp and held it. "The path in front of you and your family is not an easy one, but I can see an inner strength in you. You have a courage you haven't tapped. This will help you and your husband as he relearns certain tasks."

"What kind of tasks?" Jackson asked from behind her.

Bless him. He had the gumption to ask.

"I mean," Jackson added, "will he need to learn to talk again?" His voice cracked. Tears started down Heather's face.

Dr. Ghani released her hand and patted her shoulder. "It is hard to tell what will be lost to him and what he'll still have. So much of brain recovery is still a mystery. Time will tell. Be well, all of you. I will be back tomorrow to check on Mr. Barrington. He is in excellent care here in ICU."

With that, the Tiger Man left the room. Heather collapsed into the nearest chair. She wanted to run from the room, find a bathroom, and sob. But her kids were there looking at her – so sad and lost. Instead she wiped her face, stood, and smoothed her jeans. "I'll take the first shift with Dad. Leann, do you mind taking the kids home for a while? Come back in a couple of hours with magazines, books, and some clothes from home. I'd love a toothbrush." She even cracked a smile. She could do this; she could pretend to be in charge of the situation, her leadership a fluke.

Live
Early June, present day

Heather drove, and Tessa wore her earbuds while shooting off an occasional text to any number of her friends. Heather bit back her annoyance. The point of driving to the Brook Meadow Mall was to bond before Heather left the country for eight weeks, but as soon as they had left the house, after much harrumphing and fussing over what to wear on Tessa's part, Heather felt fatigue wash over her. The girl drained her of all energy. Having the child drift into her music/texting world seemed simpler than having even the most inane conversation about sundresses.

But Tessa was her only daughter after all, so she reached her hand out while at a stoplight and tapped Tessa's shoulder. Tessa jumped and grimaced, taking one earbud out.

"Sorry to startle you, honey." The "honey," another gesture, stuck in the air like an odd smell from outside. "What department store should I park closest to?"

"I don't care," Tessa said and slouched in the seat. "No wait, how about Boston's? I saw they have a sale."

"Okay. So we're looking for some summer clothes that will get you through my trip, especially tan pants and white t-shirts for work at Frosty Jack's Parlor."

"That is the lamest name for an ice cream place, and it matches my lame white cap I have to wear. One chocolate drip down the front and I have customers staring at my boobs for the rest of the day."

Heather cracked up. At least Tessa could do this, make her laugh unexpectedly, but when she did it these days, she always pulled back from the joke and assumed her vacant, slightly bored face she had worn for over three years. The mask surfaced, and Heather stifled her laugh.

"Right, but you need clothes, white or not. I can't believe you grew taller this past year. Most kids are done by the end of high school."

"Why does everything you say to me sound like an accusation?" Tessa said and sat higher in her seat.

"I didn't mean it that way. It's just, you're taller. New clothes." Heather remembered reading this in a parenting magazine that was geared for toddlers. The advice column said that if your toddler ignored directives, instead of repeating yourself multiple times, shave the command down to one or two words and say it in a clear and non-desperate way (not easy in Heather's mind). Though Tessa had been sixteen at the time, Heather had adopted the strategy, and it stuck. Instead of extending this conversation about Tessa's need for new clothes because she grew another freaking inch and a half after Heather believed she was done with the growth spurts, she reduced the chat to two words: new clothes.

"Here we are!" Heather said in a false voice that sounded so jolly Tessa rolled her eyes.

Car doors slammed; flips flops shuffled, and the earbuds remained nestled in Tessa's ears. Heather huffed and shoved her keys into her purse. She glanced at her watch, pretending to adjust the wristband, but really she wondered how long this excursion would take.

They made their way into the fluorescent lighting of the department store. Swimsuits and sundresses crammed the clearance racks while slim sweaters, jeans, and even winter coats adorned the manikins. Heather never got used to the seasonal express train in stores. She wanted to see the swimsuits displayed NOW because now was the time to wear them. New sundresses should flow from the androgynous manikins, not parkas. She didn't want her summer, the first she'd have in a long time, to slip away before it arrived.

"I'll be at the clearance racks, Mom," Tessa said, already heading that direction, and then she turned, making a point to look like her idea was an after-thought, something offhand and unimportant and said, "You want new sundresses and shorts for your trip, right?"

Heather nodded, warmed by the attention and Tessa's effort to seem uninterested. "Yeah, if you see anything, let me know. And don't forget to look for hiking shorts and things for yourself. When you and Jackson join me in Scotland in August, we could do some camping."

Tessa shrugged and turned.

Heather wanted to explore the racks away from her daughter, so it would give her time to think, really think, about things. She'd missed any mental space that morning, up and out with Tessa like a typhoon, so now, while taking in the distant, flowery scents from the perfume counter and pushing through hangers of unsorted spring and summer wear, did she have time to collect herself. Was it a bad idea that her children would meet her in Scotland at the end of her writing retreat? She had no idea. It had seemed like a good idea at the time, and they hadn't taken a real vacation since before Marc's stroke. Sure, they'd each had little day trips away, but the longest excursion the three of them had taken in the last three and a half years had been to California for a long weekend for Marc's niece's confirmation. And then, they'd all been plagued with guilt for leaving Marc behind with a caretaker. The entire weekend, instead of being awash with salty sea air and piercing blue skies, kept Heather jumping like a jackrabbit at every loud noise, as if Marc's voice would break the surf at any moment to request something from his automatic lift chair.

Heather shuddered and pulled out a swimsuit that could fit her, but she knew she'd be uncomfortable around the midsection. Her stomach wasn't terrible, but it definitely wasn't flat. She shoved the suit back and slipped through a range of shorts, from Daisy Duke's to capris so long they could have been floods.

"Mom," Tessa said, putting Heather on alert with her tone. "How about these?"

Tessa held up two sundresses, one blue with geometric patterns and grayish hues, and another shorter, reddish pink one.

"Try them on," Tessa said while hitching her head to the side, toward the fitting rooms. "I also grabbed a few pairs of shorts. They're shorter than you usually wear, but they're cute, and I think they'd look good on you."

"Thank you," Heather said, taking the garments with two hands and flinging them over her forearm. "Did you find anything for yourself?" she asked.

"Yeah, I'm scouting some things. I'll meet you in there." Tessa took off with a bounce in her step, reminding Heather of when she stood a foot shorter.

In the dressing room, Heather turned from the mirror when undressing. She stared up at the fluorescent lights and slipped out of her bra, knowing the straps would show under the sundresses. Tessa had grabbed a strapless bra for her, a padded 34C – Heather's exact size, and even though she still had enough breasts to do without the padding, since breastfeeding both kids for a year each, her nipples had taken on a new form, a cross between spouts and knobs, not exactly something she wanted to see jutting through the dress. She put on the bra in a rush, slipped into the blue sundress, and turned to the mirror. The neckline dipped more than she was used to, but the colors were perfect, and the material soft next to her skin, but not too silky; both dresses had a functionality she thought would be ideal for Scotland.

"How are they?" Tessa asked from the other side of the door.

"I have the first dress on, and I think I like it," Heather said, gazing at a new spider vein behind her left knee.

"Can I see?" Tessa knocked, but shoved the door open before Heather could answer. "Oh, Mom, you're stunning!"

Heather blushed. "No, that's too strong of a word –"

"No, it's not," Tessa said, squeezing through and standing behind Heather while adjusting the shoulder straps and looking in the mirror. "It suits you, Mom." Tessa smiled briefly and grabbed the other dress. "This one will work, too. I'll go get some other things for you."

Tessa dashed out and in numerous times, carting sundresses, shorts, new summer pajamas Heather would never usually wear, but in the hands of her daughter, the one who lapsed between a borderline personality, a shrewd forensic scientist (her dream job), and an average nice girl, Heather acquiesced, with pleasure. Maybe this trip would repair things.

And now, soon, she would be shed of the monstrous, suburban house, the buyers a new, growing family not unlike how Heather and Marc had been. The buyers' apartment lease would be up in September – right when Tessa left for her first year of college at UW, and Jackson would transfer his community college credits to start his third year there. Heather could live anywhere she chose. Maybe she should move to Madison to be near her kids? Would they want to get an apartment with her? Today, with Tessa running garments to her like a runway gopher, Heather believed it possible.

In the end, Heather and Tessa bought armfuls of summer gear, and one cozy fall sweater at full price for Tessa at college. They trudged back to the car in silence, fatigue from being on their feet and scanning the racks settling in; it felt much later than mid-day to Heather .

Tessa broke the silence when they were in the car and heading downtown to pick up Jackson at Green Life. "We got some significant reductions, and now we're both set for summer."

Heather wanted to stop the car and grab Tessa in a giant hug. It had been so long since Tessa showed herself for this long. Usually, "the sweet girl," the one she reserved for her brother or friends, only flashed herself like a fireworks display with the hard crackle you only see for an instant that gave a jolting boom, and then, nothing but the black sky. Tessa shifted and stuck the mask back on, one that had formed progressively after Marc's stroke, as if every damn thing had been Heather's fault.

Stop, she told herself to check her mind before speaking. She knew she was part of the problem, casting just as much blame at Tessa. Why did mothers and daughters do this to each other? It seemed so much easier with Jackson.

"You found all the sale items, Tessa. You're the pro at it. Are you sure you didn't get a full scholarship to UW for shopping and not math and science?" Heather bit her cheek. She worried the words came out wrong, that she had gone and ruined an almost perfect day. She waited.

Tess cocked her head, looking at Heather through half-open eyes. The sun caught the blue in them, sending off a sparkle Heather hadn't seen in some time. "Maybe. And maybe I'll get my MRS. Degree rather than go all the way for the masters. What do you think? Should I meet a guy and get married?" Her tone was light, but like so much with Tessa, there were layers beneath her words, or maybe Heather just took them that way. Was she referring to Heather's life? Heather knew she could take this two ways, so she decided to bend on the side of levity.

"Oh, yes, and please get knocked up like I did while you're at it," Heather said and focused on the road because it was time to cross two lanes of traffic before reaching the merge lane for I43.

Tessa's laugh rang out, the sounds so foreign to Heather she almost cut off an SUV, but she gained her bearings and merged. Once safely on 43, she glanced at Tessa and smiled. She wanted to say more, to tell her how proud she was of the scholarship, how much it eased her financial worries, but that could be taken wrong, too, so she opted for changing the subject, following the adage to "quit while you're ahead."

"Jackson said he'll be working on the new vermicomposting houses."

"Ah, gross," Tessa said and squirmed. "Let's go in and see them if we must. I suppose it's better than seeing the Jolly Green Brother sulk like a sad beanstalk. I hope it doesn't spoil lunch for us. You still want to stop somewhere and grab a bite?" The hopeful lilt almost brought on an epileptic fit of hugs on Heather's part.

They pulled into Green Life Urban Farm, a tucked-in oasis of green on the cusp of the inner city of Milwaukee. Though Green Life had satellite farms on rooftops, in community areas throughout the city, and one in a nearby town, this urban location, nestled between busy city streets, served as the headquarters. Jackson mainly worked at the headquarters, constructing things like vermicomposting "houses," taking care of the chickens and goats, running tours, or teaching classes, but often Fred, the founder, took Jackson with him to the rural farm. Heather loved to approach the farm from the parking lot and take in the exhaust with the odor of manure mixed in with the smell of herbs and flowers she could never identify, but the amalgamation of scents made her dizzy with an appreciation of nature, as if her body sensed the nutrient-rich soil and craved green leafy vegetables.

As she and Tessa got close to the doorway, a group of hulky, twenty-something men were unloading bins from a truck labeled Allison's Café. One man glanced over his shoulder and scanned Tessa. She gave a wide smile and waved. Then his eyes moved up and down Heather's legs; she felt like covering up, wishing she wore the capris she'd worn earlier, but Tessa had insisted she leave the store in her new shorts.

"Hi," Tessa said after waving. She paused.

"Let's go," Heather said, tugging on Tessa and seeing Jackson hunched over a pile of dirt. "Jackson's up ahead."

"See ya," Tessa said to the men and followed. "You're crushing my mo-jo, Mom."

"Yeah, consider it crushed. I can't handle being around when guys check you out."

"And you. I told you those shorts would look good." Tessa laughed and called out: "Hey, Jackson, what's for lunch?"

Jackson straightened and wiped his forehead, leaving a smear of mud. "Red wigglers and worm mucus, and if you wait long enough, we'll have some compost tea, which is pure liquid waste." He put his arms out wide, and to Heather's surprise Tessa walked right into the hug, even though her teal t-shirt with a dinosaur on the front now had streaks of dirt on it.

"Ugh, you smell," she said and pulled away, but she smiled, and yanked at Jackson's hand. "Come on and clean up. We're taking you to lunch."

"What? It's lunch time?" Jackson didn't look at a phone or a watch, but at the sun. "I'm not even hungry."

"Obviously not, Worm-Boy, why would you be with the smell of shit around you and all these 'wrigglers'?" Tessa tossed her hand to the mud pile. A few feet away were the new worm houses Jackson had spent so much time constructing. "Look, bro, you need to break up this Puritan work ethic a bit, because once Mom, our working government body, has left the country, it's going to be 'party all the time in the suburbs.'"

Jackson's face broke into a wide smile. He shrugged and looked at the muscled, black arms and gloved hands arranging some newspaper and food scraps on a screen between the wood slats of worm houses, "Hey, Fred, you mind if I grab some lunch?"

Fred hunched down, his face shadowed under a Green Life cap, and said, "Hell, yes, Jack, you been the mule around here for weeks, take a lunch and then some. In fact, I don't want to see your sorry face until tomorrow morning."

"But, the aquaponics –"

Fred cut him off, "Get on, you." Fred stood and stepped out from behind the wooden slats that made up the six-foot "houses." Heather thought they looked a lot like wooden scaffolding with screens of muck making the levels, like the old time Barbie townhouse she and Leann used to play with.

Fred walked toward them. "And hello to you Mrs. Barrington. I'd shake your hand for hello, but I'm filthy." Fred must have been close to sixty, but stood tall with bulging arms and legs and an almost wrinkle-free face.

"Please, call me Heather. And thank you for lending us Jackson for the afternoon."

"Absolutely, the kid needs a break. Have a good one." Fred glanced at the new delivery from a nearby restaurant. "More compost's coming."

"Fred, I can help you move that to Bed A before I go, and I planned to check the pH in the anaerobic digester this afternoon," Jackson said, moving toward the delivery, but Tessa yanked on his shirt.

"I got the psycho, Fred. Don't worry, we'll stuff him silly, and if needed, I have those large animal sedatives you gave me for occasions like this one."

"Awright, Miss Tessa," Fred said and laughed. "You got this under control, I see."

"Yep, too bad for Jackson, they come in suppository form."

"Okay, okay," Jackson said, following. "Just be quiet."

Heather trailed her children, hesitant to leave the humid, murky air of the urban farm. She watched Jackson strip off his work shirt, revealing an abdomen cut like a boxer, and slip into the new shirt Tessa must have thought to bring for him. They had both sprouted into adults, ones too well-versed in caretaking, while she addled through the last three and a half years. She couldn't hear what they said to each other, but seeing Jackson laugh and Tessa smile without a sign of her distant mask, she thought that this was what it felt like to be a typical family, one who went to lunch on a Saturday, one who picked up a son at work, and one who didn't need to be relieved by a caretaker or friend for a hurried, frazzled escape. Instead of compressing around her, today's time was opening with the day's wide blue, beautiful sky. She wanted it to last, but felt an instant pang of guilt for feeling so free of Marc. She shoved the guilt back down.

"Okay, now I'm hungry," Jackson called back to Heather. He caught her eye, and they stayed locked as if he had read her mind. His smile tightened, and Heather tried to put up her own mask, a false smile, an obvious effort. Jackson mirrored it, and the three walked on together.

Remember

April, three years ago

"Okay, Marc, now there's one small step at the top of the ramp," Heather said from behind her husband who hunched over his walker. She clenched the stability belt that circled his waist harder and rested her free hand on his left shoulder, trying to guide his weaker side to catch up.

"I'm in the kitchen, Daddy." Tessa's voice rang from around the corner. Heather could hear the nervousness in her daughter's voice, which Tessa masked with a high-pitched giggle.

Jackson clopped up the wooden ramp he and Heather's brother had constructed during Marc's long stay in rehab facilities. She glanced over her shoulder and gave a weak smile.

"I'll start unloading all of Dad's stuff. Where should I store the wheelchair?"

"I'm not going to need that wheelchair, son," Marc said, his speech clear but slower post-stroke. He stopped on the ramp, gaining his balance, as if the effort to speak and find the right words used too many neurotransmitters. Marc opened his mouth to say more, but closed it and resumed the slow climb up the incline.

Heather pointed to the garage and Jackson nodded. She and Jackson had grown so good at silent, stealth communication over the last three months. Eye blinks, mouth twitches, and slight shakes of the head – they read it all in order to keep their family moving forward. Tessa sometimes caught the cues, but many times she looked too stunned and hurt to respond, so lost in her own fifteen-year-old world that had been shocked into a newer, harsher reality.

Marc lifted his right foot, always the lead these days, up and over the step. He took a deep breath and pulled the left one along; the leg responded, hesitantly, with a stutter-step. When both feet were deposited within the safety of the walker, Heather let out a breath she hadn't realized she was holding.

"This is my home," Marc said in a tone that was more of a question than a statement.

"Yeah, Daddy, come on to the living room. We bought you this fancy lift chair," Tessa said, resting her hand on his shoulder and pecking his cheek.

"All right," Marc said.

Heather wanted to spring away from her post behind him and dodge to the bathroom to pee and sob, but she didn't. She kept her position, hand on the safety belt, and said, "Right through the kitchen, honey, see the cream carpeting. That's the living room."

"Okay," he said. Heather doubted he remembered much of the house. Mercifully, he knew all of them, right away in the hospital identifying Tessa as his "princess" and Jackson as his "scout," which was odd to Heather because Jackson had never been in the Boy Scouts, and Marc had never called him "scout" before. Then it had dawned on Heather that Marc had been a boy scout, and that must have been what his dad had called him. Heather had never met Marc's dad because he died when he was thirteen.

"Watch this, Dad," Tessa said, grabbing a remote with a button that made a blue recliner slowly crawl to an upright position. "This is service."

Marc's eyes connected with Tessa's for a fraction of a second, making Heather almost cry out, "There! There he is – there's the old Marc. I see him!" Marc had made a remarkable recovery, all things considered. He regained the ability to swallow, talk, and walk, but he was forever changed: a brain-injured, middle-aged man with withering muscles, a horrible short-term memory, and eyes that were lost. His gaze somehow tracked the world differently, often slipping into a cottony memory, pupils adrift in the past, with no more sparkle, no more connection to another human. Gone.

Tessa must have caught the brief glimpse of eyes with life because she slid her arms around Marc's waist and rested her cheek on his chest for a hug. He balanced with one hand on his walker and patted her back with the other. By the time Tessa pulled away from the embrace, her face had streaks of tears. She searched her dad's eyes again, but they held the new blankness. Heather could tell Tessa could break apart with sobs at any moment, so she leaned in and said, "Okay, honey, both hands on the walker and once you are in place in front of the chair, walk backwards into it."

Marc did as she instructed with the look of concentration on his face he had adopted since the stroke and during hours of therapy.

"Good, now do you feel the chair on the back of your legs?"

"Yes," he said.

"Okay, reach back with your right hand, keep the other on the walker and sit down," she said.

Marc sat slowly, exhaling when in the chair. "How do I make it go down?" he asked.

Tessa had recovered and placed the remote into this palm. "Here. It's really slick. This button for up and this one for down. Now don't abuse this, okay?" She smiled at Marc, but he was only focused on how to operate the chair. He pressed the button for down and the seat shifted to where he reclined comfortably. Marc sighed and leaned back, closing his eyes.

"You must be exhausted, honey. Remember, if you want to recline even more, you can. Just press this," Heather said, pointing, but he was already nodding off.

Jackson had been in and out of the house several times, carting in Marc's suitcase, the lift toilet, and other gear the rehab hospital had supplied. Tessa slipped into the kitchen and grabbed a carton of orange juice out of the fridge. Her hands shook a little while she poured.

"Tessa –"

"No, Mom, it's okay. I'm okay. Don't say anything. It'll make me cry again, okay? Just don't say anything."

Tears pooled in Tessa's eyes, but she sniffed, and wiped her eyes with the back of her hand.

"All right," Heather said. "I'm going to start puréeing things for your dad for supper. Leann sent over chicken and noodles. I'll start with that."

"I can do it, Mom," Tessa said, snaking around Heather and reaching for the blender. "So what do we do? Heat it and then blend it, or blend it and then heat it?"

There she was – the sweet Daddy's Girl. Now tears started in Heather's eyes as Tessa stood ready to pulverize food so Marc could swallow it.

"Puree first, we'll heat it up closer to time to eat," Heather choked out the words, went to her office, and leaned against the door closed behind her.

The office was the same: soft wood, large desk, her files, laptop, family pictures, bookshelves, reference books, favorite novels, and her swivel chair she'd often spin around in while working out a plot point in one of her Millicent Monvail mysteries.

Can't I just go back…please.

She'd do anything to go back, take away the stroke, forget the months in and out of rehab hospitals, and mercifully let her kids live their teen years without the drastic changes. She slid down the door and sat on the floor, quietly crying.

No, it will be fine.

The force had let Marc take an early retirement, which included a lifetime of health insurance for the family. That alone was a gift of gold. His retirement and disability insurance would cover the mortgage, and even though her income came in waves with contracts and royalties, they would be fine financially, if they lived on a budget, one that now included a part-time caretaker. She wished she could afford Ronna more than half-days five days a week, and the occasional Saturday. But the prices for in-home care were high, and she had to think about college for the kids, which was just around the corner.

Heather bit the side of her hand, then whisked away the tears. She could try to find a full-time job outside of the home, but, most likely, that would only provide enough to pay Ronna full time. It reminded her of the time before Jackson and Tessa were not in school all day – how each day had so many hours to fill, and every moment away would mean paying someone to care for them.

That was when she had really started writing because they decided not to put the kids in a childcare center, so she was home with them, all those long hours, and Millicent sprang up – an escape from the mundane. Maybe her mysteries could get her through this too. All she needed was a plan, some daily writing goals, ones she could accomplish when Ronna cared for Marc.

"Mom!" Tessa called from the kitchen.

Heather shot up and out the door, her heart pounding. Marc was up and standing within the walker, trying to move toward the bathroom.

"I have to get to the bathroom, Heather," he said. "Where is it?"

"Here, honey, right this way." She squeezed behind him and pointed to the hall off the kitchen.

"Where? It's an emergency," he said, moving forward.

She pointed again, and he started in the right direction, each step an effort to hurry. Jackson came out of the bathroom where he had just installed a raised toilet seat with handrails. Right away, in the bathroom, Heather saw the problems. The walker just made it through the doorway, but there wasn't enough room for Heather to get past Marc, so the door gaped open and he stood awkwardly in front of the toilet.

"Now what do I do?" His voice sounded confused, almost panicked.

"Here, can you turn and grab the toilet hand bars?"

"Yes, I think so. I have to go." He reached for the handle as Heather reached forward to move the walker to one side in front of the sink. Marc tried with his weaker hand to pull down his sweatpants. Heather hurried to help him, but they were too late. Shit flowed out of him in an awful stream. He gasped and fell backward onto the raised toilet, in the mess. He sighed with relief. The odor rose to Heather's nose, gagging her for an instance. Once he was on the toilet, she squeezed into the bathroom, kicking the door shut.

In another minute, Jackson knocked and said, "Mom, what can I do?"

"Did you get the shower bench set up yet?" She grabbed some disinfectant wipes and started cleaning up the side of the toilet.

Marc worked at the toilet paper roll and said, "Sorry about that, Mina, I wish you'd get paid overtime for cleaning the mess."

Heather's mind ticked through all the nurses he had had, and Mina was one from his last rehab facility. She was so focused on cleaning up the mess and Marc she decided to go with the Mina thing.

"Yeah, overtime pay would be great."

Marc chuckled, still trying to get toilet paper.

"I got the shower bench, Mom," Jackson said outside the door. "I'll bring it in."

Jackson pushed into the room, immediately putting his nose into his shoulder. Heather shifted out of the way. Jackson pulled the shower curtain open and quickly attached the bath bench to the tub.

"It's a good thing Uncle Rob installed a hand-held shower sprayer.

This bench only fits on the opposite end," Jackson muttered, slamming at the bench to get it secure.

Heather stood and dashed from the room to get paper towels and a trash bag. She inhaled her shirt sleeve to get a waft of fresh laundry scent, but the reek of shit permeated the air.

"Wait," she said to Marc.

"I want to stand," he said.

"Ah, Dad –"

Jackson nearly fell out of the tub, the rim now looking like a small mountain to Heather.

How in the world will he get his gimpy leg over the lip?

Marc stood at his walker, revealing the extent to which his sweatpants and backside were soiled. Heather choked back bile, gagging into the trash bag, but keeping her lunch down.

"Let's get you in the shower," Heather managed.

Jackson's eyes searched Heather's.

"Jackson, I'll get the clothes off, but I need help getting your dad to the shower bench."

"Okay, I'll step out, and be right back."

Heather started with guiding Marc through how to take off his sweatshirt and t-shirt.

She did a cursory cleaning with wipes of the toilet seat. "I need you to sit on the toilet again, Marc. Then I can help you get your shoes and pants off."

Marc followed the commands, groaning when he felt the smear from his sweats coat the back of his legs.

A light feeling made Heather's head swim for a few seconds.

"Ready for me, Mom?" Jackson asked from outside the door.

"I think so."

Jackson entered and they locked eyes.

"So this is Peter, huh, Mina," Marc said. "He's a lucky man to have you."

Heather shrugged, fighting tears again.

Is this how each time to the bathroom is going to be? I can't do this.

Jackson saved her. Instead of shrinking from the shit smears, the naked father, and the not- realizing-who-they-were thing, he jumped right in.

"Yeah, I'm a lucky one, Mr. Barrington. This lady's a true keeper. Let's get you in the shower now."

Live
Mid-June, present day

Heather's head lulled back and snapped up. She'd been riding in a compact car for over an hour. Her contacts at the Solace Arts Fund, Finlay and Jackie, had met her at the Glasgow airport, scooping up her bags at the luggage area and directing her into the morning outside the airport, the sky a smudgy gray.

"It takes a good hour to drive the tip of the loch," Finlay said, his brown eyes dancing. "We would have taken ye over by way of the Corran Ferry, just south of Fort William, but we thought you might like to see the loch and countryside. Also gives us a chance to talk." The lilt in Finlay's voice soothed her nerves – the accent subtle, for instance, "sooth" for "south." He must have been in his early twenties, eager with bursts of information about local writers and events. When dim rays broke through the car windows and caught his hair, Heather noticed highlights of red. "And you'll have plenty of time with the ferries and all, when you get on some excursions to the wee isles around Ardorn Estates. Have you decided on your first outing, Ms. Finch?"

Heather loved to hear only her maiden name, her writer's name, and the name she'd used when she'd danced in college. Somehow, hearing this old name, the one she'd grown up with, in this new land and from the mouth of a twenty-something Scottish boy, she felt new again, like the rolling green unfolding out her window. The scenes of pastures with puffs of sheep backs or humps of brown cows dotting the horizon made everything, every last scent of dung or burst of wind, speak to Heather in details oddly familiar but also new. She grabbed for a pen and her notebook and jotted down sensory notes she wasn't sure how she'd use during her writer's retreat, but right now, even sleep deprived and jet-lagged, she just wanted to capture initial impressions.

"And look at that Jackie, she's writing already," Finlay said to Jackie, a woman who must have been in her early forties, at least that was what Heather had gathered from their conversations. But Jackie had virtually no wrinkles, and her long, dark hair had only a couple gray strands. She pulled it back in a loose ponytail. In one email exchange, Heather had learned that Jackie's family came from India, the state of Punjab. She had light brown skin and hazel-gold eyes that flashed shapes like the swirls in marbles.

"Finn, you're so nosy sometimes," Jackie said, taking a curve quickly. Heather felt off-balanced – a little like Alice on the other side of the looking glass – with the driver on the right side as if they would veer off into cow pastures at every turn. "Let her be. Excuse the lad, Ms. Finch. He's excited. It's his first season at Ardorn, running all the writers' gatherings, retreats, or readings. I have to remind him that we cannae expect to have standing room only for the readings, that sometimes writers' circles can be small. Don't you think?"

"Please, call me Heather, and yes. I have a pretty good fan base for my mysteries, but even then, I make sure I have readings where I know I can get a certain number of people in the book store." A memory flashed in her mind of her first reading, ten years before, at Harry's Books in Milwaukee. Most of the audience consisted of Marc's coworkers from the force and Leann's friends.

"Okay, Heather, then. Be sure to call me Jackie, and Finn is just Finn."

"Finlay if you want to be formal, but only my mum calls me that."

"I have a son not far from your age," Heather said, noting how the sun finally broke through the haze, illuminating the murky-brown fields to look golden.

"Nay, that cannae be, Ms. Finch. You must be only thirty, and you couldn't have birthed a bairn when you were one yourself," Finlay said.

Heather blushed and smoothed her sweaty hands on her skirt. The road narrowed even more, and Jackie took the curve like a Nascar driver.

Finlay leaned in from the back seat, his breath hot on Heather's right ear. "Don't worry, the wynd opens up further on, so the zig-zags won't be so hard on the insides." He tapped her shoulder and slouched back in his seat.

Jackie smiled and said, "Wynd meaning narrow road, but you probably got that being a writer and all. You may need to rely on your context clues with some of the locals in Lochaline. The accents can be thick."

Heather nodded and gazed back to the landscape. She'd read so much about the area, very keen to know as much as possible about her surroundings so she'd be prepared in case of bad weather or blackouts, not that Scotland was an epicenter of storm activity, but she couldn't shake the careful adherence to predicting calamity that came with motherhood and then taking care of Marc, when each footfall could bring peril.

"So I read a lot about the Solace Arts Fund relationship with Ardorn, but can you tell me a little more about the estate, beyond where I'll stay at White Cottage." Heather yanked her hair back, her neck getting a layer of sweat from travel, and turned to be able to see both Finlay and Jackie.

"Aye, the entire estate is 5,000 acres butting up to coastline and forest, beautiful that," Jackie started, pride in her voice. "There's a farm in organic conservation that has led the way in cropping up all through Mull and other surrounding areas."

Heather's mind flashed to John Timmer who lived and worked on a nearby co-op farm. Her stomach twisted with the anticipation of seeing him, but she eased her mind because from their most recent text, he wouldn't be back in Scotland for at least another week. She'd have time to get settled and get her bearings.

Jackie continued, and Heather knew she missed something from tuning out. She bit the side of her cheek to keep focused. "Ardorn is at the forefront of sustainability. There's 1000 acres of certified sustainable forests; the wildlife is protected in the area, so you can see seals, otters, dolphins, whales, just knocking around on a kayak. Many of the cottages are rented out and there's a catering business for weddings and parties at Uihlein Hall. Many business blokes have tried to work their wee brains on how to buy up some of the land or property to get in on some more of the tourism industry, so there's been talk about selling parcels here or there, or even the White Cottage where you'll be staying, but the Ardorn Foundation seems solid. At least, we with the Solace Art Fund hope so. It's a great experience to house writers from all over the world here for retreats, and the contest you won – it's nationally known."

"Can you tell me more about the relationship between the Solace Art Fund and Ardorn Estates?" Heather asked and added in a rush, "I mean, I know the grant I won is funded by Solace Art." She trailed off, her brain soaking in the landscape and imagining misty mornings with people on horseback galloping through the channels of green, dashing into the thick bunches of woods.

"Aye," Jackie said, keeping her eyes on the road. "The Solace Art Fund is actually a branch of the Scottish National Funding for the Arts. Though the grant money given to you comes directly from Solace Art, rent for White Cottage is paid by the national fund. Ardorn is owned and run by a local business man, Steven Connolly –"

"He's the Sustainability King 'round these parts," Finlay cut in.

"Indeed," Jackie said. "Anyhow, he's all for supporting the arts, so he worked out the relationship with renting the cottage, though this may change. I'm not sure about the future of this location. We were excited to get a Yank, namely you; there are big mystery fans, specifically, big Millicent Monvail fans, on the judging committee."

"You could become the Scotland-American writer liaison, a bridge between countries!" Finlay's hand swished the air.

"See what I mean, the lad likes the grand gesture."

"I see." Heather laughed after Finlay winked at her.

They rode in silence for a few more minutes. Heather couldn't believe she was there, in another country. The only other countries she had been to were Mexico and Canada. Now, she was on another continent, and she would live here for over two months. Unbelievable. If she had a large workout room, like the studios from her college days, she'd dance to mirror her joy.

"Here we go," Jackie said. "We've entered the estate. There on the right are the main offices, and the large stone building is another one of the cottages Ardorn rents out to larger parties. We'll snake around now, through the land, and you can get a sense of how beautiful and big it is. We can give you a tour when you're ready, after you're settled in White Cottage."

As they wound through the estate, Heather caught her breath, taking in the crowds of trees in the forest and the silence, complete save for bird trills outside the hum of their car. The bruised-colored sky now cracked apart with sunlight, casting a full glow to the greenest green Heather had ever set eyes on. A pond glistened to her left with thatches of weeds and reeds poking from the surface like an old man's wiry hair. Two deer poked out of the tree line, stared at Heather with oily eyes, and darted away, quiet as cotton. Soon the car turned onto a partially paved road that had an open field on one side and more forest on the other. Peat moss, stones, and native grasses lined each side, but dots of purple and yellow shot up in patches of wildflowers and tall grasses.

"We're coming up to White Cottage," Jackie said. "Now as you can see, it's a bit of a hike for you to get anywhere on the estate, about a mile and a half walk to get to the main lodge where the Ardorn offices are, where Finn and me keep some hours there. We'll be in touch with ye, because if you be needing a car, this will be the one to use."

Heather's stomach dropped at the idea of driving a car with the steering wheel on the right side. Jackie caught her eye and let out a small laugh. "It takes getting used to, but you'll be fine."

"Or," Finlay popped up from the backseat, "you set it up with me and I'll take ye along to get your essentials. Locheline's the best bet for ye. I'll show you sights, too, if you wish it. And there'll be whole gatherings of festivals this summer from the Highland Games if you're willing to see some kilted men, there are tons of literary circles – workshops, readings, banquets throughout the summer. And –"

"Okay, Finn, she gets the idea," Jackie said. "Here we are, White Cottage, your new home for two months, Heather."

The creamy brown stone cottage butted up against another thatch of trees. Small patches of wild flowers, tall goldenrod and short tufts of blue flowers Heather couldn't name, dotted the lawn around the cottage. Heather had read it had a kitchen and small living room on the main floor and one larger master bedroom and bath on the top floor. She had seen pictures online of the writing desk in the bedroom that sat in front of a window looking out over the grounds. She'd hitched her breath when she'd seen it – the solitary place and the view reminding her of college days, before pregnancy, when she'd first read Virginia Woolf's *A Room of One's Own*, and now, all these years later, Heather was a writer herself, and for the first time in her professional life, she truly had a room of her own in which to write, one without obligations, without kids or caretaking. Tingles ran up her arm with the anticipation.

"I'll be master of the luggage," Finlay said.

"And I'll get your keys, show you the cottage," Jackie said, shaking at her tote bag until she found the ring with one key attached to a round piece of wood: so simple, so delightfully simple. Heather smoothed her travel-worn clothes and followed Jackie up the two red steps that led up to White Cottage.

The opened door revealed a cozy, yet modern cottage. Soft light peeked through the window on the main floor, casting shadows on the wood floors, painted white, making Heather think of Nantucket or Moby Dick, or lighthouses, anything nautical. A patterned rug covered the living room floor and a low cushy blue couch and a cushy chair to match angled around an electric fireplace. Heather had read that she would have all conveniences, such as DVD player, television (though only for DVDs), Internet, gas stove, and a microwave. Next to the cushy chair were a cherry wood bookcase, writing desk, and matching side table.

"Good to have the fireplace," Jackie said. "It can get nippy at night when it's rainy, even in the summer. You just may use it now and again."

"It's so cozy!"

"Aye. You want to go around on your own, or you want the pence tour?" Jackie smiled; Finlay stood sentinel next to her luggage with a boyish grin and said, "Should I take the bags up to your bedroom?"

"Thank you," Heather said. "I'll poke around on my own. Thanks, Jackie."

"I'll wait down here for ye, and then we can discuss the next couple of days to get you settled."

Heather gazed out the long window that faced one of the many ponds on the estate. She'd also seen pictures of bucolic streams, and of course, Loch Linnhe and the Sound of Mull that spilled into the Atlantic. That alone – being able to wake up and see a body of water – would do her spirit and her creative juices a world of good.

The kitchen had white walls, an iron rack with pots and pans, a black and white tile floor, and a small table at a window that also faced the pond. She imagined herself sipping afternoon tea, like Virginia

Woolf, at the little table and jotting notes in her notebook.

She left the kitchen and circled to the entryway again. This led to the one set of stairs, a curvy, low incline where she instinctively felt the need to hunch a bit as she climbed.

She and Finlay shouldered each other on the stairs.

"You're all set up there, Ms. Finch – ah, Heather," Finlay said, a blush coloring his pale skin.

"Thank you," Heather said, turning the corner at the top of the stairs to the master bedroom. Her breath caught in her throat. The bedroom, nestled under slanted light blue walls, covered the whole top floor. The same white-painted wood floors creaked under her feet. The bed had a wrought iron frame and fluffy green and blue pillows that matched a thick quilt. She opened the closet and an extra blanket and one other quilt were stacked on a high shelf. She walked to the window, again, facing a portion of the pond, and beyond that the forest sprouted like broccoli tops. Another smaller writing desk, oak wood, would position her facing the window as she composed. She could hardly wait to get writing. Here, tucked under the low ceiling, surrounded by soft, delicate things – like the porcelain vases and knickknacks painted with blue flowers that decorated the end tables and bookshelves – this very place would be her room, her sanctuary, where she could sort through the events of the last three years. Her ideas would spring from her like a bubbling fountain. She was more than ready to retreat into her writing world. Here, she could imagine and create.

Heather bounced on the bed one time and could not stop smiling.

Live
Mid-June, present day

Finally, the sun came up. Daylight started early in the Scotland summer, but Heather's first night in White Cottage lasted longer than the shadows she'd watched on her ceiling as the moon poked from behind cloud cover. She'd known jet lag would cause her system to be off, but she hadn't expected to be awake almost the entire night. Sleep had come reasonably fast, but she woke at 1 a.m., unclear of where she was, and then she'd been up since then, staring at the ceiling, thinking through plot points for the last chapters of her fifth Millicent Monvail mystery with the nagging thoughts about how many murders could happen on Madeline Island without the federal guard coming and sequestering the island for housing so many sociopaths? Millicent seemed to know what Heather was thinking and refused to let go. Thoughts of the specific way to wrap up the last chapters bounced around on jetlag of their own. Heather found herself fighting Millicent for control over ideas and where she wanted to place her attention. Each turn felt ridiculous and contrived, but she'd gotten out of bed, hammered out an outline for the final chapters, and vowed to make this book the last cozy mystery she'd ever write.

Maybe it was the fresh, salt air, or the craggy coastline she'd passed on her way to Ardorn Estates, or the absolute quiet of the night she'd just passed, or the feeling that she was now in an ancient land, but she felt like she must respond to this landscape of new experiences because something hidden called out to her to find it –

A new character?

A new story?

A new novel?

A new beginning?

She laughed at herself for thinking of that cliche. Still, Scotland with its undulating lands and wind-whipped shores could be her land of true mystery. No more would she make up her own generic ones.

Suddenly, unsolicited memories of caring for Marc collected in the corners of her mind, waiting like unearthed maggots. That image had actually popped into her mind at 3:30 a.m. Now, drinking coffee and staring out her kitchen window at the wildflowers and sparkling pond, it felt grotesque and all too apt for the myriad of squirmy feelings that surfaced when she reflected on her last three years with Marc.

Heather had two hours before she was scheduled to meet Finlay at the lodge. Instead of writing, she opened her laptop and logged on to her email. Her inbox bulged with junk, but a Facebook notification made her stomach tighten. She had a new message from John Timmer.

Hey, Heather Finch,

Welcome to Scotland! I'm sending you this message from thirteen thousand feet, just about to do my first jump of the day here in England. Free fall in the next few minutes! I hope you're getting settled. My move date from this jump zone to the one in Scotland may be getting pushed up. I'll know more soon, maybe even after I hit the ground. You just might find me in your Ardorn woods before we thought. Beautiful country, that's for sure. I'm anxious to get back to the farm house. You'll have to come and see it when you're not brooding like a good writer. Gotta go. Free fall imminent. Catch ya later, J

Heather's stomach knotted again. He'd sent the message twenty minutes earlier. So that meant John Timmer was most likely in the sky right now, or at least she assumed so. She had no idea how long it took to drop out of a plane. The thought of him fighting wind currents with his body and then with an air-filled canopy sent a miniscule adrenaline rush through her body. Thinking about the free fall would be enough for her; there was no way she would ever jump from a plane from thousands of feet above ground. She thought about her most recent text from Leann, saying: *any Timmer contact yet? Let's hope for full body.*

The text had made Heather laugh and flush with nervous embarrassment at the same time. Heather wanted to focus, eliminating all distractions from her writing. Just because John was 1) male, 2) unmarried – he had told her in one of their early chats that he was divorced with twins – and 3) soon to be in her present location on the planet, did not automatically mean anything beyond their friendship would develop. In fact, it would complicate her goals for the writing retreat. Her intent was to see John a few times, maybe he could show her some sights – the thought of venturing on her own through the uninhabited islands or even the cities intimidated her. He could be a friendly contact, but she was sure he was busy, and dating someone for that matter.

Ding.

Heather jumped. John had sent her a chat message on Facebook.

She chugged a gulp of coffee and read.

Feet planted on solid ground. Yeah, just found out from my mates that I'll be packing up. I could see you as early as the day after tomorrow, if you're keen. I don't want to be pushy, but it'll be a trip. Haven't set eyes on you since, hell, I can't remember? I could swing by Ardorn and meet at your cottage since you don't have wheels. What do you think?

Instant sweat beaded on Heather's forehead and under her arms.

How should she answer? She knew what Leann would say, *hell yes, and did you know I have a bedroom at the cottage?* She chuckled at her ardent thought, one she hadn't entertained in three to four years. Long years.

Heather wiped away the sweat on her forehead and typed words antithetical to what she had just determined about only seeing John Timmer a few times.

Hi, John,

I can't believe you wrote to me right before you JUMPED OUT OF A PLANE! Yes, my feet are firmly planted on Scottish ground. I'd love to see you the day after tomorrow. Have you been to Ardorn before? I'd give you directions, but I'm afraid you'd be better off dropping from a plane into the pond behind my cottage.

Heather smiled to herself. Did she sound fun and even flirty? Who was this emerging woman? Definitely not someone she recognized. A memory blossomed in her chest and curled down again, like a fast-forward film clip of a morning glory opening its petals and then closing for the day: she used to flirt with boys. Maybe she even flirted with Marc way back when she danced and laughed at things much more freely than she did now.

Ding.

Heather's heart jumped at the response from John Timmer. John Timmer. John Timmer –

Suddenly the name became like the horizontal scroll of news at the bottom of a television screen during CNN.

Hah! That'd be a deal. Talk about dropping in – ba-dum-bum (or however you spell the drum roll after a bad pun). To answer your question, yes, I've been to Ardorn a few times. Once for a wedding, and a few times I've led tourist groups on kayak tours around the waterways on the estate. I know Steven Connolly. He's the econ-friendly Sherpa who runs Ardorn so efficiently there's almost no carbon footprint. Anyway, I'm getting away from myself. I can swing by around midday on Wednesday if you're cool with it?

Again, Heather didn't think about the outline she'd just written for the last Monvail chapters, and the thought of starting something new got put back into the compartment in her mind. She answered.

Sounds great. Here's my cell number if something changes.

She typed the number and hit send before she could change her mind.

It's a plan, Heather Finch. See ya, J.

A plan. Not the plan in which she saw herself walking the rocky coast of Loch Linne with a notebook in hand, or hiking through the woods with a notebook in hand, or sitting outside her cottage, gazing at the pond with a notebook in hand. Now Wednesday became the pivot point of the hours ahead.

Even if John Timmer became only a friend, that would be fine. When was the last time she did something with friends besides Leann and Brian? A new friendship could help her tap into the energy she needed to write. At least that was what she told herself before she went upstairs to shower.

Two hours and two miles later, Heather strolled into the lodge to find Finlay piling pastries on a china plate from a luxurious buffet table set up in the main room, which had light wood floors and walls, ornate rugs, and low, cozy furniture circling a fireplace. Bookshelves lined the walls leading to hallways and tall windows overlooking the picturesque countryside. Heather would love to come to an office in this building every day. She wondered how many rooms branched out from the meandering halls, and what happened up the wide staircase with a hunter green runner?

"Ms. Finch!" Finlay said through a bite of scone.

"Heather."

"Aye, Heather," he said, chewing. "Might I interest you in some confiscated sweets from the buffet of some of the Mull's biggest muckety mucks?"

"No, thank you," she said. "What's all this for?" The spread was delectable with heaps of scones, cheese and jelly danishes, bagels, and coffee that tempted her jetlagged-addled brain. "Although, if it's all right, I will have a coffee."

"Help yourself," Finlay said. "This is for the board meeting for the Ardorn Estates. I think they have weighty issues to discuss, and I say this only because of the abundance of sweets. Melissa, she's with the Solace Art Fund, is in on the meeting. She'd love to fill you with sweets."

"I wouldn't want to intrude –"

"Nay, get your coffee, you look a bit pale. I assume you slept like shite. Pardon my language, but I know jetlag makes you drag ye bones, and you're far from hame." For reasons unknown, Finlay's pronunciation, "hame," not "home", gave Heather a pang of lonesomeness for Jackson and Tessa, even if things were now strained at times with Tessa.

"Yes, coffee would help, but I've already had a half of a pot. This smells so good though," she said, filling a cup and adding a splash of cream.

"The meeting people won't even know we were here." Finlay gave her a wide smile.

"So we don't have to take this to go?" Heather smiled back.

Finlay started to say something in reply, but the door to one of the conference rooms opened. The board meeting spilled out into the main room, leaving Heather and Finlay standing awkwardly near the buffet with their hands in the cookie jar. For all of Finlay's previous jokes about the "muckety mucks," he looked stymied and guilty. Heather couldn't help but feel protective – the boy matched Jackson's age after all.

She stepped forward, toward the woman she recognized from online communication as Melissa from the Solace Art Fund.

"Hi, Melissa," Heather said, putting her hand up in a wave and then extending it when Melissa came near her.

"Oh, Heather, it's a pleasure to see you here! Are you getting settled in White Cottage?" Melissa's eyes sparkled.

"Yes, thank you, and Finlay kindly agreed to take me to Lochaline to get some supplies. It really hit me how isolated I am."

"Aye, but I'm sure it will prove fruitful for your writing," Melissa said.

"So this is our guest writer," a man said as he crossed the room. He turned to shake hands with someone, but broke away from another conversation to make his way toward Heather's group.

"Hello," he said, taking Heather's hand in a firm grasp. "I'm Steven Connolly. I work here at Ardorn."

"Why that's the understatement of the century," Melissa said. "Steven here owns Ardorn, and this is indeed, Heather Finch, the writer who won the grant for the summer."

"A pleasure," he said, clasping her hand with both of his hands before letting go. Steven stood at eye level with Heather, so not tall for a man, but his presence made up for it. His light red hair had faint bits of gray peppering his temples; his pale green eyes caught the light, making them look like sea glass catching colors, depending on the angle. His arms and legs bulged with muscles like he'd been working outdoors most of his life. Heather figured he was about fifty, but by staying in that kind of shape, he looked forty.

"It's nice to meet you, Steven. I love White Cottage already," she said, reddening a little under his gaze.

His eyes swept over her intently as he said, "Want to buy it?"

"What?" she said, face even hotter.

"Wait a minute, sir," Finlay broke in, "you aren't actually doing it, are ye? You aren't going to sell White Cottage? What about the art fund?"

"No need to get upset, Finn," Melissa said. "I'll look into if the Solace Art Fund can buy it, but I cannae make any promises. In fact, I should go and work at the numbers straightaway. Nice to see you, Heather."

While Melissa walked away, Finlay waved to Heather as if to say, "hang on," and chased after Melissa. Heather turned back to Steven, not sure how to proceed with conversation. Should she bring up John Timmer? No, that would lead to more conversation, and with those eyes searching her face, she felt too much heat rising off her body.

What was going on with her? Why did every man within reasonable vicinity flick a switch in her body? Maybe Leann was right, maybe her near celibate phase was coming to an end. But if Steven was close to fifty that meant he was that much closer to stroke age. Heather stamped out the thought and realized he had said something else to her.

"I'm sorry, could you repeat that," she said. "I must have been thinking about buying White Cottage." She couldn't think of any other thing to say.

"Oh, you on the market?" his mammoth shoulders shrugged up and down, and his eyes had an impish sparkle.

"Well, yes, I suppose I am, for a place to live, that is," she started, surprised by the flirtatious nature of the banter, "but I'm American. I can't just buy a cottage in Scotland."

"Sure ye can!" he said, as if he was the master of the civilized world. "I know people in real estate, and we could work out a plan. You rent for a bit while you get your visa, and then you buy it. I cannae think of a better buyer than a beautiful American woman. The estate's stock would go up with you living on the grounds."

What in the world? Heather couldn't think of the last time a man called her beautiful. Now this cocky Scottish highlander had her in his charms; her mind flashed to the idea of living here, buying the cottage, and walking this lush land every day. *Again, what in the world?*

"But," he said, stepping closer, "ye might have a husband who wouldn't want you leaving to buy a cottage in the land of ghosts and whiskey." His face broke into a wide grin. The man had charisma oozing out of his pores.

"Yes, I did have a husband," she said, her voice breaking, even now, after all the heartache with Marc, "but he died after a long struggle, just six months ago."

"Oh," Steven said with eyes filled with concern, "you need to heal then." He took her hand again, patting the back of it, this time in a brotherly way. "I'm sorry to hear this, Heather. I've never been married, so I don't know the kind of loss you've been feeling." He let go and sighed. "I do know Ardorn is a place for healing. We work every day to heal the land, and as much as it pains me to sell White Cottage, I'm also a businessman. I need to look to the future and though I've turned some profit by renting it out to guests and the Solace Art Fund each summer, I hope to sell to buy up some buffer land to the north."

"Buffer land?" Heather dabbed her eyes after Steven released her hand.

"Aye, it's these meaty chunks of nature linking places like Ardorn to other natural settings in Scotland. You link them up, and you have a migratory nature preserve – critters, insects, native plants all have a continuum of nature to thrive in, and that's something in this day and age, where humans are occupying almost every inch of the planet. But, I'm getting away from myself. You need a place to live, and White Cottage could be the answer."

Yes, she thought, that was true – was Steven Connolly an environmental Sherpa/soothsayer? She needed a new home, but she also needed something else. She didn't know how to identify it – not yet – but something new. Her life could be a springtime blossoming before her, without a measurable way to even define it, but all she had to do was step forward and it would take – her whole life would take – a completely different direction.

"You're right," she said. "It's been a difficult time for me, so maybe White Cottage could be just what I need. I sold my house, and right now I have nowhere to live after this retreat." The words settled in her mouth while her brain buzzed, startled by sending a message to form the sentences: what was she thinking? Move to Scotland!

"Really?" he said, his eyebrows shooting up in surprise, as if their meeting rang of serendipity on both a romantic and pragmatic level. "Then I say you let me buy you dinner this weekend, and I'll convince you of the merits of White Cottage and the Highlands themselves."

Finlay walked up and stood between Heather and Steven; he snatched a pastry, chewing and eyeing the two middle-aged people in a lascivious way.

"Oh, um, I'm not sure," Heather stammered.

"How about Friday? I could pick you up about 7:30? If you'd like to sample some of the delicacies at our restaurant, Near the Loche, you will most certainly fall in love. Imagine being able to dine at such a place each weekend by sharing the estate grounds with the restaurant. So, 7:30 okay with you?"

Finlay cleared his throat and shuffled.

"All right. That sounds nice. Thank you." Heather put out her hand to shake Steven's, wanting to end the conversation before she turned the color of the jelly inside the danishes.

"Wonderful!" he said. "I look forward to it. Good day to you." Steven nodded to both of them and strolled away with a display of confidence owning the room.

When he had cleared the building, Finlay let out a low whistle. "Blimey, he fancies you a lot, Ms. – er – Heather."

Heat rose up her chest and to her face. "No, he's just being polite. Plus, he's a businessman and he sees me as a potential buyer for White Cottage."

"Whoa, I step out for a wee minute and you're all the sudden thinking of buying the cottage? I knew Ardorn has some magic in its woods, but this is fast magic."

"It's entertaining to think about," Heather said. "Anyway, let's get going to Lochaline. I don't want to take up too much of your time, Finlay."

"Nay, it's my pleasure, so take as much time as you need, and entertaining is the word, Ms. Finch, you're shaking things up around here is what I think."

Remember
May, three years ago

"Do I go to bed now, Heather?" Marc asked. Heather had struggled with his shirt, cursing once again that she hadn't finished the laundry because his pullover tops were buried in the heaps of dirty piles. Though she had gotten rid of most of Marc's button down shirts, a few lined his closet still, even though the tiny buttons proved impossible for his lack of manual dexterity.

"It's not bed time, honey. It's mid-day. Our friends Leann and Brian are coming over with their kids. We're cooking out!" Heather didn't recognize the falsetto in her voice. The cookout would be the first gathering at the house since Marc's stroke. Heather said she'd provide the meat, grill, and beer, despite Leann's protests. Leann said she and her family would bring all the sides. Heather knew that would be enough to feed the group.

"Brian. I told you about how my buddy Brian and I started a rock band in high school, didn't I?" Marc said, sitting on the edge of his hospital bed and losing his focus, his mind tracking backwards as it often did.

"Oh, yes, but you can tell me again, if you want," Heather said, pressing her palm to his lower back, their signifier that he should gain his balance and stand.

Guide, guide, guide, she told herself, get him to his electric chair with the newspaper, and get on with it.

"I don't want to bother you, but we really did cut up on the stage,

Brian and me, and the other two. Gary and Paul. But Brian and I were the real head turners," Marc said as he ambled to the living room with his walker.

Heather tuned out and went through the list of things that still needed to be done: check the marinating chicken, put ice in the cooler for the beer, wipe the deck chairs, go over the toilet and sink in the bathroom, shower, and clip Marc's toenails if she had time. She doubted he'd want sandals on outside, but she never knew what requests would come, and if he wanted the sandals, his toenails were disgusting. Finally, she eased Marc into the chair, and stood another half minute while he looped about the band again. She felt Tessa at her back.

Tessa smiled at Marc and pecked his cheek.

"Sorry to interrupt you, Dad," Tessa said, "but I need Mom's advice on the grill. Brian and Leann should be here any time."

"Heath, did you find Brian Gilmore from the band to come here today?" Marc's vacant eyes danced for a fraction of a second, but then he seemed to forget what he'd said, so Heather decided not to answer. She picked up the newspaper and handed it to him, saying, "today's paper," and walking away before he launched into another teenage memory.

Once in the kitchen, Heather said, "What's the grill question?"

"It's not really a grill question," Tessa said, her voice thick with annoyance before the cookout even began. "Please don't make me hang out with the brothers anymore."

Leann and Brian had twin boys, Carson and Elliot, ages twelve, and one girl, Ashley, age ten.

"Why?" she asked.

"Mom, they stare at me constantly and say the dumbest things. I'll go do Ashley's make-up and hair, but put Jackson on the rodents."

"Tessa! Be nice."

"Fine, I'll be nice, but I don't even want to be outside. I'll stay with Dad inside."

"No, he can sit on the deck. I think it'll be good for him."

"How do you know what's good for him?"

"What?" Heather's heart raced. She started going through her list of tasks. "I don't have time for this. Go wipe down the deck chairs."

Tessa huffed and stomped away with a scowl on her face.

Heather's body almost shook from the encounter. Tessa had grown so fiery in the last month; each thing Heather said made her bristle and bark. She started unloading the beer from the fridge and snapped off the top of a Point beer, chugging a quarter of it, and feeling instantly better.

The house phone rang once and stopped. Heather figured it was for Jackson, but a few minutes later, he nearly spilled down the stairs wearing an expression of wanting to get off the phone. He nodded, saying, "Sure, Mr. Evens, good talking to you, too. Yeah, here's my mom."

Evens? Who was Mr. Evens?

"Hello," Heather said as she scoured the sink area with disinfectant wipes where the chicken had sat. "This is Heather."

"Hi, Heather, this is Thomas Evens, I know your husband through a national police organization called Safe Night."

"Hi, um, I don't want to be rude Mr. Evens, but I don't want to make a donation at this time."

"Oh, no, it's not about giving money. Marc and I usually get together for pick-up basketball games at the conventions, and I sent him several emails about the one coming up next month. I hadn't heard back, and I thought it was odd, so anyway."

"Oh! I'm sorry, I didn't recognize the name, but it rings a bell now. Yes, Marc talked about the conventions sometimes. I didn't realize it was about that time of year again."

"Yep, every summer. It's hard to believe. Is Marc there so I could talk to him? Your son said it would be better if I spoke with you."

Heather took another sip of beer, preparing to deliver the news. "He is here, Mr. Evens, but he had a stroke back in February, and he can talk and walk with a walker, but he's not the same. He's not able to carry on conventional conversations much these days. It's more listening to him go over things in his past because his long-term memory is intact, but his short-term memory is virtually gone. He doesn't talk on the phone for that reason, and I don't know if he'd remember you. I'm so sorry."

It amazed Heather that she didn't sob at conveying this information, but instead, she spoke matter-of-factly, not out of apathy, but routine. She turned her face from the receiver and swigged her beer.

"Whoa, I'm sorry to hear this. Man, I don't understand. Marc was always in perfect physical condition," Thomas Evens said.

And this Heather was used to: she knew how to nod and sympathize now with people who related having a stroke to a more elderly person, the ones who turned ashen with the news that one of the fittest in their age bracket had succumbed to a stroke. Her shock passed with each day, and even though she had moments of fear, wondering how she'd keep up caring for Marc, Heather took on the responsibility very much like she approached motherhood; she didn't analyze it too much; she simply relied on doing. Lists stood ready to be checked off; tasks were addressed as they piled up.

Heather finished her beer just as she hung up with Thomas Evens. Her head felt instantly lighter, and she felt more capable to get on with the cookout. But before she dove in, she checked on Marc dozing in his recliner, made sure Tessa had cleaned the deck chairs, and put Jackson on lighting the charcoals on the grill. Her shower could wait.

The phone call had rattled her and made her realize she had put off going into Marc's email long enough: what if an outstanding bill notice sat waiting in his inbox? What other distant acquaintance hadn't heard about Marc's condition? The weight of it propelled her to sit at Marc's desk, which collected magazines and dust in the corner of his old office, now made their "bedroom" consisting of Marc's hospital bed and her twin bed. Marc would never climb the stairs again to reach the master bedroom. Heather shook off the thoughts and logged into his account. When she saw the inordinate amount of emails, fresh feelings of inadequacy sprung up inside of her.

How would she ever keep up with everything?

She scanned and deleted junk mail, checking the time and deciding, in lieu of ashower, she would simply slather her body in lotion and tie her hair in a ponytail. She started to click on an email from Marc's cousin in Ohio, when she accidentally went into the "Drafts" folder. Queued in the "Drafts" there was an email addressed to Heather. Specifically, the subject line read "Dear Heather."

Heather's heart pounded in her chest. Her optimistic side yearned for this to be a love letter from the old Marc (the draft date was January 1st of that year), but even that made her feel as if her head may blow off. What kind of emotional whirl-i-gig might result from getting such a letter from a husband who no longer existed? Her fearful side, the one that didn't want to unearth any family strife, worried about contentious content. Had they had a fight on New Year's Day? Heather couldn't remember. She clicked on the draft and sunk lower in the chair, reading and biting her lip to the point of drawing blood.

Dear Heather,

It's the beginning of the year and time for resolutions. This year I'm determined to tell you the truth. The truth is I've been a coward. Soon, I will send this. I've promised myself. I can't go on lying to you. You deserve better. The truth is I've fallen in love with someone else. I didn't mean for this to happen. I tried to resist my feelings by throwing myself into work, workouts, house projects, and the kids, but it didn't work. The problem is I still love you. You have been such a guiding force for me for so long I didn't know I could even imagine living without you. Somehow along the way I became this man, the man who has an affair. I am so very sorry. I don't know how to proceed, but it is not fair to you if you only have part of me, where I'm thinking too much about Erin. Though I've tried not to be in love with her, I am. We have been seeing each other for about a year. I should have told you sooner, but you and the kids are my family. I didn't want to break any hearts, especially yours and Tessa's, my girls, but I can't go on deceiving you. You will always be my first love, the mother of our beautiful children, who are so strong and beautiful mainly because of you. I cannot forgive myself for what I've done, but I know I have to move forward, and the path in front of me is something I must pursue with Erin. We should sit down and talk very soon. I

Heather stood and paced, leaning over the trash getting ready for vomit that never came. An affair? He had an affair for an entire year without her knowledge. What else did he plan to write?

What the fuck else was going to be after the "I"?

Hot tears ran down her face; she burst from the room, shot into the kitchen, and grabbed a bottle of Scotch from a high shelf, thinking inanely how silly it was to keep it up so high. If Tessa or Jackson wanted to nip some hard liquor, they could reach it.

"Mom –" Jackson said to her back. "Hey, where are you going?"

"Upstairs." She took the stairs two at a time and locked herself in her old bedroom. She hadn't grabbed a glass, so she downed two chugs in one furious swig. Her mind counted ninety seconds before one of her children knocked on her door.

"Ah, Mom, are you okay?" Jackson asked. "The Millers will be here any time."

"I know," she said, downing another gulp. Fuck this. Fuck this bullshit.

"You okay?" Normally the pleading in Jackson's voice would have melted her, but not now. Not now that adultery loomed like a gallows.

That motherfucker slept with another woman. ERIN – for an entire year!

"I'm fine. I'll be down in a bit." She didn't recognize a tinny quality to her voice. Her head spun, but she drank again. Another drink. Another year. Another bathroom visit with Marc unable to care for himself.

Where was this Erin when Marc couldn't wipe his own ass?

Heather paced the room and took two more sips, slowing down on the liquor intake out of habit. Tessa slammed on the door.

"What are you doing, Mom?" her voice harsh and her knock on the door a falling ax.

"I'm drinking. It's a party after all," Heather said. She giggled, despite her rage at Marc.

"You're drinking? What's wrong with you? Dad needs help in the bathroom."

"I got it," Jackson yelled from downstairs.

"Okay," Tessa hollered back with an edge. "Jackson's helping him, Mom, but you need to come out."

Heather flew at the door handle, yanking it open and staring at her daughter.

"Your sweet daddy loved another woman before he had his stroke. Did you know that? Is he so perfect in your eyes now, Tessa? He had an affair with someone named Erin for an entire year."

Tessa blinked and shook her head. "That's not true. You're only saying that."

"It IS true," Heather yelled, slamming her hand on the door.

"You're lying. You want to make excuses for not taking care of him." Tears tumbled out of Tessa's eyes; she clenched her fists and took a step closer to Heather. "He would never do anything to destroy this family."

"NOT TRUE!" Heather screamed in a shrill voice. "He's a lying sack of shit. He didn't care about this family." But as soon as Heather said the words, she regretted them, knowing they weren't true. Even in his confessional email, Marc's devotion came through.

"You just don't want to be married to him now that he's had a stroke." Tessa yelled. Splotches of red flared on her cheeks; her blonde hair framed her face when she shook it out in fury.

"Stop it, stop it, stop it. You don't know what you're talking about. Go look at his email. It's on his computer." Heather's scream wasn't as shrill, but her throat stung already from yelling. Her teeth started to chatter, and her head spun.

"You're lying. I don't need to see it. And if he did sleep with someone else, it was probably because you hardly showed him any affection before his stroke. You were always writing or running around thinking you were mother of the fucking year, and he was on his own."

Slap.

Heather reacted, without a hesitation. Her hand had come up and slapped Tessa's left cheek. Instantly, tears filled Tessa's eyes, and a red streak appeared on her face. Movements and sounds came from downstairs – shuffling feet, greetings, glassware set on countertops, the slow metallic click of Marc's walker on the kitchen floor.

Tessa turned and ran to her room, slamming the door, and screaming, "I hate you!"

Instead of mothering-up, apologizing, and begging forgiveness for how she'd acted, Heather swallowed one more hot sip of Scotch, and then she screamed back, "You don't need to scream that, Tessa, because I know it! You ungrateful little girl!" Then she slammed the door of her old bedroom and kicked at the covers of her bed.

Live
Mid-June, present day

Wednesday. Heather had spent the last two days not writing. She had paced her cottage at odd hours, listening to the whispery sounds of the trees outside, rearranging the dishes in the kitchen cabinet, and looking at the spines of books that lined the shelves. She had tried to walk around the estate to get her juices flowing, but she ended up wondering what Wednesday would bring, when John Timmer came over to her cottage about midday.

The clock on the shelf next to the fire place had ticked with menace at the wee hours of the morning, and now that noon approached the ticks took on an anxious clip. Would midday mean exactly noon? Instead of walking another pace route on the wood of the ground floor, Heather went upstairs to check her reflection for the tenth time in the full-length mirror.

She stood to the side and studied her backside, which didn't look awful in the new shorts Tessa had picked out. She tugged at the seam, yanking the bottoms down more on her thighs, but the length didn't expand, the shorts a fair deal shorter than her comfort required. Heather turned and studied herself in the blue-gray v-neck t-shirt; it hugged her breasts more than she was used to, so she tugged again and swore to herself: if she wanted to look like a dumpy writer, she had plenty of baggy clothes she could change into, but she wanted to look appealing for some reason. Again, not that anything would lead to anything with John Timmer; she simply wanted to appear to be more put together than she actually felt. No reason to come off like a basket-case widow with enough baggage to check a pro-sports team onto an international flight.

Knock – one loud one, followed by two quick raps on the front door of the cottage.

John Timmer.

Heather fluffed her hair, smoothed her clothes, and tried not to run down the stairs. She pulled back the curtain of the front window to confirm it was indeed John Timmer and not some wayward hiker come to stab her to death.

As Leann had suspected, John's middle school height grew into a fine 6'2". His upper body form, muscular but not bulging, was evident under his tight-fitting gray t-shirt, and his legs were long with defined slopes and tight bends.

Stop, answer the door, and stop checking out his body.

She opened the door and offered a smile that didn't have one note of pretense.

"John!" she said, putting her arms out wide.

"Hey, Heather Finch. Wow!" He hugged her back, a quick, platonic embrace between people who had grown up together. In that flash, Heather felt the firmness of his back muscles.

"Come in. It's great to see you," she said.

"Yeah, no kidding. It's been some years, that's for sure. You look great! And this place is amazing." He scanned the cottage, smiling. He had brown-blond hair that had a subtle undertone of red made lighter by the sun and fair skin, but he hadn't burned in the summer sun; miniscule freckles dotted his face, making him seem more like fifteen than forty-two. His features were all large and welcoming: hazel eyes, a wide nose, a strong jaw, and full, inviting lips.

Stop.

"Have a seat, John," she said, clearing her throat nervously. "Do you want some tea?"

"Not quite tea time." He laughed. "But yeah, I'll have a nip."

"I'll put the kettle on." The brief retreat to the kitchen gave Heather a chance to catch her breath. What was she feeling? She couldn't slow her heart rate down even with deep yoga breaths. She filled the kettle and set the water to boil. Grabbing the tea basket, she steadied her nerves by focusing on the flavors: vanilla chai, sleepy peach, arousing green-ginseng. Arousing. Arousing.

"How you settling in, Heather?" John's voice came from the couch in the living room.

"Um, okay." She breathed in and walked back into the same room with John Timmer. John Timmer. John Timmer.

"Okay, let's see your poison," he said, standing.

"What?"

"The tea flavors, what do you got?"

"Right. Sorry, I've been working on my last mystery and you said poison, which made my mind flip to the chapters I'm not writing, and someone just got poisoned." She thrust the basket in his direction.

"Ah. Like I said, I don't want to get in the way of your writing." He flipped through the teas. "I'll go for the green-ginseng."

Heather blushed. What should she say next? Was this middle school? The tied tongue was about to do her in.

"There's the kettle. I'll be back."

"Or I can follow." He followed, and Heather felt his eyes running the length of her body.

She struggled through getting the mugs, filling them, and setting them on the kitchen table.

"The view is great," John said, bending and opening the curtain so they both caught a glimpse of ducks drifting on the pond. "So why aren't you writing the mystery chapters, if I may ask. Thanks for the tea." John sat down and blew on his steaming mug.

So as not to feel like an Amazon hovering over the table, Heather slid into the chair across from John.

"I don't know if it's the jet lag or something else, but I haven't been able to write a word. I planned to finish the mystery and get a chunk of something new done while I'm here. It is a writing retreat after all." She forced a smile, but suddenly felt like bursting into tears for some unknown reason. John searched her face with an interest she hadn't seen on Marc's face for years, if ever. John's delicious mouth turned up in a half smile, and then he bit his bottom lip in a way that made Heather stop looking and concentrate on the business of cooling her tea (sleepy peach) with steady puffs.

"Jet lag will get ye," John started, sounding Scottish, "but it could be you have another story in you. Maybe. Hard to tell, Heather Finch. But since you aren't writing much yet, I won't feel like I'm keeping you from anything. How about we go out on those kayaks you have parked near the pond and take in some of this glorious day?"

"Kayaks. Yes. That's a great idea. That's a perfect remedy for writer's block – go and live, rather than think about living and writing about it." It happened again, tears pooling in her eyes.

John connected with her eyes, his face concerned. "You've had a hard time of it. Sorry about Marc. I know I wrote you condolences on Facebook, but that seems so lame. I wanted to say it face to face. I'm sorry he died, but I wonder if he would have wanted it that way. I can't imagine if he had been like he used to be, before the stroke, active and fit, I can't imagine he'd want to burden you much longer. I'd think he'd want to move on."

Finally, someone not afraid to say it. She had grown so used to people tiptoeing over the topic of Marc, now that she faced some honesty she wanted to stand up and shout, "Thank you!"

"You're right about that, John." The rest of the sentence caught in her throat. The tears rolled down her cheeks, and she brushed a few away with a quick swipe of the back of her hand.

"Hey, I didn't come here to make you cry, sweet lady. I came here to show you around. If you're keen?" John stood up and she met him standing face to face, though she had to tilt her head up to make eye contact. John reached out and hugged her again, longer than the first time, and pecked her cheek right where a tear ran. "We're school-kid friends, remember? We grew up together. I'm not going to let you flail here in a foreign land. Gulp down your tea and meet me at the pond. I'll get the kayaks ready. Sound okay?" He pulled away and Heather missed his arms on her back already.

"Okay," she said.

Once outside, Heather's eyes adjusted to the sunlight. The lawn around her cottage rolled into native grasses, brambles, and bracken at the edge of the woods. She jogged the slight incline that ran to the edge of the pond. John had the two kayaks perched on the shore next to weed tangles and shoots of water plants. John ran his hands along the tops of a spiky black and white flower that looked like a toothbrush.

"Common sedge," he said as he took the flower top in his fingertips.

"You know all the names of the plants around here?"

"Not all, but some. That patch over there," he said pointing to more grasses with purple hairy stalks, "that's purple moor grass. I know the prevalent ones for the most part. Other ones I know from the wildflower mixes we throw out in bunches for our roadside gardens leading up to the farm."

"Wow," Heather said, putting a hand up to shield the sun from her eyes. The group of ducks they saw earlier paddled off down the pond, leaving a rippling wake. "And this," she added, bending toward the mucky weeds at the edge of the pond, where her ankle-cut hiking boots sank, "this rare species of plant is called pond-weed totalis."

John cracked up and said, "See you're getting the hang of it. You're in new territory here, Heather Finch, it's all fake-it- till-you-make-it round these parts. Climb in. Your ticket to instant serenity awaits."

John took her hand and guided her into the kayak; then he handed her the oar.

"Off you go," he said and shoved the kayak into the sparkling water.

Heather twisted and started to say, "What about you?" But John had already strode into the water, hiking boots and legs submerged to his upper thighs, pushed the slim boat, and leapt into his kayak while holding onto his oar.

They paddled in near silence – the only sounds were the alternating plunk-plunk when the oars hit the water's surface. After several minutes, Heather's upper arms grew tired, but she didn't want to appear to be a wimp. So many people, at least John Timmer and Steven Connolly, were so fit, so she willed herself again to use this time not only to write, but to get in better shape.

John sidled his kayak right next to Heather, laid his oar across his lap, and hooked his fingers on the lip of her seat. "Wanna drift a bit?" he asked.

"Sure," she said, relieved. She followed his lead and did the same with her oar. "I read in some of the literature on Ardorn that this pond is about five miles long. Well, it was listed in kilometers, but I figured the conversion. Five miles." She gave a small smile and caught John staring at her.

"You grew up real nice, you know that?"

Heather laughed. "You did too, John." She almost added "Timmer" because in her mental world she often put the names together, almost like they were still in grade school, their names listed on year after year of classroom photo sheets. She could still picture John Timmer as a second or third grader, his eyes bright and a little wild, his smile lighting up the page.

Feeling a blush rise under his scrutiny, Heather switched topics. "Tell me more about the farm where you live."

John sighed. "It's great, a big old stone farm house Claire runs as lodging. Chickens, a stream with trout, and fifty acres where we grow our own food, all seasonal stuff she and her employees sell at local markets, but tatties, er potatoes, are the bulk vegetable. She has a good supply of strawberries, red currant, tayberries, and blackberry brambles, so visitors can come and do a pick-your-own thing, which is another revenue stream for her. Claire's a shrewd one; she also boards people at the farm house and has them work for reduced rent. I'm a regular when I'm stationed in Scotland, so she always keeps my room for me. Right now she's boarding two other guys, brothers, with Skydive UK. She takes in travelers who book ahead and runs it like a B&B."

John had mentioned Claire in messages, but hearing him say her name gave Heather a twitch of jealousy.

"You're making a face," John said, braiding his fingers through a strap on her seat. Heather felt heat coming off his skin and the weight of his arm on the semi-circle seat around her back.

"I didn't realize I made a face. What kind of face did I make?"

"Like this," he said and twisted his mouth in a nervous grimace, not at all becoming.

"Oh, god, that's awful. I hope I don't make that face a lot." Heather forced a smile.

"No, but, maybe you want to move on? We could paddle some more."

"No, let's drift a little more," she said, surprised by how quickly she answered. She liked John's arm on the back of her seat, and the way the pond reflected in his eyes, which looked true hazel in the sun, like the murky depths beneath their kayaks.

"Drifting is good," he said, and they fell into silence again.

John's legs somehow fit into the front of the kayak, even though they were long. A ring of wetness seeped into the fabric where he had submerged in the water. Heather switched her gaze from John's legs to the opposite shore, where bunches of goldenrod grew in yellow-tipped crowds.

"I know that one, goldenrod, right?" she asked.

"Uh, hmmm," he answered, his voice faraway.

"Did I break your reverie?"

"No, I like talking with you. I always looked forward to our chats on Facebook." He readjusted the oar on his lap, letting go of her boat for a few seconds.

"Don't let go," she blurted without thinking, and a true blush followed.

John's eyes lit up. He smiled a sexy half-smile and said, "Don't worry. You won't drift away." His hand went back to its spot behind her back.

"Sorry," she said, and then wondered what she was sorry about.

"No worries."

Heather decided to try to get back to the conversation. "Chatting with you really helped me through some hard days."

"Yeah, I got that. It's an ass kicker to take care of someone 24-7. My mom took care of my dad for seven years while he battled cancer. I still wonder if it took some years off her life."

"I remember you mentioning that. I'm sorry both your parents are gone."

"It's weird, and I think about them a lot, but I guess we're around that age, maybe a little young, not to have parents knocking around still. I wish my kids had known them better. Mia and Graham are fourteen now, but they were only four when my dad died, and then seven when my mom passed. But my parents were older than ones in our grade, if you remember."

"I do," she said, fiddling with the oar by rolling it between her palms as if flattening out a pie crust. "How old were the twins when you and Celia divorced?'

"Eight. Not a bad age for it, from what I read. Kids that age are still very much into being kids, and if their needs are met, and the parents aren't fighting like cats and dogs, it can build some resilience. I remember going to this god-awful parenting class that was required in order to get a court date, and the guy talked about how some kids self-mutilate, turn to drugs and shit to deal with their parents' split, but those cases mainly happened when the parents badmouthed each other and things dragged out in court. I was resolved not to let that happen." He paused, squinting at the sun, maybe collecting thoughts. "But Celia and I didn't fight much. I think we fell out of love. It wasn't long after we divorced that she married Paul, and they have two girls – four- and two-year-olds who are adorable. Paul has always been great with my twins. Can't complain about anything."

"It's good you like him. I always thought that would be hard for me, you know, if Marc and I ever split, for him to have another wife who would be in my kids' lives like a parent. I didn't like that thought," she said.

"It made me burn for a while, especially because I suspected Celia had a thing with Paul while we were married. But I let it go. It doesn't do anyone any good to let things fester."

For reasons unknown, Heather spoke in a rush, "Marc fell in love with this woman Erin and had an affair for a year before his stroke. I found an email he was going to send to me, telling me about how he was sorry, and it wasn't me, and he had tried to resist her, tried not to love her. Anyway, he never sent it. He had the stroke, and then after that, he didn't remember her. I wanted to divorce him, but what kind of a bitch divorces a forty-year-old stroke victim? He'd probably have to go to a nursing home, or worse, one of my kids would feel compelled to take care of him. So I stuck with him and took care of him, but every day, I fantasized about him being well and me slapping him and taking off, starting a new life without him." Hot tears spilled out of her eyes. Heather wiped them on her sleeve and bit her lip to stop from crying again. Who would want to hang out with such a crybaby? "Anyhow,

I'm not sure why I told you all that. You're, like, one of four people who know that. Jesus, I'm going to scare you away from hanging with me." She hoped it wasn't true. She didn't think it was, not by the way John had pulled her kayak closer to his own, or how he leaned in, his cotton t-shirt showing the curves of his lean, muscular torso.

"That was a kick in the head, the affair," he said. "His loss. He was a fool to cheat on a woman like you, Heather Finch. His brain must have been misfiring well before the stroke. I mean, come on, you! No, he's a first class loser for doing that. You should have divorced his ass. Let what's-her-face take care of him. Really. To hell with what the rest of the world would have thought." John's smile infused Heather with laughter. She started to giggle, hunching in the kayak and nearly losing her oar. John's words and tone reminded Heather of Leann, or those old friendships from childhood that were purer than the rest because reactions were based solely on picturing a child-self dealing with adult shit, and the kids won out, like a pick-up game of kick ball at dusk, on a summer night.

"Forget about all that. We're gonna have fun today. Grab your oar, sister, let's hit the shore and do some exploring."

John broke from her; both giggled as they stroked to shore.

Live
Mid-June, present day

Friday evening. Heather had plans for Steven Connolly to pick her up at White Cottage for dinner. Her nerves split her psyche between excitement and betrayal. Why should she feel like she was betraying John Timmer? They weren't dating; they had one chaste day together, "knocking around," as he had put it. She had no evidence whatsoever that he had any interest in her besides being old friends with a renewed friendship. And yet, Heather had done little else than relive moments from her Wednesday with John Timmer. After kayaking, John had driven her all through the estate and beyond, taking her to Lochaline for a late lunch at a pub, where the proprietor's accent was so thick she'd needed John to translate for her. They'd walked the shore and chatted about, what? Nothing and everything. And then he'd driven her to Cabrach where her writing life had since been transformed because there she'd found a setting, a place she now knew she had to write about: a stone crofter's house.

Since visiting the ruins in Cabrach, lush meadows with an isolated half-standing stone home, called a crofter cottage, Heather had become obsessed with learning everything she could about the Highland Clearances. John had taken her to the abandoned, crumbling crofter cottage. Her feet had made a dusty trail in the same spots some weeping Scottish family had squatted in after they had been driven out of their Highland home and forced to a smaller piece of land, paying healthy rent sums to British landowners, decimating the clan system for good.

As Heather had sat on a rotted log, breathing in the fields of wildflowers and grass, the dirt smell of dead wood and squirming bugs, a voice came to her. A new character. A woman – a Scottish woman who had been raped, her husband sent to the coast to harvest the iodine-rich kelp to make a living, and left in this stone home, carrying the baby of the British soldier who had assaulted her. Heather had taken out her pocket Moleskine notebook and pen and scribbled ideas down at a frantic rate while John had explored the ruins, the fields, and faraway trees, his hunky silhouette giving Heather shivers when she had finally looked up from her notes. A new idea had formed, one not mired in overused characters and plot twists, and she'd wanted to hop up and skip over the rotted stumps as if skipping across stones in a stream.

When John had approached her, he'd glimpsed the gleam in her eye and said, "I think you like it here."

"I do," she'd said and hugged him quickly, "you've brought me to my setting. I could kiss you."

"All right, then." But instead of taking John in her arms and really kissing him, she'd squeezed him in another hug, pulled back, and pecked his lips. Once, twice, and even a third time, but it hadn't led to anything else. Since then, Heather had thought of little else than those three light kisses on the lips.

The way Heather was thinking about it now, on the Friday of her dinner with Steven, one would think they had passionate sex in the meadow outside the crofter ruin. But that was only in her imagination. What did she feel for John Timmer? Her question of if she would be attracted to him answered in the electric pulse that ran the length of her body whenever he stood in proximity. She had fun with him, laughing easily, and feeling immediate comfort by his presence. But she wondered about how he felt about her. There had been ample opportunities for physical contact, but he didn't pursue it, even with the magical three kisses, pecks really, in the crofter meadow. She feared her attraction to him was one-sided, or stemming from her minus-zero sex life for the last four years. Somehow her stay in Scotland served not only as a spark for creativity, but an ignition of sexual drive; every male remotely close to her age seemed fair game. The emerging feelings were both tantalizing and anxiety-producing because she worried about how her fragile emotional world would take any form of rejection.

Her phone buzzed, but as had become routine, Heather glimpsed the incoming number or name, but when she tried to connect, the call failed. The information packet on White Cottage and Ardorn Estates had warned about intermittent-to-no cell phone coverage, but they had decent WiFi for Internet connections, so instead of talking to Leann, Jackson, or Tessa, Heather chatted on email or Facebook. Tessa had also set up for Heather to utilize WiFi to text when she didn't have phone service – a perk of having a tech-savvy daughter. The lack of her phone freed her somehow, and she reveled in the silence, hoping the quiet would allow her Scottish crofter characters to speak to her.

After the call failed, Heather read a text from Steven who let her know he'd be at the cottage in five minutes. Heather decided to grab her blue sweater and meet him outside. She glossed her lips, wiped most of it off, and locked the cottage.

Evening outside of White Cottage almost undid her each day she had been in Scotland. Sunset happened at about 10 p.m., so 7:30 brought the dusky feeling of her childhood, even though the bracken near the woods, the glistening pond, or the circling eagle (yes, she had spied sea eagles already) were not any of the makings of one of her childhood memories. But the moment she stood onto the red step and breathed in the scent of almost-rain, she thought about walking back to her house with her brother, Leann, and other neighborhood kids after long hours in the summer sun, "knocking around." She sank to the step, chin in her hands, and realized she missed John Timmer. What was he doing on a Friday night?

In exactly five minutes, Steven's car crawled down the gravel lane. He parked in front of the cottage and hopped out of the car, moving like a fast-moving mink, a mammal Heather had spent an inordinate amount of time reading about because they were prevalent in the Ardorn woods, and she longed to see their silky pelts undulating beneath the scrub brush near her cottage.

"Good evening, Heather," Steven said, approaching and taking her hand in his. He gave her a quick hug and a peck on the cheek. They pulled away, eye level, and Heather blushed from his sharp eyes taking her in. He wore fashionable khaki pants and a button-down shirt that showed his hulky arm muscles. Heather noted that though Steven was not tall for a man, he was perfectly proportioned; the word statuesque popped in her mind; even his facial features could have been carved in stone, down to the perfectly cropped hair. John Timmer's prominent features, his tall, muscular frame, and his easy manner were quite different. She couldn't place the word for him. She stopped herself from thinking of one man when on a date with another.

"It is a lovely evening, and thank you for inviting me to dinner," she said.

"Shall we, then?" he asked, turning toward the car.

"Yes."

Steven opened her door and half jogged to his side before sliding into the driver's seat. Each time Heather sat on the left side in the front seat of a car, things seemed off-kilter; she wanted to lean in at every curve or grab at an invisible steering wheel to navigate her way. Steven must have noticed her unease because he said, "Not feeling comfortable with the opposite seating, are ye?" He glanced at her with half-open eyes, the sea-green twinkle flashing.

"Not at all," she said. "I don't think I'm going to drive while I'm here. Walking is fine." She smiled, not knowing what else to say.

"We could have walked to the restaurant since it's on the grounds.

Usually I do, but on a date, it seemed proper to pick you up at your door," he said, smiling.

Date. No ambiguity here, no uncertainty of if this was a date or not, like Heather's question of her Wednesday with John. Steven put it right out there. Nervous sweat started under Heather's armpits.

"And it smells like rain," Heather said.

"Aye."

They drove in silence for a few minutes, and Heather ran through topics in her mind: Ardorn Estate, his childhood, why he never married, but all three led to places she didn't necessarily want to broach. The Ardorn topic made way for the discussion of Heather buying White Cottage, which seemed like a crazy fantasy; his childhood seemed fine, but what kind of question kicked off that discussion without sounding like an interview, and the why he hadn't married – that one spoke for itself.

"What kind of food do they serve at Near the Loche?" she asked and blushed when his eyes lingered on her face and then scanned her body in the time of two blinks.

"I think it's a grand menu, but I may be a wee bit biased. You probably don't want to ask me about self-sustainability – eating what you grow and all that – because I'll bore you to tears well before dessert is served. But at Ardorn, I've tried to set up this model, so even the menu at our restaurant follows suit, for instance, if you order a hen dish – say the 'Valley Chicken with Beetroot and Orange,' the chickens are from our stock of corn-fed ones, or from nearby organic farms. The whiskey-smoked salmon or trout fillets are from our ponds or rivers. You get the idea. Are you a vegetarian?"

Heather couldn't help it. When Steven mentioned the nearby organic farm, she wondered if he meant the one where John Timmer lived. When Steven asked if she was a vegetarian, Heather thought about how John was a vegetarian.

Stop it.

"No, I'm an omnivore. I don't eat much red meat, though."

"Good girl. It's not good for ye if you eat too much." Steven turned into the gravel parking lot of the restaurant and hotel and turned off the ignition. The silence in the car made Heather want to blurt something, but instead she nodded like an elementary student agreeing with the bad idea of red meat.

"If you were a vegetarian, we have a nice assortment of farm fresh meals. I should stop boasting and get your door."

Before Heather could protest, Steven had done his jog thing and materialized at her door, opening it with a bow.

"Here we are. Have you seen the place yet?" Steven gestured to the large cream-colored stone building that looked like a Victorian mansion.

"I have from the outside, when Jackie and Finlay gave me the tour of the estate. I haven't been inside yet."

"Then you're in for a treat."

They walked the wide stone stairs to the vestibule of the hotel/restaurant, reminding Heather of movie shots of Pemberley from Jane Austen's *Pride and Prejudice*. Once inside, Heather couldn't help but gasp at the splendor. The floors were carpeted with red. Tapestries with rich earth-tone colors draped the walls. A spiral staircase circled up to a balcony that Heather assumed led to the hotel rooms upstairs. Waiters and waitresses in black and white uniforms bustled into the dining room carrying full trays on their shoulders. Though a hostess stand blocked the entrance to the dining room, Steven nodded to the woman at the door, and she signaled for the two of them to go to a far table near tall windows that overlooked a swath of green rolling into woods, patches of heather, and then a stream that snaked through more trees.

Heather glanced at the other diners in the room, and many wore more formal attire. She tugged at her light blue cardigan and smoothed her simple patterned skirt. Should she have worn nylons? Her feet began to sweat in her sling-back sandals.

Steven pulled out the chair for her and as soon as he sat down, a waiter appeared with a bottle of white wine.

"Your wine, Mr. Connolly," the waiter said, showing the label to Steven.

"Very good, Michael. Heather, I went ahead and selected a wine from our cellars for tonight. I hope you dinnae mind."

"Not at all," she said, relieved she wasn't the one doing the sample tasting of the wine because she felt so incredibly nervous all of a sudden.

After the glasses were filled and the waiter departed, Steven raised his glass and said, "To Heather, our visiting author!"

They clinked glasses and Heather drank a gulp, not a sip, and saw Steven had sipped his, so she vowed not to take another drink until his glass had diminished some.

"So," he said.

"So," she said, and they both chuckled.

"You like the view, Heather?"

"Aye," she said, and they both laughed. She went for her wine, but stopped herself, and said, "the grounds are amazing. Every time I look out a window, I imagine leaping into the greenery."

"If you leap out this window, you would roll down that brae and into a burn, you know," he said and drank another sip. Her wine still settled below the level of wine in his glass.

"Translation," she said, "I'd log roll down a big hill and into a river."

"Aye, you're getting the hang of things here, but a 'burn' is more of a stream, though we do have some fast-moving rivers leading out to Loch Linnhe and the Sound of Mull. Are you thinking of doing some fishing or boating when you're here?"

"I haven't thought that far ahead," she said and thought that she'd stop comparing her glass to his; she was nervous as hell and needed another sip. Heather tipped her glass back, pursed her lips tightly to keep from gulping, and spoke again, "How long have you owned Ardorn?"

"Since my parents died, so twenty years and some days." His eyes searched her face. Maybe he didn't know what else to say to her? When he looked at her, Heather felt heat run through her body, but she also wondered if she was imagining the connection simply because she was out of practice and years away from having any game at all in terms of reading date cues.

"Tell me about this buffer land you mentioned," she asked.

"You sure about that? I could go on and on," he said. "Shall we place our orders first? If there isn't anything on the menu you like, I can have the kitchen fix you something special."

"Oh, no, that won't be necessary. Let me see."

They opened their menus and Heather wondered what to order; she didn't want to take too much time deciding, noticing that Steven glanced at the list for about thirty seconds and snapped the leather casing shut with his unending supply of confidence. Heather quickly selected the oven-baked smoked haddock and shrimp and placed her menu on top of his.

The waiter came right over and took their order, refilling Heather's water and wine glasses before he departed.

"So, the buffer land," she said, longing for him to talk a while so she wouldn't have to.

"Morvern – the greater area the estate is in and the sea around it – provides a wide variety of habitats for birds, mammals, and sea life. Elevation wise, the land goes from sea level to 500 meters. We have sheer rock faces along the sea, underlying rocks such as granite, basalt, some schists, then there are wide stretches of bare wet heaths, mires, and drier patches of bracken and heather. North of the estate, there is some land that, when I purchase it, will provide a continuum of natural land where all these habitats can simply exist, without human construction. In fact, the human intervention will happen simply to observe nature and preserve it. Though I'd love to keep White Cottage, I need the sale in order to buy the land without taking on any debt. I get moderately obsessed with reciprocity, where you only take what you give from nature, and I already went on about the self-sustainability model – I think this way so much that it infects my business mind. I only purchase what I can buy without accruing debt. It's helped keep things running smoothly, and I'll only sell the cottage to a buyer who will sign an environmental agreement. This eliminates a lot of buyers who would love to replace the cottage and the surrounding land with a more tourist-centered venue. So if you'd sign such an agreement and buy the cottage, I only see a winning scenario. Then we could have more dinners like this one, looking out on the burns of heather." His eyes sparkled and stared.

Heather smiled and shook her hair out. "I don't know, Steven, I said I'm looking for a place to live, but buying the cottage? It's kind of a fantasy."

"It doesn't have to be."

The food arrived, and though Heather had done a spontaneous order that she didn't expect to love, the smoky smell of the fish, and the crisp snap of the vegetables that laced the edges of the plate, melted in her mouth. They ate in silence for a few minutes, and in that time Steven finally finished his first glass of wine. Instead of refilling his own, he topped off Heather's glass with a generous gurgle; he reached for his water glass the next time he drank. She hated that the full glass of wine brought relief.

"Is the Solace Art Fund an interested buyer? I would rather that the writer's grant be able to continue. If they are a serious buyer, I will definitely stop entertaining the idea," she said, surprised that she was back to talking about purchasing White Cottage. For real.

"Nae. Melissa got back to me the day after I saw you last. The foundation cannae swing it. So that leaves one other interested party, a businessman, Niles Graham, who is also eco-friendly. I think he wants to get it as a present for his kids, a place for them to live when they aren't in school, or whatever they do. I'm certain he'd sign my environmental agreement."

"It sounds like you have a deal already. We should stop talking about this. You'll make me want to do this the more I think about it, and it's a crazy idea." Heather started on her second/third glass of wine, feeling she needed the slow burn of the liquid in her stomach, and it tasted so good with her meal.

"Shall I order another bottle of wine?" Steven asked, wiping his mouth with the corner of his linen napkin, looking like a person who was accustomed to the finer things.

She wanted so badly to say 'yes,' but she doubted he would drink much more, so she shook her head and answered, "no, thank you."

"Heather, if you want the cottage, it's yours. And if you want the writer's retreat and contest to continue, what better way than to buy it? I dinnae think Niles will continue it if he buys. You could keep the tradition going, and I'd offer you a fine deal on staying in the hotel for the duration of the visiting writer, or better yet, go on holiday when the writer comes. You'd get some income from the Solace Art Foundation."

The man was smooth. He made everything sound simple, logical, and accessible.

"You have the plan in place," she said with a smile.

"I'll send you some numbers, and you can look at your finances. How about that? Then I'll stop hounding you, and we can have dessert. The chocolate caramel cake is delectable."

"Okay, send the numbers. And the cake sounds excellent."

It was a good thing Steven Connolly didn't live on Heather's shoulder, or she thought she'd be swayed to do whatever he said. A drizzle of rain started and made specks on the wide window.

The dinner finished with cake and coffee that left Heather feeling full and ready to sleep. Gearing up for the date, discussing the cottage, and drinking wine made her head spin. She longed to crawl in her down-covered bed in the tucked-away upstairs of the cottage and sleep off the surreal of her new world.

They ran to the car, trying to race through the rain. Steven still opened her door and jogged to his side, heaving a wet sigh when he slammed his door, closing off the pounding of water streaks against the window.

"Looks like the rain came in droves, and do you think that would make me remember to take my umbrella into the restaurant." He bent and pulled one out from under his seat. "I'll walk you to your door under this, though you're already soaked."

Heather shook and folded her arms over her stomach, trying to warm up. As they drove slowly through the estate, the rain turned into a storm, breaking the sky with light again and again; the intermittent flares of lightning between booms of thunder illuminated the woods, making the tree branches look like upturned hands reaching for the stars shrouded in storm clouds. Heather loved summer storms, and her first in Scotland gave her an excited thrumming in her chest. She also worried about a possible kiss at her door.

When they stood on the red step of White Cottage, under the hood of Steven's umbrella, Heather couldn't determine what the goose pimples on her arms meant. Was she cold or did she yearn for Steven's lips, her first real kiss since Marc.

"Good night, Heather," Steven said, leaning in and kissing her gently on the lips, slowly at first, and then deeper.

They pulled from each other, and Heather smiled, but winched at the sound of thunder cracking open her gray world with a crash followed by zaps of fiery light. She said goodnight to Steven and turned quickly to her new haven, dashing upstairs, gaining a better purview of the flash and crackle of a summer storm in Scotland.

Remember

Mid-June, three years ago

"Are you ready to try the Double Dog with me, Heather?" Leann's ten-year-old daughter Ashley asked.

Heather shut the novel she had been reading and adjusted her one-piece swimsuit. "I don't know, Ash, I think I'm a chicken."

Leann stood next to Ashley, soaked from her last chlorinated splash after her tube ride down one of the water park slides. She grabbed a towel and started dabbing her body dry.

"Take it," Leann said, handing the two-person inner tube handle to Heather. "I know I said if you came with us to Water Land you could do whatever you wanted all day." Leann paused, glanced at Ashley, and then mouthed the words "except drink" to Heather. Then she continued out loud: "But I need a break from that Double Dog ride. Multiple times up the stairs, while carrying the tube, are making my legs shake, and I almost wet myself this last go. I know this place is a hermetically-sealed cesspool of germs, but I just couldn't relieve myself in the pool. I need to find the bathroom a.s.a.p."

Heather smiled and stood, worrying that her stomach stuck out too much. She and Leann had kept up on their walks in the last six weeks, but her staple of wine or beer in the evenings had made her more fleshy. She hadn't done one yoga stretch, Pilates workout, or dance move since Marc had come home.

"Okay, Ash, lead the way," Heather said.

Ashley's face lit up. She took the other handle of the inner tube, making the two into a lop-sided train, and guided Heather through the crowds of parents, children, and life guards. A horn suddenly blared from overhead, causing Heather to stop even though she had heard it countless times since arriving at the indoor water park. A waterfall spilled out of hanging barrels to the delight of a group of six- to eight-year-olds below it.

"That barrel water is cold," Ashley said over her shoulder. Ashley was a miniature Leann, with hay-colored hair and sparkling brown eyes. Her teeth were uneven in that school kid way – mismatched adult and baby teeth battling it out between her lips. And Ashley's body had the same war happening: at ten she still had the straight waist of a younger girl, but under her suit Heather could make out the hints of adolescence. Tears came fast to Heather's eyes when Ashley smiled again at her and said, "The water soaked me, but then Jackson took my brothers and me to the hot tub. He only let us stay in ten minutes because we're kids."

That was just like Jackson, always looking out for other people, especially kids or the disabled (Marc). And Ashley reminded Heather so much of the younger Leann, and then Tessa, and then herself at ten, she could have sobbed into the plastic blue inner tube, inhaling the synthetic scent and wiping her nose on her bare arm. She got control of her emotions (this was supposed to be a fun break from care-taking, after all) and headed up the three flights of stairs to the Double Dog slide.

They had to pause three-fourths of the way up and wait. Ashley rested her end of the tube on the railing and Heather did the same, trying to blend.

"I wish Tessa could have come today," Ashley said. "What's she doing again?"

"She had plans with her friend Mia. They were going to the mall, a movie, and then she's spending the night at Mia's." Heather almost added that Rona, the woman who cared for Marc part-time while Heather wrote, was taking excellent care of Marc, but she bit her lip. Ashley hadn't asked, and Heather wanted to stop defending any moment she took away from Marc, the lying adulterer now turned invalid that he was.

Stop, she told herself while staring at the happy families laughing at their kids as well as the haggard families with moms or dads who wore expressions of mental retreat cropping up when watching their children slide or swim or shoot water at each other. The solidarity of parenting, something lost to Heather on two levels, made her want to go home and crawl under her covers. She pictured Marc before the stroke, before the affair, before – now. He wore swim trunks like a model; his body fit. His attention to the kids at places like this outdid any other husband. In fact, she had never been to a water park. Marc had been the one to do things like this while she did what? Wrote. Stewed. Cleaned. Scheduled. How much time she had wasted! How much frittering away of precious moments! Did they even have a bar in a place like this? They had to – it was a hotel in addition to being a water park.

"Well, have you Heather?" Ashley asked, wide-eyed.

"I'm sorry, Ashley, my mind was wandering. What did you say?"

"Have you ever had foxes or deer in your backyard like we have?"

"Oh." Heather couldn't keep back her smile. "No, but remember, your house is closer to the nature preserve. My subdivision is only close to a strip mall."

"One time, I think it was on New Year's Day, not the one where you stay up late, but the day-day, two foxes curled up in the snow in our backyard and slept there. My mom took a million pictures of them. They were so cute. I really want to be a large animal vet, or work at a humane society, you know, helping hurt animals. Once we found a dying mouse in our yard, and I really wanted to take it to a place for rehabilitation, but my dad said it was better off if it just went. He said it looked like the little guy had a breathing problem. I stayed with it until it started getting dark outside. My mom took me inside and made me a huge banana split to make me feel better. My dad stayed with the mouse until it stopped breathing, and then we buried it in the morning next to the vegetable garden."

Heather made *oh* sounds as Ashley told the story. Heather also knew the backstory from Leann. In the real-life version, minus fresh-faced Ashley who wanted to save every bleeding stray or wild animal, Brian had put the mouse in a pillowcase. He and Leann had downed about three shots of tequila a piece, and then Brian had clubbed the mouse for mercy's sake.

What about real-life mercy for an adult male, age forty, who had morphed into another human entirely, whose mind was gone, whose body was broken? So often she returned here: what would have happened if she had slept late that fateful February morning and woke to Marc dead of a stroke on the kitchen floor?

She hadn't thought this way right after the stroke, or in the rehab hospitals, or when they first got home, but after finding out about Erin, Heather's mind often drifted to those ugly thoughts.

"We're here," Ashley said. "You need to sit in the back because you're bigger. It's the rules."

Prickles of silly fear danced through Heather. A larger boy, probably the same age as Ashley, turned with his inner tube from the circular whirlpool area that served as an entryway to the slide. He squished through the line of people and headed back down the stairs with his inner tube slung over his shoulder. Ashley took a step closer to the start of the slide. One more pair straddled the pool and slid the inner tube down. The lifeguard, a bulky teen with spots of acne and giant eyes, blinked and rattled off a phrase he must have said fifty times a day, "If you're in the back, hook your feet under the front person's arms. Have fun." Google eyes cracked a smile at the girls who were getting ready to plummet, and then he gave them a shove. Their screams burst through the hum of flooding water.

"That one boy who just passed us chickened out again. He turned around at the body slide earlier today. I wonder where his parents are?" Ashley said.

Probably at the bar where any sane adult should be.

"I don't know, suddenly, he seems like the smart one," Heather said. "I'm ashamed to say I'm nervous."

When had she become so afraid of the most inane things? She used to not get jittery when she tried something new. Back in college, before Marc, she had even gone spelunking in a cave in South Dakota with her friends. Her suit dampened between her legs and under her breasts from sweat.

"You'll be fine," Ashley said. "We're up next. Remember to hold on." She added with a giggle.

Heather wanted to make a bee line to follow the chicken boy, who to Heather, seemed like a level-headed kid. Why risk a neck injury while your parents got cozy at the bar?

Without thinking, Heather followed Ashley to the kiddie-sized pool that swirled benignly, but the drop of the green slide beyond it made Heather's stomach flip. She started to step backward, but something vaguely miraculous happened. Little Ashley glanced back, caught her eye, and in a fraction of a second seemed to understand her vulnerability – that at the moment Heather did indeed believe something really horrible, like Ashley flying off the tube mid-slide, or some kind of neck break for either of them could happen. And Heather knew all too well how one instant, the blip of an abnormal artery in the brain, could change everything. Ashley reached back and took Heather's hand, not unlike how Heather used to take Tessa's. And in her kid-go-along-with-it way, said, "It'll be fun, you'll see."

So Heather stepped into the tube and flopped down without grace.

The bulky lifeguard said something to them, probably his foot-hook line, and gave them a push into the green vortex. Heather would have motioned for the boy to stop them, but her hands bled white holding onto the black handles. Ashley giggled and yelled, her whoops infecting Heather with laughter and her own uncontrollable howls. They lurched and whizzed down the flow of water, careening in a controlled way, every turn causing a dip in her stomach and peels of howls from both of them. And in a flash, the ride was over and they emerged from the tunnel like a newborn whale sent adrift. Ashley laughed and kept patting Heather's right foot, saying, "That's so cool, right?"

Heather could only giggle and paddle the tube to the ladder. She wasn't sure why she bothered trying not to submerge her body in the water at this point. Her hair and body were drenched; her chest had a light, airy feeling.

"Wanna go again?" Ashley asked.

"Sure," Heather answered. She and Ashley snaked through the clusters of people, seasoned and confident, and proceeded to climb the steps and plunge down the Double Dog at least another six times. Heather lost count. Each time, the lift in her body came; the anticipation for the drop, and the sheer thrill of curling her toes beneath Ashley's bony arms never failed her. Heather didn't think about anything else for the seconds it took to slide through the glowing green tunnel. The only things she and Ashley discussed were how to get more lift on the dips in the tunnel, or how to lean into the curves to get more *umph*, as Ashley called it.

Leann sat back in the white plastic chair and sipped an iced tea. Each time Heather and Ashley passed the table, Leann lifted her eyebrows, asking if Heather wanted to go another round. Soon Jackson and the boys joined in on the Triple Trouble slide. Sometimes one of them opted to put his body in torpedo formation and shoot down the yellow body slide. That left two others for the Double Dog. Heather asked

Ashley if she'd rather go down with her brothers or Jackson, and Ashley said, "I'm with my dumb brothers all the time, and I'd be too embarrassed to have Jackson's feet under my arms." Ashley's milky skin turned crimson. She added, "Anyway, I like going down with you."

That comment led to another three slides, after which even Ashley appeared tuckered out and requested they get something to eat from the snack shop. Heather grabbed two small towels from the stack near the lifeguard stand, regretting that she forgot her own beach towel. She slung one over her shoulders to cover her chest.

Leann pulled money from her purse and handed it to Heather. "My treat," she said. "I owe you a blue Slurpee for going down the slide with Ashley so many times."

Heather laughed. "It was my pleasure. I can get my own."

"Naw," Ashley chimed in. "I like to pay."

Heather smiled at the girl, once again warmed by her presence, and followed her bobbing head through the crowds to the snack shop. Right away, Ashley grabbed a candy bar, nachos, and a red Slurpee. Heather's stomach growled and her mouth salivated at the smell of grilling burgers; she glanced at the clock, saw it was about lunch time, and picked up a hamburger in a red and white cardboard container from under warming lights.

"I'm waiting for the next batch of pepperoni pizza," Ashley said.

Heather nodded and wandered to the refrigerators with cold drinks: on the right, sodas and juices, on the left, bottles of beer and wine coolers. Here it was – the alcohol. She eyed the beer, craving a bitter lager so much, but reached to the right-hand cooler instead. In the last six weeks she had become what would be categorized as an "at-risk" drinker (she'd learned this term from a woman's magazine). Instead of having one drink a day, the magic amount that was touted as healthy, Heather's daily intake had crept to two or three, sometimes four. On weekends, she sometimes pulled out a bottle of something harder when

Tessa and Jackson were out with friends. She would tuck Marc in early on those nights, his concept of time lost, and she'd hunker down with her bottle and a movie, or she'd cruise Facebook, envying the lives of other people.

"Ready?" Ashley asked while rearranging the food on her full tray.

"Ready."

Heather felt the pull of the beer fridge as she left the snack shop. She could always pop back in later in the day. But she had promised Leann she wouldn't drink.

Once they were seated and eating in silence, Leann left with the boys to get their own overpriced, greasy food. Heather and Ashley wolfed down their lunch, and as soon as Heather had swallowed her last bite, Ashley said, "How about we go on the Lazy River while we digest?"

The girl was just as sensible and charming as Leann.

"Sounds right up my alley."

The Lazy River curved through the water park at a crawling current. Ashley found a two-person inner tube and took Heather's hand.

Once they were at the stairs that dipped into the "river," Ashley dropped her hand and slid the tube next to the railing.

"We could take two single ones, but then we'll get separated, and we aren't supposed to make a train like the boys who just went past did."

"The double one is good," Heather said, almost overcome with emotion. She had passed up beer after all, and now Ashley wanted to be close to her. When was the last time someone wanted to be close to her? They would be in proximity. What a delight!

Heather sank into the rear end of the tube and held the rail while Ashley bobbed under water and popped up in the front.

"Now we get all lazy," Ashley said, hanging her feet over the edge and resting her head on the back.

Heather pushed off, and the meandering current took them. She leaned back, taking in the fake, potted ferns and the hum of artificially flowing water. She closed her eyes and thought this would be Day One of going back to "healthy" drinking. Already she felt the divide between herself and Tessa. Her daily dose of alcohol-induced oblivion wouldn't help the child through adolescence. And Jackson – how much slack was the poor kid taking on for her? She could tell, in her better observant mother moments, how he was retreating further into his own mind and being less social.

Day One. Life had had many "day ones," and this would be no different.

Ashley tapped her shoulder and said, "You can go ahead and take a nap if you want, Heather. I'll steer the ship." She giggled.

Heather nodded, a lump in her throat from the child's mercy, and put her head back, wondering what other epiphanies would come to her in such a place.

Live

Late June, present day

A week had passed since Heather's date with Steven. As promised, he had sent the numbers for the sale of White Cottage to her email address, which he must have acquired from Finlay or Jackie. With the sale of her house, Marc's retirement, income from her freelance work, her steady royalties from her Monvail mysteries, and the fact that both of her brainiac children had partial scholarships and work study for college, Heather could easily buy the cottage and still help her kids with extra school expenses. Maybe things were turning for her? Had the charms of Steven Connolly misted their way into Heather's world?

Her morning had been productive, starting at 4 a.m., eyes opening and mind whirling with scenes from her new novel, one so different from anything she had ever written. Megan, her protagonist, kept seeping into all of her thoughts, and her voice woke Heather before the sun that morning.

I've come to deliver myself. This line ran through Heather's head again and again all morning. How did it work into Meg's story? Had she fled the rape scene and made her way to another crofter's house? Did she come upon a skirmish between a British soldier and a clansman, was she nearly killed herself, and had she fled to safety? Heather was not sure, but she knew she had to write scene after scene until she made it to this line of dialog.

For over an hour, Heather had sat at her kitchen table, the overhead light casting a soft glow on the black and white floor tiles. Usually, with her mysteries, she kept to her regimented four hundred words a day, rarely more or less, but with her Crofter story, she looked up from her keyboard and two thousand words were tabulated on the bottom, left-hand corner of her document screen. She had missed the sunrise, and now as she rose from her perch, her neck stiff, she filled her coffee mug again and bent to gaze out her kitchen window. An arrow of black birds darted up and over the sun-sparkling pond; another bird trilled from the tree outside; Heather's eyes watered from the glare off the pond.

Instead of returning to her chapter, Heather logged on to Facebook. She had a message.

From John Timmer.

He'd sent it five minutes ago. Apparently he was another early riser.

Heather clicked on the red message symbol, her heart pounding with anticipation.

Hey, Heather, you up? Claire has us rising with the sun to pick strawberries today so she can make some preserves to sell at next week's Farmer's Market. You busy writing, or you want me to pick you up on my next break? I can be there in 30-40 minutes.

As soon as she finished reading the message, her phone buzzed with an incoming text. She jumped, splashing coffee on her robe. She touched the phone and read.

Wanna pick strawberries at the farm with me today? Pick u up in 30 min?

She had accomplished more than she had planned that morning, and she had the whole day ahead of her. Her body tingled with the idea of seeing John again.

She texted back, *Yes*, and ran upstairs to shower.

At first she dressed in one of the pairs of shorter shorts Tessa had picked out, but when she practiced squatting or crouching, a position she remembered from taking the kids to pick strawberries at a farm in rural Wisconsin, she slid out of them and put on her longer cut-offs.

The mornings in Scotland often carried a chill, so Heather trotted down the stairs and popped outside in her bare feet to test the weather in her cut-offs and t-shirt. On the walk in front of the cottage, something caught her eye beneath a cluster of goldenrod. She stepped closer and a small animal slipped out from the scrub and dashed over a pile of decorative stones near the garden bench and into the woods.

"A mink!" she shrieked with excitement. The small mammal waggled its sleek body as if to answer her. Then she realized it was a pine marten, a similar ferret-like creature, and followed it to the edge of the trees, craning her head to the forest sounds. The pine marten nosed at moss, its shiny pelt catching the sun that filtered through the spots of fern. It stopped at tree roots, sniffing and twitching, but when Heather stepped up to the thin path that started at her patch of lawn and then snaked into the wood, the quick, chocolate-colored mammal darted off, disappearing in the brush. The grass cooled her feet, making her dance from foot to foot to warm up. She would definitely need a sweatshirt this morning. Twigs cracked and acorns thudded the ground one after another when the wind blew. She lifted her head to the sky and inhaled the fresh air, feeling ebullient from a morning of writing, the pine marten sighting, and the lush Scottish countryside. Wheels crunched the gravel path behind; John's car, no doubt. Heather turned and waved even though the glare from the sun made it so she couldn't make out his expression as he drove in.

"Hey, you thinking about going for a barefoot walk in the forest, Heather?" John said when he got out of the car.

She glanced at her feet, smiling. "I wanted to see about the weather, and then I saw a pine marten. Can you believe it!" She threw her arms out as if to hug the air; she let them drop to her sides and said, "And here I am."

"Yes," John said, his voice husky. "Here you are." His long legs shrunk the distance between them until they stood inches apart.

Was this it? Did his intent gaze mean he planned to kiss her? She wanted to step closer and reach up to him, but his warmth quickly left, replaced with a sudden aloofness. This infinitesimal change made her remain in place, yearning for him to lean down to her lips, but the moment passed.

John cleared his throat and said, "I'm afraid you need shoes, and we better get going. Claire runs a tight schedule. She was glad to hear I recruited an extra set of hands for today. I think that was the only reason she let me leave to come and get you."

Right. Claire.

"I'll run in and get my shoes. Back in a minute." Heather ran off and felt like a toddler who runs to every destination. Where did this new energy come from?

She raced through the cottage, grabbing her purse, but leaving her phone (she didn't want to feel obligated to answer if Steven should call), and shoving her feet into her hiking shoes. After a fast glance at her appearance, which was tolerable, but not stunning by any means, she locked her cottage and left, wondering what the day would bring.

In the car, John didn't say much. He immediately asked about Heather's Crofter story, and she surprised herself with talking almost the entire way. Before she knew it, fifteen minutes had passed, and she'd given him plot, character, and possible twists, including her new idea of introducing a ghost to her story.

"Well, you're in the right place for a ghost story, Heather," he said while she caught her breath.

"I know," Heather started up again, so relieved to talk to someone other than herself. She'd spent a fair amount of time reading pages and talking out plot points to the white walls of the cottage. "I've been researching these ghost sightings in the Highlands. Did you know, not far from Ardorn, there is said to be a ghost of a woman who chucks potatoes and other vegetables at passers-by? Or more toward Inverness, there is a house with a gray lady who walks on misty evenings. She supposedly murdered her baby."

"How do you think a ghost will play into your novel?" John seemed genuinely interested. She'd picked up on his curiosity for stories during their Facebook chats over the last couple of years.

"I'm not sure yet," she said. "It's a bit murky still." She paused and bit her nail. "I'm sorry, it's barely morning, and I'm talking your ear off," Heather added. She'd even turned sideways in the seat to offset the wrong side of the car feeling and also to face John better.

"Not at all," he said. "It's really interesting to me."

"Really?"

"Really really, Heath. You got a knack for storytelling," he said with a smile.

Of course, she did. She was a mystery writer after all, but this felt new. The Crofter story propelled her into new territory; the trajectory felt like sailing.

At a wooden sign on the side of the road that read "Claire's Organic Farm: B&B Available," they turned down a dirt lane.

"The thing is, John, I'm nervous about trying something new – this historical stuff takes so much research. I can't possibly learn everything that is needed to be fully immersed in the time period," she said, biting her lip.

John glanced from the road to her, and his eyes lingered on her lips. The fraction of time his eyes stayed on her lips flickered, and he focused back on the curves of the lane and said, "Just write it. You can always fact check later if need be."

"That's more than well-said. It's spot on," Heather said as she absorbed the view out her window. Patches of wildflowers lined the roadsides. Gold and green meadows rolled to distant trees and fenced areas where wooly-backed sheep grazed. Ahead, a long, stone farm house poked up from the valley. Maple and oak trees stretched up on the sides of the house, and beyond it, rows of cultivated land created a patchwork to frame the valley.

"It beautiful!" she said.

"Aye," John said in his Scottish accent and gave a dazzling smile. Warmth filled Heather's chest. Again, she wanted to lean in and kiss him, but what if his smiles and eyes on her didn't mean he wanted to kiss? If memory served, he had always had a warm, open manner as a child. She made a mental note to observe him today with the other strawberry pickers, especially Claire.

After parking in the gravel drive and picking up baskets, they headed toward the strawberry fields in silence. Walking beside John, Heather wanted to grab his hand and say, "thank you!" It seemed that every time she was with him, his presence filled her with creativity: renewal burst forth from her mind and body, just as the yellow-headed daffodils clustered in a dip of land they strolled past. Their green costumes of leaves crowded like a troupe of miniature painted people. She wanted to skip off the path they were on and pick some, but she didn't say a word; she let the fresh air fill her lungs, and the sensation of light wind tickle her hair. John walked with his head bent, his stride longer than hers, but he slowed to match her gait. Walking side by side – so natural, so filled with possibility.

"Down this hill, see the strawberry rows?" he asked.

"Yes," she said, more breathless from being with him than the walk. He cocked his head at her and smiled, a wide, white-toothed smile, and Heather had an instant desire to lick his teeth.

Where was this coming from? She hadn't had thoughts like this in a lifetime.

She added, trying to calm her racing pulse, "Let's go. It'll be fun."

"Come on." Then the miraculous happened. John took Heather's free hand and tugged at her like she was a kid. She almost lost her footing, but she steadied herself and took off to match his run. Their baskets caught the wind, making wicker kites of friction. She laughed when the hill sloped downward and there was nothing to do but sprint and hope her feet didn't catch on a root or rock. Heel over heel, knees pumping, hair wild and eyes watering, Heather screeched with delight and John pulled on her hand more, laughing too, and whooping as they reached the bottom, slowing their feet and stopping. He let go of her hand, leaving heat and sweat in her palm and tingles in her body.

A stocky, fit woman with long, golden, braided hair that was tied under a blue bandana stood with a basket of strawberries between her legs. She wore cargo shorts and a short-sleeved shirt, her legs and arms tight with muscles, her skin fair, but slightly tanned. When they approached, Heather saw Claire wasn't a conventional beauty. She had uneven teeth, small brown eyes, and spots of freckles, but she was very pretty in an earthy, unyielding way. She smiled at them and said, "Hiya, 'bout time ye showed back up. Took your time, dinnae you, Timmer."

"Oh, pipe down, Claire, you woke us before the sun, riding those two boys, and now you're on me? Come on," John said.

"I also fixed y'all a fabulous breakfast. I dinnae hear you complain about that, did I?"

"Fine, fine. You're right. Topic change, this is my old friend Heather Finch. Heather, this is Claire Fletcher."

Claire stepped out of her strawberry row, wiped her hands on her shorts, and extended it, "Pleasure, Heather. Thank you for helping today. I've had preserves on my mind and now's the time to pick."

Heather shook her hand, feeling Claire's energy and warmth, and said, "I'm very happy to be here. I couldn't pass up a chance to be outside in this gorgeous weather."

"Aye, that was another reason. It's meant to rain later this week." Claire motioned and shouted to two younger men hunched over a far row. "Come meet our guest, boys." She turned back to Heather and said, "I know they aren't boys, but now I've hit forty, anyone in their early twenties, like these two, are boys to me."

"I know what you mean," Heather added "Sometimes I look at the skin of a twenty-something, and I can't remember mine ever being so smooth."

"Absolutely. Being in the sun makes my face look like prune," Claire said. "And don't get me started on the freckles."

The two young men, who were obviously brothers with the same features, dark hair, and green eyes, strode up. They even wore the same wide grins and carried their stocky bodies with duplicate wide-armed stances.

More fit humans in the Scottish Highlands, Heather thought.

"You must be brothers," Heather said, shaking their hands. "I'm Heather Finch."

The slightly taller one said, "I'm Mick Graham, and this is my brother, Carson." "Brother" sounded like "broother," making Heather smile.

"These two work with me when I'm here in Scotland," John said.

"With Skydive UK?" Heather asked. She wanted to pay better attention to John's life, especially after prattling on about her new novel in the car.

"Aye," Carson said. "Timmer set us up with Claire to bunk. In return, we're basically indentured servants, doing her bidding at the wee hours of the morning, before we even head to the drop zone."

"You all have to go to the drop zone later today?" Heather asked, instantly disappointed that she didn't have a whole day ahead of her with John Timmer.

"Yeah, but not until after lunch," John said. "I thought you might like to tag along and see the hanger?"

"That'd be great," Heather said, blushing.

"Now we have that settled," Claire said. "If everyone gets three large baskets a piece, then I'll make you a scrumptious, garden lunch, and when me preserves are done, Heather, I'll send you some at White Cottage."

"White Cottage?" Mick asked. "Do you mean the one on the Ardorn Estate?"

"Yes, that's the one," Heather said. "It's lovely."

"Heather's not saying it," John said, "but she's the author in residence there this summer. She won the Solace Art Fund Grant."

Heather reddened by the pride in John's voice.

"Hearty congrats to ye!" Carson said.

"Thank you."

"Okay, everyone," Claire cut in, heading back to her basket and row of berries. "Let's get to work."

The brothers left, and the way they leaned into conversation in a conspiratorial way made her miss Jackson and Tessa.

John must have noticed, too, because he stepped toward Heather and said, "Being around those two makes me want to see my kids."

"I was just thinking the same thing." Heather squinted to the sun, which poked out from behind clouds and streamed down onto the rows of strawberries, casting a shimmery glow on the wet leaves. John licked his lips, and Heather felt heat in her body again. She wondered how she'd make it through the day constantly imagining kissing him. She smelled a faint scent of weeds and sweat from his skin.

"Shall we?" he asked and motioned to a nearby row.

"Yes, definitely."

Heather took John's lead and bent over the end of one row while he worked at the one right next to her. Once in a while, he'd stand to relieve his back, and Heather did the same, bringing relief to her lower back, but causing her feet to fall asleep and her legs to cramp. She alternated bending and squatting, picking in silence and trying to identify the bird calls from the nearby spruce trees. Nature sounds, smells, and textures were her entry point into the new novel. Certain plants and trees had populated the Highlands for hundreds of years, so the same spruce could have been standing during the time of her novel in the 1700s. For a span of time, Heather let herself listen to the lines of dialog cropping into her head or imagine the smells in the kitchen of her main character's Crofter home. She wasn't sure how much time passed before she reminded herself that this morning she intended to learn more about John.

John's basket held almost twice as many berries as Heather's. She hadn't been paying enough attention to his system, so now she paused, stretching her back and observing his method. John's hands worked through the bushes in quick motions where he picked three or more fingertip-sized berries at a time. Then he dropped them into the basket at his feet. His large, calloused hands moved with delicate accuracy. He hardly made a sound, and when he slid the bush's branches to the side to see if there were any berries on the underside of the plant, Heather didn't see one.

"Wow, you didn't miss one berry! I feel like I need to go over my row again to be sure I got each one."

John stood, twisting his back and stepping out of his row. He jumped up and down twice, and Heather giggled.

"What's so funny?" he asked.

"I don't know if I've ever seen an adult jump up and down like that."

"Gets the blood moving. I noticed your feet must have been falling asleep when you squat to pick."

"Yeah, not sure how you knew that, but go ahead Mr. Psychic."

"You kept switching positions and when you stood up, you moved your feet around to wake them up. So I'm not psychic, just observant when it comes to women's bodies."

Flirty, definitely flirty. Now what? Heather's mind was blank. She wished a quick, sexy comment would come to her mind; instead, she reddened and stammered a choking sound, something between an otter bark and coffee pot gurgle. Then she said, "Have you seen otters in the river Aline, where it enters Lochaline?"

Complete humiliation washed over her in new, uncomfortable floods.

"What?" John shook his head, but he whisked the confusion away as quickly as he picked strawberries and followed with, "Yeah, I've seen otters there. I'll take you if you want to see one. But what made you think of that?"

Heather sighed and stepped out of her row and closer to John. She smelled his sweat again mixed with strawberries and leafy dirt. She took a step back, not because his scent repulsed her, but because she was too turned on to be picking strawberries. This buried world of desire had been turned up like garden dirt; the trowel turning and turning, and she opening and opening. The yearning so great she could hardly breathe.

All she managed to say was, "I don't know. I didn't want to ask about otters." Her voice sounded breathy. She hoped it came off as sexy instead of asthmatic.

But John carried the surplus on sexy. He brushed his sandy hair out of his large, hazel- almost-green-in-the-morning-light eyes, and said in a low voice, "What did you want to ask?"

Now she was on the spot. What exactly did she want to know? But she knew, deep down, what she wanted to know, and she simply had to voice the words.

"Are you with Claire?" She paused and adjusted her stance, trying hard not to cross her arms over her chest in a defensive, protective position.

John's thick eyebrows went up, and then a mysterious smile broke out, causing creases to all the lovely corners on his face.

"No, I'm not with Claire. But I'm not going to lie, she's been my Fuck Buddy in the past."

"Fuck Buddy?" Heather hated how squeaky she sounded, so motherish, so prudish.

"Yeah, once in a while, if we haven't had anyone for a while. Well, let's just say we help each other out. But that hasn't happened in some time because she's dating a woman from Fort William."

"A woman?" Oh, God, please take her vocal chords to spare her the humiliation of her Puritanical voice!

"Yeah," John said with a smile. "Claire's bisexual, probably more toward the woman side of things. So, anyway, we haven't slept together for over six months."

"That's nothing, try four years," Heather blurted out before she could control herself. She hoped the ground would swallow her and end her misery.

"It's been that long, Heather?" John's voice was soft, his words like chimes.

"Yes," she said, her voice a breath. What else was there to say, but the truth?

They stood in silence for almost a full minute. Heather would have counted in her head had it not been spinning as her body burned from the electricity between them. John held her gaze for the time a bird trilled and chirped, trilled and chirped, from the spruce. But he broke the moment by bending down again to his strawberry row. She stepped away from the magic pull between them, afraid she'd imagined it, and went back to her basket.

John hadn't let the moment plummet into awkwardness; she decided he was too much of a gentleman for that. Then he said, "Heather, you need a Fuck Buddy. You need to get back out there."

"Really?" She started picking again. Again, what else was there to do? The kiss from Steven had come so easily, his intentions so clear; this ambiguity made Heather's confidence soar and dive in seconds.

"Yeah. You're too beautiful not to be getting any," he said, eyes on his berries, hands wind-milling through the plant.

"Well, let's just say, men haven't been knocking down my bedroom door since Marc died."

"It's because your door's not open. You gotta open it, and believe me, they'll come."

"Maybe I'm not ready," she said, suddenly so nervous she squished a strawberry between her fingers. She popped the remains in her mouth. John stopped picking and stared at her mouth again. Her Brave-Self wanted to say, "Will you be my Fuck Buddy?" But that Self was holed up in the closed tomb her heart had become.

John ran his hand through his hair, keeping his eyes on her lips. He wiped his mouth with his fingertips, touching away miniscule beads of sweat.

"Sweetheart, you're more than ready. You're ripe, baby, you just need to get picked." He laughed then, the whoop-holler he had done down the hill, but switched gears again, so fast, Heather's hormones couldn't keep up. "Anyway, the reason my plants are so bare is because I'm totally anal retentive. Most skydivers are. We like the ritual of gear maintenance, putting on the gear, how we jump, the list goes on. I cannot help myself from finding and picking every berry on this plant." John bent back to the plant.

Heather stood speechless, her head in a whirl of too many thoughts. She wanted to get back to the topic of being a ripe berry. She wanted to tease out information from John about how he saw her, what he saw for her future. Did he fantasize about her? Instead she went back to picking, realizing she had gathered information about John Timmer. But just as she learned more answers, more questions came to her mind. And then, of course, the word ripe, ripe, ripe kept scrolling through her mind with each plucked strawberry. Suddenly, the morning's hungry, physical tension shifted to a strong curiosity in the next row. Did she want a Fuck Buddy? No strings, no commitment, just sex? What was John Timmer to her? She stopped herself from overthinking and went back to listening to the dialog of the imagined world in her head.

Remember
January, two years ago

Heather pulled their car into the handicapped spot at the Glenview Police Station. Her hands shook when she turned off the ignition and hung the disabled-parking placard on her rearview mirror.

Imagine getting ticketed on a day like today, she thought.

"So what's the schedule of things, again?" Tessa asked from her slouched position in the back seat. Despite her occasional zings and her mood swings due to adolescence and her rocky relationship with Heather, she still had an organized mind, one suited for working a math problem or a chemical equation until perfection; this mind wanted to know the system for the day.

"Chief Wilson said we'll be in a back room while he gives a brief introduction to the police officers and staff. He'll introduce your dad and give him the award. It will all take place in what they call the 'meeting room,' which looks like a cafeteria. They have a buffet lunch afterwards." Heather was used to giving the run-down of specifics to Tessa since she was a toddler and less likely to meltdown if she knew what to expect.

"What's the bathroom situation?" Jackson asked, his voice hoarse from saying so few words. Had he grown even more bookish and taciturn these days? Heather vowed to pay better attention.

"All on the same level with handicap-accessible in both the women's and men's rooms, so I can help him," Heather said.

"No!" Jackson said quickly, asserting the protective, male authority he sometimes did with his dad. Heather usually quailed when he did, feeling small and sad about emasculating their father. Then she resented Jackson for making her feel that way when all she wanted to do was spare him from having to help his dad in a public toilet. Thus the cycle of their care-taking family dynamic spun between the three of them like a murderous game of fast-moving handball.

"Where are we, Heather?" Marc asked.

It had taken her twice as long to help him get ready for this retirement party. The pants, button-down shirt, and tie he used to slip into, looking like an Adonis-come-lawyer, now took an excruciating amount of time, and helping him into the suit and its accoutrements this morning gave Heather a dull ache in her lower back. She knew she did too much for him in the occupational therapy sense, but if she waited for him to zip his pants and put on his socks, they would still be in their bathroom at home.

"We're at your retirement party at the police station," Heather said for the twentieth time that morning.

"The police station! Did someone get in trouble?" he asked with genuine shock on his face.

It took all of her strength to suppress the urge to roll her eyes and say, "Are you fucking kidding me?"

Instead, she took a cleansing breath like her re-adopted yoga routine demanded and said, "No one got in trouble, Marc, you may not remember, but before your stroke you worked as a police officer."

Jackson and Tessa were already out of the car.

"Oh," Marc said, his vacant eyes drifting off as he placed his hand on the car door handle. Jackson and Tessa stood ready with Marc's walker. Heather grabbed the tote bag with extra underwear, pants, socks, and another adult diaper if Marc soiled the one he wore. Jackson and Tessa directed Marc out of the car, guiding him to the walker and up the ramp. Heather hurried ahead to hold the door open. She brushed stray hairs out of her face and held her coat tightly to her chest. Thankfully, no snow or ice lined the sidewalk in front of the door, but the wind blew with bitterness, and no sun broke through the hazy gray of the sky. She had put off the retirement party for two months, saying it would be better to wait until after the holidays, which were dull and depressing with the new, brain-damaged Marc. She had rallied, cutting back on alcohol since last summer, having only one drink a day at most; at least she had kept that up until Christmas Eve, when she couldn't resist the whiskey bottle in the cabinet because she had been so sad and alone.

The real reason she wanted to put off the visit to the police station: Erin. She assumed the mistress still worked there. She dreaded seeing her in person.

Chief Wilson greeted them at the door.

"Heather, hello!" he said, taking her in his beefy arms for a hug she thought might crack her back.

"Chief, thank you for doing this," she said once released. Marc made his way up the ramp, eyeing Chief Wilson suspiciously. Chief Wilson – Kip – clapped Marc on the back and turned red with emotion.

"Marc, it's great to see you," Kip said, slapping Marc's shoulder and then taking Tessa in a hug, then Jackson. The chief had tears in his eyes, and Heather knew Marc had no idea who Kip was, his eyes lost in the past, his mouth about to open and say something Heather knew would be completely out of context. She couldn't stand to put Kip more at dis-ease, so she cut in.

"Where shall we wait?" Having been to the station so many times before the stroke, she knew they had to walk about a hundred yards to the office off the meeting room. Not once had she seen Erin, why? It dawned on her that Marc and Erin had started their affair one year before his stroke, and in that year, Heather doubted she had gone to the station. Their lives had become so distant and separate. She bit back guilt, struggling to wrestle the fear down, that destructive, evil root of a thought: she had made Marc have an affair because she'd been so cold since they lost their second child.

No, no, no, not now!

She focused on the back of Kip's uniform, his crimson neck bulging over his tight collar, instead of reliving emotions that had driven her to drink more and care less about life.

Once in the office, Heather saw that if Marc sat in any of the chairs, it would take both her and Jackson to hoist him out. The same thought must have ticked through Jackson's mind because he said, "Dad, stand for a while, okay? The chief is going to introduce you, and then we'll walk in with you to get your award. Got it?"

Marc stared at Jackson for a full twenty seconds, not registering what was said. Tessa put her body in front of Marc and said, "Daddy, you were a police officer before your stroke, so they have an award for you. Isn't that great!" Her voice cracked.

"An award?" Marc said. "What the hell for? Does this have something to do with the band?"

Heather stepped in, trying to save Tessa from breaking into true tears. Jackson's face was beet red with anger, and Heather understood why. Though not at all fair or compassionate, it became so easy, like slipping into a drinking routine, to get really mad at Marc for being lame. The worst annoyance she struggled against was being upset with his mental incapacities. She would do anything to spare her children these thoughts. If only she hadn't had Jackson call the ambulance, then Marc would have died, and his children could mourn a real dead dad rather than a lost one who had morphed into a body of need.

"Marc, how about you follow us in, take the award, smile and say thank you, and then we'll sit down for lunch," Heather said, wrestling down her wishes of his death and knowing she had given too many directives. She modified the directions: "Follow me into the room, and I'll tell you what to do."

"Okay," Marc said, leaning on his walker; his once muscular frame, still strong to some degree, but different. His muscles had shifted; he had a good appetite, and with an inability to keep up with a rigorous exercise routine, he had developed a bit of a paunch. More gray hairs dotted his temples, and more lines scratched at the corners of his eyes and mouth.

Heather softened to him as she always did. She leaned over and pecked his cheek. "You look very handsome, Marc. We're proud to be here with you."

Two tears slipped out of Tessa's eyes, and she quickly swept them away with the back of her hand. Jackson rubbed Heather's back and gave her a fast hug. Instantly, the tensions repaired themselves like a fresh skin enveloping all of the family in one body.

Chief Wilson poked his head into the room. "We're ready. Are you set?"

"Yes," Heather said. "Marc, this way. Follow me." Jackson and Tessa flanked Marc.

When they entered the meeting room, all of the officers stood at attention and saluted. Something must have clicked in Marc's memory because he paused and straightened his body. In a flash, Heather recognized his other eyes, the ones connected with his life. Marc's throat made a gasping sound, and it seemed his face registered all the moments, all the movements, all the relationships he had lost, and Heather could hardly bear it. She put her hand to his face, looked him in the real eyes, and said, "You're all right. Follow me, darling."

Marc nodded, composing himself; after one tear slid down his cheek, and he had reached the podium, he seemed to know to take the placard from Chief Wilson, shake the man's hand, and say, "Thank you, thank you all" in his old, booming voice. Surprisingly, Heather didn't cry, but both Tessa and Jackson were sobbing quietly on the side. Heather motioned for them to sit down, and she guided Marc to his seat of honor at the table.

The rest of the ceremony blurred from short speeches to brief remarks, and soon Chief Wilson directed Heather and her family to be the first to the lunch buffet.

"Mom," Tessa said, standing, "do you want me to get your plate and Jackson gets Dad's?"

"Yes, that would be great," she said. "Just get me whatever, and Jackson no –"

"I know, nothing he can't swallow," Jackson said, softening his voice, telling Heather he was sorry for his earlier tone without saying the words.

Tessa and Jackson made their way to the buffet, already leaning into each other's shoulders, consulting about what food to get their parents.

"This is something, Heather," Marc said. "We must have really wound this group of cadets up last night."

Right, back to the band.

Instead of correcting Marc for the umpteenth time, Heather smiled and patted his hand. He took hold of it and laced his fingers with hers like he used to; the gesture shocked Heather, making her feel adrift instead of anchored.

A woman approached the table, and Heather knew it was Erin. Erin stood at average height. Heather had expected a knock-out, someone to match Marc's striking good looks, but Erin had a fuller build, long blondish-red hair, and a rather uneven face. Her eyes, though, were the color of sea glass, and when she spoke, a soft, luxurious voice broke through the clink of silverware and mumbles of conversation like a Siren song luring sailors into the deep.

"Mrs. Barrington," she said. "I'm Erin Murphy. I work here as a cadet trainer. I worked with your husband." Tears filled Erin's eyes; her hands shook. Instead of a uniform she wore black slacks and a white, button-down blouse. Marc glanced up from his chair at Erin without recognition or comment. His fingers picked at the peeling fake wood on their table top. Erin started to speak again, but closed her mouth as tears slid down her cheeks.

Here was Heather's moment to say all of the things she had rehearsed to herself for the last seven months. What a whore Erin was! Where was she now that Marc had a stroke? How could she break up her family? But now that Erin stood there, looking so young and vibrant and obviously wrecked with lost love and guilt, Heather's molten emotions flowed away and were replaced with a calm understanding. What good would it do her to attack this girl?

Heather imagined herself at twenty (Erin was thirty-five at most) in a dance studio and practicing a ballet. She twirled on soft feet and leaped; she could feel her pulse, her vitality. She imagined this girl when she spoke to Erin: "It's so nice to meet you, Erin." Heather took her hand in both of hers and added, "If you ever want to come to the house to visit that would be fine. Marc remembers more about his younger years, so don't feel bad if he doesn't remember you. It's the nature of his brain injury. But he does enjoy the moment, and you'd always be welcome."

Erin choked back a sob and nodded. "Thank you, I'd love to come and visit, and if there is anything you need, please let me know."

Tessa and Jackson approached, setting down paper plates with mostaccioli, garlic bread, beef, and salad for Heather, and a full plate of mostaccioli and cooked carrots for Marc. Erin stepped to the side, wringing her hands.

"Kids, this is Erin Murphy," Heather said. "She trained cadets with your dad."

Both Jackson and Tessa juggled their plates and shook hands, offering smiles and pleasantries that sounded like muffles to Heather. She could ask Erin to go into the office and bombard her with question after question about the affair. Did they love each other? (Of course they did; this was evident in the email and the weepy girl before her.)

Did she plan to marry Marc? (Did she really want to know that? That would have made this woman the kids' stepmother.) Where did they meet up and have sex? (What good would this do, after all the many months washing and wiping Marc?)

Tessa sat down to eat while Jackson stood next to Erin making small talk. Heather cut in during a lull in the conversation, asking, "Would you like to join us?" It was disguised as a well-mannered offer, but Erin declined and excused herself, throwing a furtive, sorrowful glance back at Marc who plowed up his pasta like he hadn't eaten in days. (Heather had made scrambled eggs and bacon that morning for everyone.)

The family ate in silence; the low din of the cafeteria was reassuring in an after-the-funeral kind of way. People came up and said something. Many patted Heather's shoulder, a gesture she knew well, expressing their pity for her plight. Tessa and Jackson offered smiles and went up for chocolate cake. Heather sipped her decaf coffee, feeling grateful she had lied to Tessa after their big row last summer, after Heather had found the email about the affair.

The day after that drunken BBQ, where Leann had taken over and put Heather to bed on a tear-soaked pillow, Heather had lied boldly to Tessa, saying her dad had not had an affair. These words had actually crossed her lips, "You were right, Tessa, I was stressed and couldn't face the day." Tessa had given her a mysterious look, and Heather still didn't know what the child believed. At least now, the fabric of pretend had been hung in place. At least now, they could eat in peace, without the true acknowledgements of betrayal. At least now, Heather had sidestepped the confrontation with some grace.

And another day passed like rain.

Live
Late June, present day

Heather's feet throbbed, her right foot raw on the heel from a blossoming blister. The true pain didn't begin until she finally sat down in the hard-backed chair in the Riverside Restaurant, which overlooked the River Ness in Inverness. Steven, the Energizer Bunny himself, chatted with the restaurant staff while she waited for her after-lunch latte. She would have given her right foot to have a shot of scotch rather than vanilla syrup in her espresso drink.

Steven knew so many people throughout Inverness, their date destination. It had been days since her strawberry picking day that had become a magical memory of luscious berries, quiet moments next to John, and a delectable farm-fresh lunch made by Claire. The brother skydivers had been eager to learn about Heather, her stay at White Cottage, and even her new novel idea, a topic John had introduced with pride. Thus far, this date – yes, Steven had officially asked her on another date of sightseeing – was shaping up to be an antithesis to the strawberry day. Steven had picked her up before 7 a.m., driven her to the village of Drumnadrochit, the closest habitation to the legendary Loch Ness. They'd walked the grounds around Urquhart Castle, the ruins perched on a promontory above the murky lake. The day announced everything Scotland to Heather: intermittent rain, lush, green rolling hills, pewter-colored stones of a crumbling medieval castle, a light mist blanketing the oily waters of Loch Ness. Heather had wanted to stare at the water and imagine undulating humps of a green-gray monster or see boats that let out low moans from their foghorns, announcing their approach from foggy distances to rocky shores.

Instead, they'd spent more time in the visitor's center, listening to a tour guide, and chatting with the proprietor at the castle café. Steven did a nice job of including Heather in the conversations, but she often found her thoughts drifting out to the loch, wishing she could take a moment to be alone and collect her emotions.

Once in Inverness, Steven led her through the streets of the city, pointing out theaters, historic buildings, local businesses, and introducing her to some of the business people at the shops. She'd decided on a knit, sleeveless travel dress and flats because of Steven's height, a choice she regretted now because of the foot pain. She had thought they could have at least paused on a bench overlooking the River Ness or in a cherry wood pew at the Church of St. Andrew, but Steven had prodded her through the Scottish Episcopal church, chattering about the gothic arches, stained glass, and the angel font – a beautiful sculpture that had captivated Heather, making her want to stay in the soft, orange sunlight filtering through the windows and surrounding the piece. Instead, she had only been able to glance for about thirty seconds at it, leaving her with a pit of loss that was soon replaced with hunger and fatigue.

At least he had agreed to caffeine and some nourishment before moving on to the next thing: Culloden Battlefield. Heather couldn't wait to visit the moor with a visitor's center that documented the battle between the Jacobites and the British on April 16, 1746, after which the British Lord Cumberland systematically decimated the Highland clan system. She wanted to imagine the smoke of the battle as she gazed at a soft mist over the heather-coated fields she had glimpsed online. She wanted to imagine the screams and blood because here new characters could be born. She hoped Steven would stop talking long enough to allow her to listen.

Steven approached with to-go cups for their lattes. As he handed Heather her cup, he started to pull out her chair for her.

Time to go, she thought, wishing her feet would stop throbbing.

"The restaurant doesn't usually do a paper cup, but I know the owner. She made an exception because we're on a tight schedule," Steven said, already one step ahead of Heather.

"Great," Heather said. "Now, we're heading to Culloden Moor; I can't wait."

"Aye, it's a powerful place." He turned and took her hand once they reached the sidewalk. She hadn't held a man's hand, at least a man who could walk on his own, in four years. Then again, it may have been longer. How much did Marc hold her hand while he was sleeping with Erin? Heather's memory had become a thick fog, with moments or horrors surfacing like the humps of an elusive monster.

"Is it all right?" Steven asked, nodding to their hands as they approached his car.

"Holding hands, you mean?" She was forty-two after all; why be led all day like a lamb. "It is kind of strange for me. I haven't dated anyone or held a man's hand in a long time."

"I can let go, if you want," he said, his accent dropping the "t" in "want," his eyes catching hers. Heather had a surge of emotion and yearning, for what she wasn't exactly sure, but her insides turned and her skin chilled. Here was a man, an attractive, intelligent man who wanted to hold her hand, no ambiguities or unknown motives. Why let go?

"No, don't," she said with a smile.

Steven gave her hand a quick squeeze then released it to unlock the car.

"Good, then, but I need it for now, to let ye in." He opened the door, bowing with a smile.

"Thank you," she said. Forget John Timmer, she told herself. He hadn't called. There had been no good-bye kiss on the strawberry-picking day. Of course, despite the fact that her body had been tingly and charged next to him all day, by the time John had driven her home, she'd fallen asleep in his car. He'd brushed hair out of her eyes and touched her shoulder to wake her, but no lean-in for a kiss. She'd stumbled out of John's car in a sore-muscled daze.

Stop. Her mind kept veering to John Timmer. Again.

Steven maneuvered his car out of the tight spot and effortlessly guided it into traffic. As soon as they were on A82 and heading east to Culloden, Steven reached over and wrapped his hand over Heather's and both rested on her knee. The weight and reality of his hand sent shivers through her body. He glanced at her, quiet finally, and gave a sweet smile. She felt buoyant all of a sudden, realizing he was attracted to her. Now what? She had vowed to respond to any seductions. As Leann had said in her most recent email, after Heather had admitted her confusion over both Steven and John, Leann wrote, "Just make a point to get laid, Finchy. Nothing more, nothing less. Get. Laid."

The thought gave Heather an out-of-body feeling, like this person could not possibly be she. What alien species had come and snatched her body and replaced it with the one driven by sexual desire?

Steven squeezed her hand again and gently ran his thumb over the back of her hand. Even this small gesture made her feel light-headed and quivery between her legs. She crossed her feet, knocking her blister and not caring a bit, and focused her mind on conversation. Her mind raced, aware of the electricity between them; maybe Steven sensed it, too, because he let out a long breath after puffing his cheeks. The other clue was the fact that for the first time all day, he was silent. He didn't point out roadside plant life or the type of woodlands and how they differed from the birch-dominate Ardorn forests; he didn't prattle on about the whiskey distilleries or sport in the area. He grazed her skin with his thumb tip and drove with only his right hand, steering the car through the curving streets. Only at the roundabout to exit onto Old Perth Road did he let go. Heather instantly missed his hand on hers. The day was looking up.

The squat visitor's center at Culloden Battlefield was the only sign of the human world with the purple-hatted heather tufts and brown-green fields surrounding it. As if on cue, a light rain started again as Heather and Steven approached the entrance. Heather's pulse quickened for two reasons. First, she wondered if Steven would want to sleep with her that night. Second, she wondered what characters or scenes would emerge as she walked the battlefield.

Steven held the door for her and said, "We can see what you want to see here; you've been such an accommodating lass today, letting me lead you to every corner of Inverness."

"It was fun, but thank you. I do want to take some notes," she said, already drawn in to the charcoal-colored floor tiles and small displays in the entryway. She was in her element. She took out her notebook and pen and walked the front area, reading facts and jotting down ideas as they came. But she felt disorganized, her mind a chaotic jumble of her own desires and the need to bring some order to the battle, some reason for researching it. Did she want her protagonist's husband to die here? Meg, her lead girl, was taking shape, and she had knocked out a rough outline and started the first draft, but her research kept leading her back to this battle, a quick, bloody skirmish that changed the course of Scottish clanship for centuries. But did she need it in her story? The thoughts made her feel uncomfortable, like a child struggling over homework, or a mother scrolling through troubles with an infant's eating or sleeping habits. The resulting feeling was the same: discontent and an unmoored need for something.

But what?

After an hour of wandering the exhibits, they entered a room with walls of videos showing battle reenactments. Steven stood like a soldier himself, staring from image to image. Instead of gaining fodder for her novel, Heather felt overcome by sights and sounds, so finally she tucked her pen and notebook away, and did something she hadn't expected: she took Steven's hand. His eyes lit up and he squeezed it back, and then out of nowhere, he leaned in and kissed her, a real kiss on the lips. Another switch, one deep in her womb, flipped on, causing her to lose her balance. This kiss was better than the one after their first date. His free hand rested on the small of her back; his mouth worked slowly with hers. She pulled away first, simply because the vertiginous feeling was too much for her already muddled mind.

"Do you want to walk the battlefield, or would you rather we head back to the Estates?" he asked, his voice low and humming like a Scottish folk song.

"I read about the Old Leanach Cottage with the heather-thatched roof that actually survived the battle –"

"Aye, it did. And it's been restored many a time."

"I thought I'd want to see that and the clan stones and other memorials, but I think maybe…" She drifted off. What did she think? Get laid, get laid, get laid? She almost shook from raw nerves.

"We can do all those things if you want," he said, again dropping the "t" on want with his lilty accent.

"I do, I think, but I'm also so tired and confused about if this battle will fit into my story, or maybe it won't. The whole thing feels so confused right now, maybe it's best I take a break."

"Then I'm your escort; I'll get you back to White Cottage. If you're hungry, I can pop out to the restaurant and bring something back to ye."

"Will you join me?" There, right there, was the younger Heather emerging, the one who had lured and caught the likes of hunky Marc Barrington, back in the day.

"It would be my pleasure," he said. And they were off again, back on the curving roads, through the hills dotted with pockets of puffy-butted sheep grazing, thickets of woods, and bracken. Usually, the Scottish countryside triggered imaginings about being a woman from a different time period who worked long hours keeping a farm. Where these thoughts came from, she didn't know, but now the landscape blurred a brown-green stain behind her eyes. A repetitive thought ticked through her mind: she may actually sleep with another man for the first time in about twenty years.

It felt like the Second Coming.

Remember
July 3rd, two years ago

July 3rd. It could fall on a Tuesday or a Friday; it could be sunny and hot or rainy and humid; it could be a day of travel before the Fourth of July. For Heather, it would always be the day she gave birth to a baby who was dead. Every year she could not help but mark the day like a bloody etching beneath her skin.

On this July 3rd, Tessa was out with friends, and Jackson had to work late. By late afternoon, Heather wanted to drink so badly that she packed Marc in the car for a drive to Milwaukee, with the excuse to watch all the people pitch tents along the lakefront for the big fireworks display over Lake Michigan, but her real agenda was to stop casually at the liquor store on the corner for a six pack of her favorite summer beer. It was a holiday after all.

After getting Marc dressed in khaki shorts with the smallest button hole on planet Earth that took a good four minutes to fasten, and then allowing him to put on his t-shirt, and then pulling on and attaching his sandals for him, she grabbed the tote bag of back-up goods and walked in their painfully slow locomotion to the car.

"We're going to the fireworks?" Marc asked while perched over the shotgun seat.

Sweat beaded on Heather's forehead. She sighed and answered, "No, the fireworks aren't until tonight. I thought you might like a drive by the lake. Remember how people pitch tents all day to watch the Lake Michigan Fireworks on July 3rd?" She bit the inside of her mouth; of course he didn't remember.

"They do? That seems…" Marc's voice drifted off. He had been having more trouble finding the right words lately, and sometimes his moods shifted quickly, from vacant and complacent to angry, almost volatile. Heather had mentioned this to his doctor at Marc's appointment last month. His doctor had given her support group information and said that the personality changes don't always happen immediately, but they are common with stroke victims. Heather had tucked the information away, thinking there was no way Marc would get so aggressive she'd feel unsafe. More than anything, the moods and odd reactions were tiresome, very much like how the endless questions from a toddler wear on a mother. Just as Heather was the repository for blame and annoyance for her children, she had started to serve that role with Marc as well.

Instead of giving Marc a word to complete his sentence, she guided him into the seat and shut the door, sighing with palpable relief at being free of him for the seconds it took to lock the house and walk back to the car. Marc gazed out the window, his good hand tapping his knee to a song Heather didn't recognize. It was probably one of the old tunes the band used to play. She started to put on the radio, but stopped herself. Recently turning on the radio while he hummed had caused him to have a vicious mood swing. Heather backed out and enjoyed the silence, save for Marc's tapping and low hum.

Driving to the lake proved ill-advised at the late afternoon hour. Traffic backed up from I94 to the lakefront exit, so Heather imagined Lake Avenue, which snaked along Bradley Beach, packed with cars and lined with people in tents who were settling in for the display at sundown.

"Marc, do you mind if you skip driving along the lake today?" she asked.

"The lake? Why the hell would we want to go there anyway?" Marc turned his face to her, his blue eyes flashing a purple hue in the light, his drumming hand suddenly in a fist.

"We don't have to," she said, breathing slowly to calm her nerves. "Shall I exit and head back toward the house. If you'd like a pretty drive, we could go through the nature preserve."

The stormy visage softened again, and Marc said, "okay," like a small child.

The closet exit was downtown, near Lumiere University, where Heather had started college on her dance scholarship. She circled through the campus, one nestled in splashes of green space west of downtown proper, and the buildings, mini-fountain, and maple trees took her right back to her college days. Seeing the hill near Davis Hall, she shuddered with the memory of telling Marc she was pregnant with Jackson. They both had cried, but then Marc hugged her and asked her to marry him. Pregnancy was such a journey, a curvaceous tunnel leading Heather further into her own body, until the burgeoning life melded with her own. Heather had been shocked to learn of her second pregnancy while she breastfed the infant Jackson. Secretly she didn't want the child, but she never voiced this. Now her eyes stung with fresh tears thinking that she had somehow cursed the baby, killing the boy, Gerard Nathan Barrington, making him dead upon arrival.

"Are you crying, Heather?" Marc asked suddenly.

She wiped her eyes quickly, shocked he noticed something about her.

Before she could answer, he asked, "Why are you crying?" in a clear voice.

"I," she started, but stopped herself. She wanted so badly to have the old Marc back on this day, one they had always marked by visiting Gerard's grave, but this was the second year in a row she hadn't taken Marc to the graveside. She had never brought up their dead son since the stroke, and Marc seemed to have no memory of him. But what if he did?

Marc's eyebrow was cocked upward, his eyes both distant and engaged in his new manner of being; he was trying to connect. Why not try, too?

"Marc, you may not remember this since the stroke, but we had a baby boy, Gerard Nathan, who was stillborn. Today is his birthday." Her tongue stuck like a fly to tar paper on the word birth in the compound word birthday.

"What?" Confusion washed over his countenance. Heather clutched the wheel and got back onto the highway toward their suburb; she would definitely get some beer and put Marc to bed early. Why had she started this with him?

Heather accelerated to change lanes, and once in the right-hand lane, she slowed to the speed limit. She couldn't wait to exit. Maybe if she didn't answer right away Marc would forget the thread of the conversation. The car in front of her drove exactly the speed limit. She didn't want to go around the car because their exit was next. She glanced over to Marc – his hands shook, but he tried to steady them on his knees. He hunched over and Heather did this horror-show viewing between Marc and the road, glancing back and forth, afraid to look at him, yet fascinated to see he was weeping. He remembered!

"Marc," she said and grasped his hand for a moment, grateful for the cautious driver in front of her.

"I, I –" he broke off and wiped his face with his sleeve. Tears poured and he made a gasping sound while he sobbed in a way that Heather had only heard one time in all the years they had been together, and that was the moment he held Gerard after Heather had decided to deliver the boy, even though they knew he had died in utero.

Heather exited and turned off the road into a gas station parking lot. She reached over and rubbed Marc's shoulder.

"Marc, honey, it's okay," she said, even though it wasn't okay, not at all, that Gerard suffocated from the life-giving umbilical cord that became the rope on a gallows.

Marc's shoulders crunched forward as he cried. Finally, the tears slowed to where he could speak through gasping breaths. "Heather, cage it, cage it!"

For a wild moment, Heather wondered if some animal had ambled out of the nearby nature preserve, so she looked toward the edge of the parking lot, which met the woods. Then, it hit her; he meant she needed to cage his emotions, contain them. He had used abstract thought, something completely absent from his present mental abilities; even sarcasm (thank goodness) flitted off into the conversational air like dandelion puffs. *Abstract thought!* The momentous instant passed in a blink because she realized he would never "get better" or enter into remission from his brain damage.

"It's okay, I know, it hurts. He was so beautiful, so lovely. I wish he had lived," she said. Her own tears poured down her cheeks. The car idled in the lot. Marc's sobs quieted to whimpers. He rubbed his eyes and smoothed his hands on his shorts.

They sat in silence for several minutes, gazing out at the weedy growth spilling onto the air pump for tires and the dumpsters. Someone had missed the dumpster when throwing in a bag from a fast-food restaurant and didn't bother to pick it up. A gargantuan American flag snapped in the wind on a high pole. People paid at the pump, staring off next to their SUVS or looking at phones as their tanks filled. A group of teens holding sodas took off on skateboards. No helmets. Heather wanted to stop them and tell them to spend some time with her husband, and that would be enough to convince them of helmet use. But they had moved off, leaving with the tick-click sound of their wheels over cracks in the sidewalk.

"Do you want some leftover lasagna for supper? We could eat on trays and watch the fireworks on television," Heather said, her voice far too chirper. No fun, leftovers, or TV trays on the anniversary of their child's death, but it was something to do, something to say.

"What?" Marc turned to her.

"Do you want some leftover lasagna? We can eat and watch the fireworks."

"I'm not going back down to that mess," he said.

"I know, no, I didn't mean eat the lasagna at the lakefront. I meant at home. On TV trays."

"Oh."

Several seconds passed. The car made a whirring sound. She should really move on or turn it off.

"What do you think?" she asked.

"About what, Heather?"

"About dinner."

"Oh, I don't care. How about a hotdog?"

Again, maybe in the recesses of memory, Marc knew the Fourth of July loomed, and hotdogs and barbeques were the norm.

"How about lasagna, honey?" she asked.

"Sure."

Heather pulled out of their spot, wondering if Marc had already forgotten his breakdown and Gerard. She popped into the liquor store and bought a six pack of her summer beer, the cool bottles protruding from the cardboard case so invitingly. Many minutes and excruciating motions with Marc would pass before one touched her lips.

It happened, though; she helped him to the bathroom, and once he was sitting, she closed him in the bathroom and broke open her first, taking a long swig and feeling relief. She checked on Marc and downed the first half.

Peeking in the bathroom, she said, "I have your pajamas. I thought it would be cozy while we ate."

"Okay."

The ass wiping, twisting, and guiding of Marc into the pajamas went faster than she had expected, or maybe the beer on a partially empty stomach made it more tolerable. She helped him to his lift chair, set up his tray, stopped to finish her beer, and hurried to heat his lasagna plate.

Beer number two, lukewarm lasagna she didn't bother to re-heat, and televised fireworks: Happy Fourth, she thought, drinking more than eating. Marc ate in his methodical, follow-the-rules way he had re-learned in occupational therapy. Heather tossed half her meal and went for beer number three. It had been months since she had more than her allotted one drink a day. She didn't want to slip back into this routine, afraid she'd totally give in to making four or more beers a day her norm. Who would have ever predicted that she, Heather Finch, healthy young dancer would tiptoe in soft shoes around alcoholic beverages each day. But here she was, helping Marc to the bathroom again, smelling his shit when it hit the toilet, and surmising that his loss of sphincter control after the stroke, the incontinence and cleaning, was the worst of his care. But she wiped again, both silent, and helped finish up.

"Bedtime!" she said in a resurrected voice, the mother voice used on toddlers who had no intention of sleeping. The good thing was Marc complied because his concept of time had disappeared as well. She settled him in and pulled the drapes by 7:20 p.m.

"Want me to play some music to help you fall asleep?"

"What? Ah, sure, something…"

She waited for forty-five seconds, and then knew he had lost his answer.

"How about some soft music, Marc?"

"Yeah. Thank you," he answered, staring up at the ceiling with his covers tucked up to his chin, a gesture that always broke her heart.

"Good night." Heather kissed his forehead.

"Good night."

On beer number three, Heather went to her office and logged onto Facebook.

"And now," she said aloud, taking a long gulp, "let's get really depressed by seeing what all the happy fucking families are doing for the holiday."

Flags, parades, kids dressed in red, white, and blue. Smiling, well-built husbands with their arms wrapped around their wives. She finished off her beer.

Ping.

Heather jumped in her chair. John Timmer, a boy she had grown up with and had "friended" her last week, sent her a message on chat.

Hey, Heather Finch, Happy 4th. It's July 4th already here in Scotland, where I'm living now. Thought I'd pop in on my Swan Princess, wondering how things are for you. It's been years (I hate to count how many) since we've talked. How are things?

What! These words sent a jolt of tingles through her body: *my Swan Princess.* John Timmer remembered she had danced as the Swan Princess as a freshman in her high school performance. She didn't even remember he had gone to see the play, and now twenty-six years later he used the possessive pronoun my! What in the world should she say to him?

She didn't think too long, the beers making her confident and calm. Relief and possibility filled her with a distant happiness because someone had reached out to her on this most awful day.

She typed.

Hi, John Timmer! It's great to hear from you. I'm okay. A lot has happened in the years since we've seen each other. I'm not much of a Swan Princess these days.

Send.

The words "John is typing" sent chills through her body.

Ping.

Sure you are. You just need to find her again. What's up?

Heather smiled and "live" chatted for the first time with a friend.

Live

Same day in late June, present day

"Love the poems of Gerard Manley Hopkins, do ya?" Steven asked. He sat on Heather's couch in White Cottage, their date day in Inverness and Culloden over. Steven had fetched delicious orange, berry, and spinach salads, home-baked bread, and wine from Near the Loch. But now, their light meal was complete. Heather's stomach dropped with the possibility of physical contact with a man; did she forget or get worse at sex after having no practice for a long period of time?

"What?"

Steven leaned over and picked up two books off of the coffee table. "Hopkins. You must love his poems. You have two books on display."

"Oh, no, I mean, yes, I love Hopkins, but no, the books aren't for display. Open them up and you'll see all the notes and markings. I read and re-read his work, especially when I'm working on a first draft."

"So he inspires you."

Heather sat in the cushy chair across from Steven rather than with him on the couch. Even leaning back in a relaxed pose felt suggestive, so she sat up straight and sipped her wine.

"Yes, inspiration and comfort, that's Hopkins for me," she said.

"That's very good," he said in that low Scottish-Highlander-come-home-from-wandering kind of way that made Heather need to cross her legs to suppress a desire she had forgotten.

The brass clock on the fireplace mantel ticked. Birds settled outside, their chirps and trills calling from the woods. The quiet of the cottage, all of its sounds, had become a known background to Heather. She had even grown used to the occasional wrestle of shrubs from the tree line, most likely a mink or a marten, during the nights or early mornings. Now, another human, a man human with the power of speech, had entered her hermitage. In addition, he certainly wanted to sleep with her; she wasn't so outdated to miss the desire in his eyes.

"Do you want more wine, Steven?" That broke the air of sexual possibility. Maybe she could get out of this somehow; retreat to her pajamas and bed alone. But she didn't want that; she wanted to feel someone else's skin, to be touched, to be held, and yet, getting her body to move in that direction felt like trying to steer a kayak over the frozen tundra.

"No, thank you," he said, running his palms over his knees. "Heather, I dinnae want to pressure you or anything, but when you kissed me at the battlefield, I haven't felt that way in some time. I get so caught up in this place, always working, always thinking on the next thing, it's not something I look for."

"What something?"

He gave a quick laugh, "A beautiful woman, kissing her, and being with her."

"Oh," she said, her face hot embers.

Steven stood and crossed the room like a sleek-moving marten. He stood in front of her chair and took her hand in his and at the same time taking her wine glass from her other hand and setting it on the table.

"I want to kiss you now, love, I cannae hardly stand it." He pulled her up and kissed her gently at first, his tongue exploring her mouth, his hands holding both of hers. Heather felt stiff and too aware of her lips at first. She responded, though, and moved closer to his chest; she let him work his hand on the small of her back without tensing up.

When they pulled back from each other, she said, "Steven, I'm horribly out of practice. I think I've forgotten how to do this."

"No, love, take it from me, you have not forgotten how to kiss." He smiled, pulled her into his arms, and kissed her neck.

Heather stared up at the ceiling, noticing a crack that ran a solid two feet. When his hands moved over the outline of her body, she moaned, unable to quiet the stirring inside of her. Her body, she surmised, had been in a state of hibernation, put to sleep and turned off to desire for so long, every touch became an electric jolt; every kiss, an awakening to sensations long buried.

Move your hands, she told herself. They moved. They felt Steven's solid frame, his chest and arm muscles like sculpted marble. His nether regions still terrified her, and at this point, even he didn't put his hands under anything, only rubbing on the outside of clothing, gently over her back, her backside, then to her breasts, causing her to moan again and nearly buckle.

Steven put his head on her shoulder, and inexplicably she thought of the Colossus of Rhodes.

Stop thinking, said her inner voice, one she couldn't manage to turn off, evidently even during PHYSICAL CONTACT.

Steven started to sway, a subdued dance. "Will you go to the ball with me on July 3rd?" he asked.

Heather's head spun because the word "ball" made her think testicle, which made her think naked. The thought of seeing and touching a naked man again, one who wasn't Marc, caused a spasm of sorts in her brain. Then the date, July 3rd, the anniversary of Gerard's birth/death. This made her stomach drop. Then her mind skipped again. Was "ball" some kind of Scottish slang for sex she was unaware of? Maybe he wanted to put it off for a few days. This idea appealed to Heather because the thought of getting naked in front of a man made her feel nervous beyond repair.

"Um," she said. Her body tensed, and Steven must have felt it because he pulled back and looked her in the eyes.

"Do you know we put on a ball every summer as a fundraiser? We hold it at the hotel. It's simply grand. I'd like to take you as my date, if you'll have me." His Scottish accent, soft and singsong and welcoming, broke her tension, and the tone of his voice was cautious, expectant, and yes, somewhat nervous. How could she say no?

"Do I need to dress like Cinderella?" She smiled.

Steven laughed. "No, but you will need to be in something very fetching. Did you pack dinner wear?"

Of course she hadn't. He was serious; she knew image mattered to Steven. If she went, she'd have to buy a suitable dress. How?

As if he'd read her mind, he said, "I can have a lass help you shop, if you'd like. Take you to a place in Fort William. I'll buy it if you need."

"Oh, no, that won't be necessary. Wait, yes, it's necessary that someone help me get to a shop, but no, I'll buy it."

"So it's a yes, then?" His sea green eyes sparkled.

"Yes."

Slowly, they hugged again and swayed, a motion so much like sexual thrusting that Heather said, "Do you want to go upstairs?" against the voice of her mental editor, the one analyzing her every move and word. *Get laid*; Leann's voice rang in her head. She felt a cosmic push from her friend across the ocean. So many times in their friendship Leann had guided her. Why not now, when she really needed to feel loved? It had been so long since she'd felt a man's skin next to hers.

"Aye," he said in a low tone. He took her hand, and they made their way up the curving wooden stairs, which creaked underfoot, a sound that had become a "home" sound to Heather. This made her think about buying White Cottage, and her mind reeled again. What if she slept with Steven, things went badly, and then she bought White Cottage, or maybe he wouldn't want to sell to her because of their history together.

Two more steps to the bedroom.

One more.

Into the attic bedroom, which glowed with moonlight.

"Here we are," he said.

She didn't know what to say, so she kissed Steven again, smashing down the voice of worry.

They did an awkward walk to the bed and lay down, Steven on top of her.

His hands swept over her breasts and stomach, but instead of being tantalized, she wondered if he liked how they felt, and she worried that once the bra came off he would dislike the odd shape her nipples had taken on after breastfeeding two babies.

"Shall I undress you?" he asked.

"Um," she said in a shaky voice, "yes."

Within seconds all garments were off – hers and his; she thought it would have gone slower, but too quickly she was naked beneath him, and feeling too bright in the moonlight. She glanced down to his groin and was not disappointed, but it also struck a thin wave of desire and nervousness throughout her body, like she was given a fancy kitchen utensil she couldn't identify, one made for gourmet cooking when she was more a day-to-day functional cook of comfort foods and baked goods. What was she to do with it?

He kissed her face, neck, shoulders, breasts; his hands were calloused and all over her body. She urged her own to respond and caress his body, avoiding his groin, the elephant in the room.

"Ah, Steven," she said.

"Aye," he murmured between kisses.

"I, I'm very nervous. I haven't done this in so long."

He lifted up, leaning on one elbow, and looked in her eyes. "You're doing great."

"Well, thanks, but do you....I don't know, do you want to, you know, go all the way?"

Oh, no. How inexperienced did that sound?

He smiled and brushed her hair back. "I'll do whatever you want."

"Well, I can't get pregnant because I've had a tubal ligation, but I'm not sure I'm ready for everything. I'm so out of practice."

"You don't seem to be."

"Believe me, I am."

"Let's go slowly," he said, kissing her lips softly, leaning in and working his hand in tiny circles between her legs, making her sink into the pillow, relax a little. Her mind finally shut off, her body calmed, and her hand moved down his body.

"Okay," she said, kissing his chest, then shoulder. "That works for me."

**

A woman stood in the moonlight in the bedroom of White Cottage. She wore a long, woolen skirt and blouse, both blood-soaked and tattered. Her auburn hair hung in wet streaks framing her pale face. Heather sat up in bed and tried to scream, but no words came out. She looked down at her bare breasts and the tip of her triangle of pubic hair peeking out from under the sheet. Where was Steven? She was alone.

Her throat felt filled with cotton. This had to be a dream. Was this Meg, her character? Never had she had such a vivid dream about a character before, never had one materialized out of the fog.

"Meg?" Her mouth formed the name in the dream, but there was no sound. In return, Meg opened her mouth to say something back to Heather. Heather leaned forward.

Clink. Clink. Tink.

Heather's eyes flashed open.

Steven's arm linked over Heather's stomach as he slept. She shot up to a sitting position, sending his arm to the bed with a thud. Shadows danced on the wall. The clinking sound came again from outside the cottage.

"Meg?" she whispered, this time with a real voice.

Her body tensed. What was it?

Clink, cla-clink, cla-clink. The noise touched the air like a wind chime and then drifted off. It was 2:10 a.m. Heather's mind raced to the imagined perimeter of the outside of the cottage. Was there a metal bucket or some other implement an animal could be batting about? No, nothing came to mind, and she'd spent an inordinate amount of time walking around her little haven, staring off at the pond or tree line, as she thought about a plot point or character tick.

Tink, tink, tink, tink.

Her heart quickened. She grabbed her robe and dashed downstairs.

Ta-tink, ta-tink. Then, nothing.

Heart thundering in her chest, she crept into the kitchen, realizing the sound came from outside the window over the table. Slinking along the wall, trying not to be in view of the window, she moved toward the pane. She paused, her body erect along the wall next to the window, and listened. The birds were quiet at this time of night; a slight wind whistled; an animal, something plunking in the pond, sounded in the distance. But this metallic pinging was new – foreign, haunting.

She shook her head and pulled back the curtain; her heart raced; her body felt taut, ready to spring. She peeked through and saw the outline of her wild flower patch, the shadow of the woods, the phantom image of her garden bench, almost glowing in the moonlight. She stared, afraid, yet compelled to study the area because she knew something had to be out there. Nothing surfaced.

Heather's head swam with images of Meg from her dream; a dizzying vertigo overtook her body, so she steadied herself with her hand on the window frame. Sometimes her left ear rang due to having a bad ear infection when she was younger, and now it resounded with a high-pitched tinging that engulfed her head. What was wrong with her?

Then – a flicker of light! Not from a flashlight or flare, nothing recognizable, just a tip of illumination that flashed through the window, caught her eye, and disappeared. Heather froze and ducked down, shaking. What was it?

She dashed out of the kitchen and up the stairs, slipping without grace into the bed next to the still-slumbering Steven. Maybe she was hearing and seeing things because of her wrecked nerves. She couldn't underestimate how intimacy with a man had shaken her. And then, the dream: never had a character been embodied in her dreams so vividly before; Millicent showed up once or twice, benignly writing in a notebook or stirring tea. Heather needed to sleep, to forget the clinking and the flick of light, which was probably just the moon. She lay awake, staring at the ceiling and listening for long minutes. Finally, she got up and rifled through her drawer and found the bottle of over-the-counter sleeping pills, a crutch she fell on in the years since Marc's stroke. She popped one in her mouth, not caring if it made her groggy in the morning. No more clinking sounds broke the air, or she didn't hear them because she drifted off into a dreamless sleep.

Live
July 3rd, present day

"Give me the details, Finchy," Leann said. Heather's cell phone crackled and cut off.

"Damn it!" Heather knocked the phone against her hip. "Not now!" She paced her living room, holding her cell up, trying to make a signal appear. Nothing.

Stomping to her kitchen, glancing out the haunted window as she'd come to call it and glimpsing a flock of barn swallows circling out beyond the pond, she sighed and fired up her laptop, resolving she'd have to Facebook chat with her best friend to get dating advice. It was already late afternoon, her "ball gown" hung upstairs, and she'd had to have a glass of wine to calm her nerves. Her hand went to the bottle, ready to pour another glassful to gulp during the excruciating minutes it took to log on to Facebook, but she hesitated and then put the bottle on top of the fridge. She had a feeling Steven wouldn't approve of a tipsy date.

As soon as Heather logged on to Facebook, Leann pinged her.

Tell me!

Heather sat down; her hands poised over the keyboard. What was there to say? She knew exactly what; her fingers flew over the keys, detailing how she had gotten through the date days with Steven and the uncategorized days with John. She left off right when Heather and Steven were alone at White Cottage just a few days ago, and following that description she wrote about the interminable days of writing and walking that felt like weeks. John Timmer hadn't called.

Heather didn't know how to put it, even with Leann, the only person she was relatively open with. She's had some sexual contact; she blushed at the idea of going into detail. What to write? Gratefully, she read the words, "Leann is typing," and felt relief, knowing her friend would guide her.

Answer this. Did you get laid?

Not officially.

Details.

It's embarrassing. You know I'm not comfortable talking about this stuff. I feel like nuns are looking at me from the light fixtures. By the way, I think the cottage is haunted. I heard strange clinking sounds the night Steven was here, and I saw a weird flicker of light out my kitchen window. I may have had a vision of a ghost or one of my characters.

She hit send.

Hah, to the nun comment. Haunted? Just your narrative imagination. I know you've been cooking up Scottish characters. That and add some male contact, and your mind is making that up. What I am interested in is this bit, "the night Steven was here." What did you do? Please don't tell me what you ate for dinner.

Heather laughed aloud because that was exactly what she had planned to write. Finally she typed, *I can't write this for real. I'm too used to fiction.*

Then give it to me in fiction.

Too difficult to cast the characters, the setting, the mood. I'm on a time crunch. I have this "ball" – a real freakin' ball to go to tonight with Steven.

A few minutes went by before Leann typed again. *Sorry. Had to put the chicken in the oven. Okay, here's an idea. Don't go into the whole made-up story, give me the "activities" of the night in a nutshell. You know, just the title or something pithy.*

Heather thought about this. The afternoon sun streamed through the kitchen window. She loved this time of day and longed to stay home in her cottage. Even though she now took a sleeping pill each night because she was ashamed to admit the "haunting" of the other night had spooked her silly. In the last few days, in between checking for messages from John, she'd started a late afternoon routine where she'd walked in the woods around her cottage, or around the pond, always with a notebook in hand, to think and take notes about Meg and other characters or plot points.

Ping. Heather jerked back to reality.

Come on, Time-crunch Girl. Get out of the ether and tell me. Give me a title of what you did with Steven.

Heather stared at the screen, smiled, and typed.

Hand jobs, Blow jobs, and Orgasms: How to Gain a Fuck Buddy as a Widow

"Leann is typing" showed up immediately.

Hee, hee! LOVE it. Good for you, girl! I do hope he was not the only one to have an orgasm?

Heather considered and then typed, *Me too. I think I could have come off with a swift wind to my groin, it's been so long.* She chuckled and hit "send." She could almost hear Leann's hearty laugh across the ocean.

Way to go, Finchy! Now, how are you feeling about tonight?

Nervous. Extremely nervous. If things progress, we'll sleep together, really together this time – you know, real intercourse. And don't get me wrong, it's nice. It's just that I'm not sure how to do this! I'm also interested in John, but then again, he hasn't called for over a week, and in this Scotland timeline, where every day feels like two or three, I'm ready to write him off.

Don't do that. Leann typed after a couple of minutes. *He has kids. He's working. Life happens. Have you contacted him?*

No.

Well, there you go. He may be giving you space. Will he be at the ball?

Heather's heart quickened. There was a very good chance that John would be there because of the farm. Claire did business with the restaurant and catering business at the hotel. If Claire was there, given her Fuck Buddy status, so would John. The thought made Heather's body tingle.

Instead of going into detail, Heather typed, *Could be. Thanks for listening, Leann. I better go get ready. XO, Heather.*

Have a great time, Cinderella!

Heather signed off. As she walked through the living room, she grabbed one of the books by Hopkins and sat on the couch. She flipped to one of her favorite poems, "Pied Beauty," and read,

> Glory be to God for dappled things –
> For skies of couple-colour as a brinded cow;
> For rose-moles in all stipple upon trout that swim;
> Fresh-firecoal chestnut falls; finches' wings;
> Landscape plotted and pieced – fold, fallow, and plough;
> And all trades, their gear and tackle and trim.
>
> All things counter, original, spare, strange…

This was one of her favorite poems, though it was hard for her to choose. She hugged the text to her chest and "dappled" sounded in her head, making her see John's image in her mind's eye. "Dappled" fit him, just as "statuesque" fit Steven. Which man fit her? She went to put the book back on the coffee table but decided against it. She tucked it under her arm, ran upstairs, and once there, placed Hopkins on the nightstand next to her bed. She made herself imagine Steven in bed with her there, but John's image appeared, his long frame taking up the length of it, his hands reaching for her. Tucking a bookmark on the "Pied Beauty" page, she wondered what the night would bring.

***

Steven took Heather's hand right before they entered the Ardorn Hotel. The night was clear, with a dusky orange sun on the horizon. Potted roses lined the wide, stone steps. Hand-made metal lanterns, with blue light bulbs shimmering within, hung from poles. Heather breathed in the scent of flowers she couldn't identify from the gardens to the right of the hotel. The air, the expansive pink and yellow sky, and the open door to an entryway with a glowing chandelier gave her a hitch in her throat. For the first time in a long time she felt she was a woman of possibility, a woman in an iridescent blue dress, the color of the inside of a clam shell, and she actually felt beautiful. That in and of itself was remarkable – something she should jot down in her notebook with the date and time.

"I have to tell you one more time; you look great," Steven said, leaning up a little to speak in her ear. Heather didn't want to regret the pumps; she'd bought them because they matched the dress so well, but in them she stood a half inch taller than Steven.

"Great" was his word of choice to describe her. Sometimes, he used "grand," like most the Scots, and she preferred that of the two. Though she really hoped for "beautiful" or "gorgeous" or "iridescent."

"Thank you," she said. "You look very handsome." He did look dapper in a traditional tux top and hunter green-patterned kilt. His hair had been buzzed since she saw him last, his face was clean-shaven and smooth. His eyes danced in the dying light.

"Shall we?" He bowed toward the entrance and led Heather through the doorway before she could answer. Heather had seen the posh hotel one time before, when Finlay and Jackie drove through the circular drive and paused in front of the Victorian-style architecture, a building from a different time that transported her into a realm of luxury. Marble floors sparkled from the chandelier and lantern light. Fresh-cut flowers spilled over ornate glass vases. A winding staircase led to a high balcony, a view Heather felt drawn to explore. Her eyes drifted up the wooden steps, taking in the men and women in fancy clothes who sipped drinks and mingled in the large entryway. People surrounded Steven already, and while he turned to introduce her, he clasped her hand and pulled her to his kilted hip, a possessive gesture that sent a surge of excitement and nervousness through her body. At this proximity, she did regret the shoes, despite the perfect match.

"Aye, I'd be in on a bracken maintenance and management plan at Ardorn, and I'd push for it in other areas as well," Steven said, releasing Heather and snatching two champagne flutes from a waiter's tray. This was a sunset ball, so only appetizers and drinks were served. After taking three long sips of her champagne, Heather's head felt light, reminding her she hadn't eaten anything substantial since lunch. Steven had broken away, completely engaged in the bracken discussion, so Heather scanned the room again. She saw Finlay, Melissa, and Jackie from the Solace Art Fund and smiled when they beckoned her to join them.

"Sorry to interrupt," Heather said, leaning into Steven's conversation with as much decorum as possible, "I'll be over there, Steven." She signaled across the room.

"Aye," he said in a deep voice and licked his lips.

He wanted to kiss her. She had started to recognize the changes in his tone right before he made a move. She smiled and crossed the room with heat on her cheeks.

"Hey, Ms. Finch!" Finlay grabbed her in a bear hug. Heather felt so much relief to be with familiar, friendly faces. "So you're here with Mr. Connolly, aye? Like I said, he fancies you if you haven't already picked up on that."

"Finlay," Jackie said, knocking him hard on the shoulder. Her brown eyes caught the light, and her purple dress hugged her fuller frame. Heather put her arms out for a hug, taking in Jackie's scent of lilies, so grateful for her amiable nature. Heather realized now what a disaster the night could be: listening to Steven talk sustainability and business, trying not to drink the entire champagne fountain, and not having a soul to talk to. Now with her three writing compatriots, Heather couldn't control her relief.

Melissa excused herself, moving off to join a group of kilted business men. Finlay snagged a waiter and ordered a pint of local ale. After handing her wine glass to Finlay, Jackie nibbled from a plate of seafood appetizers. Heather smiled and downed the rest of her champagne, allowing the bubbles to warm her throat and chest.

"Would you fancy another glass, Ms. Finch?" Finlay asked.

"Um, I don't know," she answered.

"Would you want some wine or beer instead?" Jackie asked. "They have quite an excellent open bar, and the food is delicious."

"Shall I get you something?" Finlay asked when the waiter returned with his beer.

Under pressure and dying for a drink, Heather said, "yes, a glass of chardonnay, please."

The waiter nodded and retreated.

"How you getting on with the writing?" Finlay asked. His lanky build swam a little in his suit jacket, and a tightened belt squeezed his kilt over his slender hips.

Before Heather could answer, the manager of the hotel, a put-together woman in her fifties, stood on a portable podium next to the staircase. She tapped a microphone and smiled at the crowd, scanning her eyes over the faces like one accustomed to holding the attention of a room.

When the group settled, drinks meeting lips, the manager said, "Hello, everyone, and thank you for attending our yearly fundraising ball. Many of you have found the buffet of appetizers and the open bar in the lounge. In the common room, which is decorated with paintings and tapestries from local artists – all of which are for sale – there will be a silent auction throughout the evening. The winners will be notified at the end of the ball. And the key event, the dancing, will take place in the upstairs ballroom. The band will begin in half an hour. Thank you again, and enjoy an amazing sunset view from the ballroom after 10 p.m."

The waiter materialized with Heather's wine, and she sipped, trying not to gulp the sharp, almost buttery apple taste. This was not from a two-buck bottle of chardonnay from her corner liquor store.

"So, your writing?" Finlay asked, picking up the conversational thread like one much older than his early twenties.

"Well, I'm writing a great deal and doing research. My head is swimming, filling up with new characters." Heather's face felt hot.

Jackie's eyebrows went up, perfect arches over her dark eyes.

"I cannae wait to read it in print." Finlay finished off his pint and smiled widely. If Heather stuck with him during the night, they could go toe for toe with the drinks.

"You may be making our resident writer nervous with your eagerness, Finlay," Jackie said, her Scottish accent subtle, her vowels rich like traces of cinnamon baked into warm bread. "All we care about is that you produce while you're here at the retreat. Many of us on the selection board, myself included, loved your Millicent submission, and I'm a big fan of your other Millicent books. I'm sure we'll be equally enthused with what you're working on now. Care to share some details?"

"It's historical fiction," Heather started, feeling nervous and uneasy for some reason. Jackie was nothing but pleasant and open. Why did she feel like she was doing something wrong?

"Blimey," Finlay said. "That's Jackie's favorite genre!"

"Really? Great!" Heather said with false excitement; now she was really nervous that her story line and writing sucked, that she would never stand up to their expectations. Steven made his way across the room, holding his first glass of champagne, and sidled up next to

Heather. He shook Finlay's and Jackie's hands, asking both if they were enjoying themselves.

The conversation hit a lull. Steven reached over and took Heather by the elbow; once again, the gesture was more than friendly; she felt the possession in it, how his eyes honed in on her face and body like she was his for the taking. She flushed in the milliseconds before he spoke, feeling Finlay's smile in her periphery.

"Are you hungry?" Steven asked her.

Heather started to answer, but someone caught her eye. To her right, where the entrance gaped open to dusky shadows and lantern light, and the scent of jasmine (yes, that was the flower she hadn't been able to identify upon arrival) wafted into the hall and to her nostrils, there, in the doorway, stood John Timmer. His face seemed tentative, but open, with wide eyes taking in the room. He wore a suit, not a tux or kilt, something tailored, hugging his fit body beautifully; the tie was smoky blue, almost like he had intended to match Heather's dress. His hunky shoulders filled in the jacket, the contours drawing Heather in, making her imagine stepping up to him, grabbing him by the shoulders, and kissing him hard on his full lips.

Her answer to Steven's question caught in her throat; her body tingled with anticipation and magnetism, for as soon as John saw her, a line of energy stretched between them, drawing his eyes to hers. Claire and another woman entered the room with John, but their outlines were blurry shades because John's frame took up Heather's sight. She flushed for the millionth time that evening, croaking out a "yes" to the question of food.

Steven hadn't noticed the gravity shift, or he ignored it. Instead he said, "I'll get you a selection then." He strode off to the buffet, leaving Heather standing and staring at John who stared back, a smile materializing on his face. He tapped Claire and pointed to Heather and her group.

The seconds it took for John and his group to cross the room gave Heather a window to catch her breath, collect her lascivious thoughts, and smile like she did to all the guests. Her face felt false and foreign because her insides reeled with excitement to be in proximity to John again. This was not good. She was on a date with another man after all.

"Hey, Heather," John said, taking her in his arms in a warm hug. She wondered if he could feel her throbbing heart against his chest. He lingered in the hug longer than he had the first time they saw each other at White Cottage. His palm seared heat between her shoulder blades where it found the backless design of the dress and rested during the seconds of the embrace. The entire moment went too quickly for Heather; she would have loved to stay in his arms longer. But it was time to pull away and say hello.

The introductions seemed to take place underwater. Jackie introduced herself; John introduced Claire and her girlfriend – Hannah – who was tall with cropped hair and near perfect features. After everyone said hello, Hannah took Claire's hand to go in search of champagne from the fountain. At least that was what Heather surmised. The interactions floated into the ether because she had a hard time not meeting John's eyes.

"I'm having another, right-o Jackie, so grand of you to drive my arse around tonight," Finlay said, tracking a waiter.

Jackie laughed and said, "So John, how is the summer season at the farm this year?"

Hearing his name, John's eyes broke from Heather, and he turned to Jackie, saying, "It's going well, almost too well. Claire has all the boarders, me, and two other skydiving brothers, working our tails off. Don't get me wrong, she can cook up a storm, feeds us off the land like a goddess, and Hannah, too. She can really cook and throw down." John rubbed his hands together and glanced at Heather, almost nervous. About what – was it that he mentioned his Fuck Buddy's name?

"I could use a beer. You ladies want anything?" John asked.

"I'm off to catch what Melissa is saying to those blokes over there," Jackie said and excused herself.

"Heather," he said once they were alone. His voice broke and cleared. His hazel eyes looked brown tonight, like the depths of the pond near her cottage. "You look so beautiful. I mean, really, really amazing." He stroked the area around his mouth where small smile lines had formed.

"Thank you," she said, feeling beautiful and awash with pleasure from hearing the word from him. "And you look amazing, too. Very handsome." Her face and hands blazed with heat. She downed the rest of her chardonnay.

"Let me get you another," he said. "You want another…"

"Chardonnay. Yes, please," she said. She glimpsed Steven making his way toward them, and her stomach dropped.

"Hello, Timmer," Steven said, nodding because his hands were full. "I'd shake your hand, but I had to get sustenance for my lovely date."

John's face fell; Heather couldn't take it. Crestfallen. She finally understood what that word meant exactly, and in that moment she wanted to stuff a crab leg in Steven's mouth to shut him up.

"Date? Really?" John said, adding a touch of surprise to his tone. The shocked expression flicked off, just as fast as his aloofness could surface.

"Aye," Steven said, cocking his head. "Don't be so surprised, Timmer, I have been known to go on a date once in a while. And this one is our third."

John jerked his head back, his face a little red, and his chest inflating.

What in the hell! Would Steven please shut the fuck up? Heather felt her lips tightening.

"Here, I'll take my plate" was all she could say. She bit into a cracker with some kind of fancy pate and said "yum," which was muffled in a high-pitched sound from her throat.

"Third time's the charm, they say," John said, gaining confidence? Cockiness? Heather wasn't sure; she downed more crackers, chewing nervously and watching the two roosters puff out their chests.

"What do you mean by that?" Steven said with a fake smile. His jaw twitched in a not so attractive way.

"Just a saying, you know, when something has run its course," John said. Before Steven could respond, he added, "I'll be right back, I was just about to get a glass of wine for Heather and a beer for myself. You want another champagne, Steve?"

"No thank you. And I can –"

"No, you have your hands full with the food. I got the drinks, mate," John said, leaving.

When John was out of earshot, Steven said, "Runs its course, what the bloody hell does that mean?"

Heather had taken the opportunity of John's departure to eat the shrimp on her plate, even though she didn't like shrimp. She chewed and nodded, chewed and nodded, hoping that the conversation would shift before she swallowed.

But it didn't.

"You mentioned you knew Timmer," Steven said, "how's that?"

Heather gnawed the last bite of shrimp, worrying it down to the veins, but finally had to answer. No businessman talking bracken habitats would save her from the conversation.

"We grew up together. Of all things. Strange how we reconnected on another continent," she said, popping in another pate cracker, wishing for more wine.

"Reconnected?" Steven asked. He had set his plate, untouched, on the tray of a passing waitress.

Heather locked eyes with Steven, trying in a peculiar way, not to give something away, even though not a thing had happened with John.

Somehow, she worried Steven could tune in to her thoughts and desires.

She had to answer, think of something benign to say. "Yes, we're friends on Facebook so when I won the grant, and I knew he was in Scotland for part of the year, we corresponded. It was nice to know someone when I was leaving the country for the first time in ten years."

Steven's relief was palpable, but then John arrived, handing Heather her wine, which she couldn't help but gulp, making Steven glance at her tipping hand with the glass a little too long for her liking.

"Thank you," she said, glancing and mindfully looking away from John.

"You're more than welcome, Heather," John said in a deep voice. She couldn't help it; she had to chance one glance at him. Sure enough, he was staring at her in this way that made her insides quiver and her groin burn.

Steven coughed and finally finished his champagne.

"Ready for another, Steve? The champagne fountain is flowing," John said. His voice was definitely cocky, with a strain of condescension. Heather hated to admit it, but she wished Steven would leave for a few minutes, just so she could talk with John alone. She squashed the thought. What would this accomplish? She was, in fact, on a date with Steven, a man who had made his intentions very clear, and if she played her cards right she may actually get laid, real intercourse, with a penis inside of her. It had been a very long time.

"No, I'm fine," Steven said. The twitch started up again.

Long seconds of no conversation went by; Heather wouldn't look directly at John, for fear of gazing at him the same way he was at her.

Mercifully, orchestra music came from the upstairs ballroom. Guests turned and started toward the stairs with drinks in hand.

"Sounds like the dancing is about to begin," John said. "Could I snag your date for a dance or two, Steve?"

Heather finished her wine, her head floating, and ditched her food plate and glass on a tray they passed while walking with the crowd in slow motion to the stairs.

"Aye, if you can peel her off of me," Steven said, taking her hand.

Heather gave Steven a look, one she hoped communicated that she didn't really like the possessive comment. John caught it, smiling with satisfaction and leading the way up the curving, wooden stairs. Steven's hand sweated in hers. She broke away and wiped her palm discreetly on her dress. As she followed John up the stairs, she watched her feet, trying to calm her pulse and clear her tipsy head.

The ballroom looked like something out of a fairytale. The glossy, polished wood floor led to a wall of windows overlooking the estate grounds. The pink and orange sky dusted the green hills and black streams. A small orchestra played softly as people filed into the room. A group of men in kilts wore bagpipes on their chests. People gathered around the band, and the conductor announced that they would start with a traditional hymn.

As they made their way toward the orchestra, Steven was greeted by a number of people. In and out, Heather weaved, all the while being fully aware of John Timmer's form to her right. At first he was in front of her, then he slipped back, and Steven had been positioned with a few others toward the front of the group. The band started with a low bagpipe sending off a mournful bellow, but then it stopped and strings picked up a folky tune. The music took Heather away for a moment. She was relieved to have some distance from the two men who had suddenly started jostling for her attention. She had no idea how to proceed, being so unfamiliar with the dating world, especially in this foreign country, an unknown culture where she was supposedly older and more seasoned, but where she only felt broken and defeated before even beginning.

Heat curled up her back while the band added more percussion, low beats that met Heather's heart. Without looking, she knew John had moved closer to her, standing directly over her shoulder, sipping his beer quietly. When she closed her eyes, she felt his breath on the back of her neck as his bodily presence sent a jolt through her entire body, where her knees nearly buckled from the pull. Hardly able to swallow, she did something that sent a new storyline in motion, she stepped backward, just a touch, but an inviting movement she knew John would recognize because he leaned in, his lips at her left ear.

"I'm going to slow dance with you tonight, my Swan Princess,'" he said.

Her throat clogged with emotion and desire, but after a few seconds she nodded and said, "Yes."

Live

July 4th, present day

Heather and Steven stumbled up the stairs of White Cottage. She had forgotten to hit the hall light, and clouds obscured the 2 a.m. moon, so no light filtered through the window of her attic bedroom. Steven had asked to come in, and Heather, dizzy with drink and a night of dancing, couldn't refuse him, especially with her hormones raging as if she were a teenager again.

When they reached the top step, Steven kissed the back of her neck. Heather's hand automatically went to switch on the light, but she stopped herself, feeling blanketed and more secure in the darkness.

"I want you so bad," he said in her neck, turning her around and kissing her throat and lips. Shockingly, her body responded. She kissed him back, allowing her tongue to explore with his, trying not to think too much about where to put her hands. Her mind flashed to the two dances with John, being in his firm grasp, feeling his muscles beneath his jacket. She kissed Steven harder. She tried to make her thoughts stay on Steven's body, his firm arms and chest, but each touch brought her mind to the image of John at dusk, the sun blazing orange outside the high ballroom windows, the light casting a glow behind him, and his voice, husky and thoughtful, asking her questions about if she liked where his hands rested, if she wanted another drink, how she liked the music or the flowers, or what she was thinking – as if she were the center of the known world, or the center of multiple worlds they could inhabit simultaneously with each ticking of the clock.

"Can we?" Steven asked; his eyes were as bright as gems. His hands rested on her shoulders, and Heather surmised they were exactly the same height: 5'7".

At first, she had been so lost in the memory of John's voice and image, Steven's question didn't register. Did he mean put on the light? No, of course not – he meant could they do it. Do it, do it, as she and Leann used to say in high school and college.

"Um," she said, biting her lip. This was her moment to say "yes" and maybe tonight she'd gain a Fuck Buddy, but something gnawed at her brain, the teeth of worry telling her she shouldn't string him along; he was a nice man, and she couldn't possibly sleep with two men. After tonight with John's stares and comments, she knew John wanted to sleep with her as well.

Steven's fingertips played with the ends of her hair. He traced her collar bone, waiting for her response.

"Yes," she said and kissed him hard on the mouth. He pulled away and smiled, his white teeth looking ghostly in the shadows.

"Aye," he said and guided her back to her bed.

Heather's head spun and her mouth went dry. She willed her hands to move to Steven's groin, and he responded with full force, kissing her, and pulling up her dress, sliding his hands up her legs. Fully aware of his erection and her slow start, she yanked at his belt, making him groan with anticipation. His fervor and vulnerability did turn her on, but she couldn't help her mind from having two layers of thoughts: one worked at the physical level and reacted to his touches, but the other layer analyzed her reactions too much, as if to say, "ah, you feel clitoral sensations, but your pussy is not very wet, Heather, try to work that out before he's there." All of this happened in seconds, and before she could catch her breath, Steven had slipped on a condom and entered her, thrusting, his tight bottom flexing, so she grabbed it, almost forcing herself to do so.

Heather kissed, moved her hips, and moaned, too, but she knew he'd be done well before she would be close to having an orgasm. It didn't matter, she told herself. She felt a bubble of accomplishment inflate inside of her chest when he came. She smiled to herself; it was over, and she had done it! The jaunty tune, "Back in the Saddle Again" played in her head. Steven's full weight had collapsed on the length of her body, and the assurance of it made her sigh with relief and happiness. Shadows fanned like fingers on the wall; a slight breeze of fresh night air wafted in the open window. Steven went up on his elbows, tenting her with his frame, and brushed his lips with hers. He smoothed back the hairs that had fallen around her face.

"Sorry that was so fast, Heather. You turn me on so, I couldn't help but come off fast."

"It was good, very nice," she said, feeling grateful for being beneath a real live man again. "It's so great to, you know…"

"Have sex," he finished for her and smiled, holding her eyes. "Anno," he added, sounding sleepy and Scottish.

"Yeah," she said, smiling back. Her body felt electric and pliant, like she could dance the rest of the night. She'd love to go on a moonlight walk, or to grab the wine bottle on her fridge and drink and talk until the sun rose.

After getting up and throwing out the condom, Steven returned to bed and took her hand. Side by side, they stared at the ceiling. Heather pulled the sheet up over her body. Noticing the movement, Steven tucked himself next to her under the covers, pecking her exposed shoulder and nuzzling into her neck.

"I'm knackered," he said. "I'm so sorry, Heather, but preparing for the ball has done me in, and you're so wonderful, so grand. Anyway, being with you has been great."

"Yes, it has. Thank you for the evening." She hated how formal she sounded, but the words were out and the tone set.

The room went silent. Heather tried to think of something else to say. Though she wanted the wine or the walk, she figured Steven wouldn't agree, so she settled her thrumming nervous energy by imagining a calm river flowing. Soon she did long yoga breaths, and her pulse slowed. Minutes ticked on, and by the time the digital clock read 3:01 a.m., Steven's chest rose up and down in waves of deep sleep.

Heather disconnected from Steven's side slowly, trying not to cause the bed to creak. She decided to make her way downstairs for water, not wine. She steadied herself by placing a hand on her night stand, taking her free hand and feeling along the top for her book light, which she planned to use as a flashlight. She clicked it on, head foggy, and skimmed the top of the night stand, thinking she'd read some Hopkins once back in bed.

Nothing. The book was gone! Hadn't she left it there?

Heather's heart kicked up to high speed. She thought she had left it at her bedside; she'd tucked in her book mark on "Pied Beauty" after thinking of John as "dappled." Where the hell was the book? The dim glow of her book light cast a small orb of light she maneuvered over every inch of the stand. Then she went down on hands and knees, flashing the light under the bed and beneath the stand, all the while her pulse quickening and her armpits soaking with sweat from nerves.

Had Steven picked it up and moved it? No, they hadn't been apart since they returned from the ball. She'd had to pee so badly before they'd left that she'd had to stop at the hotel bathroom. Once they reached White Cottage, and he'd asked to come inside, they'd touched and kissed and made their way to her bed.

On her feet now, she held the book light like a sword and descended the stairs, arming herself to what she wasn't sure. If an intruder had entered her cottage while she'd been away, maybe the person still lurked in the darkness? But how utterly ridiculous this thought was: why steal a book of poetry? She doubted the thief remained in the cottage, so curiosity propelled her forward.

She streamed the tiny light along the wooden floor and let it lead her to the kitchen. No one crouched in the corner between the refrigerator and wall, or in the nook near the window. She turned and went back to the living room, flicking the lamp on and wondering why she hadn't done that right away. No one jumped out at her from behind the chairs or couch or curtains. The lamp cast a soft, comforting glow on her cozy room, which remained as she had left it before the ball: laptop, camera, and a stack of books on Scottish history sat innocuously on the coffee table. Mindful of tidying before Steven had arrived, any random items, like her make-up and her coffee mug, were still in their places. Nothing had been disturbed.

Where was her Hopkins book?

Instinctively, her eyes scanned the cherry bookshelves in the living room, the ones that had been stacked with an eclectic mix of titles before she'd arrived. Though the books weren't alphabetized, they had been arranged by genre: large photography books on Scotland took up the expansive bottom shelves; travel guides were grouped together, and novels made up the bulk of the titles, and these seemed to be grouped by genre. There, tucked between Dickens and Eliot, sat her missing copy of Hopkins's poetry. She jerked it off the shelf, flipping through the pages at a furious pace, verifying that it was her copy. No one had stolen it, but it had certainly been moved. Had she moved it and didn't remember? Heather collapsed to the couch, wanting to fall asleep, but knowing she would be up for the rest of the hours until dawn. Her stomach twisted with nausea, partly from the lack of sleep and wine intake, but mainly from the burgeoning idea she'd tried to suppress, the one everyone from Leann to Tessa to Jackson had laughed off: she believed, within her bones and sinew, that White Cottage was haunted. The question on her mind now was if the ghost had anything to do with her emerging characters?

"Meg," she said aloud. "Did you move my book?"

No answer came, and no apparition appeared.

Remember
November, two years ago

"It's still okay if I go?" Tessa asked. She wore her favorite jeans and a blue turtleneck sweater. Two of her friends had asked her to the movies on the Saturday after Thanksgiving. Heather stood over the kitchen sink scrubbing a pan caked with the remains of their turkey enchilada dinner. Jackson and Marc watched football in the living room. Heather wanted to tell Tessa the truth – that she couldn't bear for her daughter to leave her, even for a few hours. One member of her wolfpack would be missed beyond reason, leaving Heather to sniff out her scent in every corner of the house until she returned. Heather chuckled to herself with the image and thought of an advertisement to fit her mood: Too dependent and attached to your children? Just practice care-taking manipulation and get them to stay home forever.

"Of course," Heather said, glancing over her shoulder and taking in the blue of Tessa's eyes. "Why wouldn't it be okay?"

"Dad's just been, I don't know, he seems more agitated lately," Tessa said. She creased her brow and fiddled with her purse strap.

"Yeah, that's true. But, honey, you need to get out. I don't want you to worry so much that you stay home all the time." Heather dried her hands on a towel and chanced a hug. Tessa folded into her arms, resting her head on Heather's shoulder like she used to.

"Jackson is staying home tonight, right?" Tessa asked into Heather's shirt.

"Yep," Heather said, pulling away and looking at Tessa, trying to reassure her. "It'll be football, leftover pumpkin pie, and bed."

"Sorry to miss it," Tessa said, sarcasm thick. She seemed grateful for the pass; her eyes lit up as she took the car key off the hook and skipped out of the kitchen. Heather watched her lean in and peck Marc on the cheek. She slapped Jackson on the back of the head. In a flash he stood and retaliated with a slap and hair tussle, which made Tessa dash away giggling. She was out the door, leaving her lotion's kiwi-scent in her wake.

Heather left the pan to soak some more and approached Marc and Jackson.

"You two want some pie?"

"Sure," Jackson said, staring at the TV.

Marc didn't answer right away, so she asked again.

"I heard you," Marc said in a bark. The tone jolted Heather and made Jackson flinch.

She let it pass and waited. The mood flashed and receded as it usually did. Then Marc answered, "sure, honey."

Heather sliced and scooped three pieces of chilled pumpkin pie on plates. She gave each a dollop of whipped cream. Balancing the three plates in her arms, she entered the living room with its hum of sports announcing and low-watt light bulb light.

Jackson took the pie and started scarfing it down without taking his eyes from the television. She helped Marc with a TV tray, knowing he couldn't hold the plate and eat with his nearly paralyzed side. After Marc started his slow process of pie eating, Heather sunk into the folds of the couch and ate. Relief seeped through her body: the day was almost over, and soon the holiday weekend would be complete. She sighed, wondering when she would stop wishing her holidays, and all of her days, away?

After pie, Heather finished scraping the enchilada pan. A corked bottle of merlot beckoned her from the corner of the counter, but she refrained from unstopping it and pouring herself a healthy glass of wine, the mere thought of the reflective blood-burgundy shine calmed her. Alcohol dependence? She wondered, amusing herself. Bedtime would be soon, the turn of a corner or two, some bathroom rituals and clean-up help for Marc, and then she would tuck him into his hospital bed and go back to the couch to read a romance novel.

"Mom, you need any help?" Jackson asked. He stood and stretched his long body, almost touching the ceiling with his fingertips.

"No, I'm fine. As soon as your dad finishes eating, I'm going to help him get ready for bed."

"Okay, I'll be upstairs. Come get me if you need help," Jackson said, eyeing his father. An unreadable expression flickered with his blue eyes hardening and softening in a flash. Heather knew the look well: they all had it. Even a year and a half after the stroke, the disbelief came and went in waves, as if they had entered a parallel world where things were similar, but changed, unworldly, and at any given time, Marc would metamorphose into the vital Marc again. All they had to do was blink and stare at the broken Marc long enough to draw out the old Marc like sucking poison out of the wound after a snake bite.

Seconds passed with nothing said, but that parallel world had been made known to both Heather and Jackson in an instant. Jackson would not go far, in case Heather needed him, especially with Tessa out for the evening. These were the newer caretaking terms since Marc had started being more unpredictable and moody. No one went too far away for too long. They moved as a pack, nudging each other forward, ears alert to any peculiarity or danger.

"Night, Dad," Jackson said, giving a small wave, making Heather's heart burst and contract because he looked so much like how he did as a toddler.

Twelve seconds later, Marc said, "Goodnight."

Heather turned off the television before the news started.

"Okay, honey, I'm going to help you get ready for bed," she said, taking the remote for his lift chair and pressing the lever to make it rise. With the other hand she slid the tray out of the way and positioned his walker in front of him, readying it for him to stand safely.

"I got it," he said. He grabbed at the chair's remote and shoved the lever in the "up" direction.

"Okay," she said. She stepped back, went to the front of the walker, and waited. She had grown used to his mood swings connected to trying to assert more control over his movements. Other times he stood docile as a kitten being groomed by its mother.

Marc dropped the remote and snatched at his walker. He tried to yank it away from Heather, but she stopped him and said, "Just let me get out of the way."

"Yeah, you better," he said, his tone sharp as a knife stab.

Heather let the words pass over her like a swift wind kicking up brittle leaves in autumn and fading to stillness. She hoped his mood would flare, diminish, and resurface more kindly.

Heather moved behind Marc, her hand hovering over the safety belt around his waist, making sure not to touch it so he would feel more autonomy. Marc breathed in and blew the air out like he was at the doctor. When he got to the kitchen and had the choice to enter the bathroom or the bedroom, he paused and craned his neck to Heather. "Which one?" he snapped.

"Bathroom," she said. The hair on her arms stood up from the cold, or his tone – she wasn't sure. Once in the bathroom, she tugged at his elastic waistband, lowering the adult diaper and his pants, and said, "Go ahead and sit on the toilet while I get your pajamas."

"Okay." The docile kitten emerged again.

As much as she could, she rushed through the bedtime routine, guiding his arms through his pajama top rather than letting him navigate the armholes; she skipped mouthwash after he brushed his teeth. While Marc shuffled behind his walker and into their bedroom, Heather flicked on the humidifier and dimmed the lights. She scooted in front of him to lower the arm rail on his hospital bed so he could turn around, clear the walker, and sit down in one fluid motion. Then she helped him swing his feet up and under the covers. Grateful for the silent mood, she felt the freedom of the evening ahead of her, just in the other room. Maybe she would enjoy one glass of merlot while she read.

"Good night, Marc," she said and kissed his cheek.

"Good night," he answered in a mimicked voice.

She turned the lights down and switched on the night light in the outlet next to the door. Clicking the door shut brought on a balloon of relief in her chest. Heather poured a glass of wine, grabbed her book, and tucked herself beneath a blanket on the couch. She sipped and read for almost an hour before she heard banging from Marc's room. She sprang up and dashed to the bedroom.

Marc sat up in bed, clanging the hospital bed rail with the alarm clock that had been on the nightstand.

Heather's heart jackhammered in her chest.

"Marc," she said, trying to use a calm voice. "What are you doing?" A silly question. It was clear he was banging a clock to a rail, again and again. His face distorted in anger. His arms and chest looked massive, like he had been lifting weights in his old body, but that must have been a trick to Heather's eyes. "Marc," she implored, "please stop. You're going to break the clock."

He paused for a moment, connecting with her eyes for a fraction of a second.

"You're my wife?" he asked, but didn't wait for a reply. "You should act like a wife." At least the clock banging stopped while he tried to formulate words. Heather took two steps toward him.

"Yes," she said in a soft voice. "I am your wife."

He clutched the clock awkwardly in his lame left hand. "You don't touch me like a wife." His voice was hollow, empty like a tin bucket.

Heather didn't register the comment at first, but then it clicked. He meant sex, an act that had drifted away into oblivion like space rocks floating. She had become celibate, only masturbating occasionally, but even then, she had ignored those urges as well, and he, after the stroke, didn't seem to realize he had ever been a sexual being. She stood immobilized and anxious, her body tense and taut, ready to spring and snatch the clock away, but she didn't want to make his mood worse. If she waited it out, maybe he'd forget what he was talking about.

But no, he bit on the topic like a tiger tearing flesh.

The clock went up in the air, balanced on Marc's palm like a waiter's tray. "Stroke my dick!"

"What?" she said. "No, I –"

"Be my wife," he yelled and slammed the clock to the rail. It hit metal and bounced out of his hand, cascading to the floor and cracking open.

Heather stooped down to pick it up and tried to gather her thoughts. What should she do?

"Touch me!" Marc lurched over the hospital rail and grabbed the back of Heather's shirt, pulling her up to him. She was surprised by his strength. He yanked at the neck of her shirt until he had a purchase on her upper arm. He drew her to his face, a distortion of lines and shadows. His breath was hot on her cheek; it smelled sour. He slammed his lips to hers and pulled at her hand with his lame one, shoving her fingers to his groin.

"No!" she tried to pull away but his strength was too much for her. They fumbled in an awkward struggle over the hospital rail. Marc sat up straight, an ominous soldier, and looped his good arm around her neck. She squatted and pulled her weight away from him, breaking free of the neck hold, but just as she broke away, Marc drew his arm back and punched at her jaw, connecting on the cheekbone and sending her flying across the floor.

The lights flickered over her. The room went black and then spotty, as if ink had been poured behind her eyelids. She crab-slid backward, toward the opposite wall while Marc shook the arm rail and yelled, "You better fuck me, you whore. Who have you been sleeping with, you fucking cunt? Tell me!" Jackson charged into the room, looking stunned and sick.

Heather cradled her swelling cheek, but couldn't speak. Tears rolled from her eyes, blurring her vision.

"What the hell?" Jackson said. He flexed his hands in and out, in and out. "Shut up! Shut the fuck up, Dad!"

"That cunt needs to fuck me like a husband. Who the hell are you?" Marc screamed. Spittle flew from his mouth and landed on the rail. From there events slowed for Heather: the fight words flew between Jackson and Marc. Marc yelled and pointed at Jackson, then at Heather. Jackson yelled back and then he loomed over Marc, shaking his father by the pajama top and slamming him to the pillow.

Heather heard Jackson shout, "Stop it!" And then he slapped Marc. Hard. Enough to see a fan of redness bloom on Marc's cheek. The room went quiet then. Marc slumped back on the pillows, his face shocked and crimson. Within seconds he started to sob. Between gasps, he reached for Jackson, and then Heather, and said, "I'm sorry. I'm so sorry."

Jackson cried, too, but didn't approach Marc as if his father were a wild animal shut in a trap, one writhing for control but immobilized. Heather raised herself up. She tasted the warm iron of blood in her mouth and realized she must have bitten the side of her cheek at some point. She felt her cheek swelling and burning with pain. Once Jackson saw her stand, he went to her side and shook his hair out. His face was blotched and wet. Jackson pulled Heather to his chest and squeezed, and then he cried into her shoulder, shaking with sobs while his father did the same into his pillow. Heather didn't cry. She stroked Jackson's hair and imagined herself as a river flowing away. Constant motion of waves ribboning through lands, never stopping, going around every fallen tree or other obstacle: Heather flowed with it.

Away.

Live
July 5th, present day

Steven leaned across the gap between them in his car and kissed Heather lightly on the lips. She smiled at him and gathered her small overnight bag. Goose pimples rose on her forearms, not from the kiss, but from her return to White Cottage. After Steven woke on the morning after the ball, the Fourth of July, he had invited Heather to his place for the day. She had wanted to be home, to process the events of the ball and the events in her bedroom, but she'd been scared to be alone in the cottage. So she'd said yes, feeling untruthful, but grateful to be leaving her haunted home.

But here she was again, having to face the white walls, shadows, little clinks or lights out her window again. What spirit drifted there? What soul in unrest banged?

"I've had a great time with ye Heather, I can hardly put it to words," Steven said. Brown-purple bags circled his eyes. The lines in his face seemed deeper.

"Me too," she said, feeling some guilt because though she'd had a good time, her ulterior motive loomed in the air like a fresh lie. "I'm going to try to get back to work. I've been in a fairytale these last couple of days." Not totally untrue, she thought. This fairytale had spirits, Scottish woods, and moving books.

"Aye, I have so much to do I'm starting to feel antsy."

Heather took that as an urge out the door. She gave a little wave and left the safety of the car.

He pulled away before she reached the front step. Dew glistened on the tips of the grass surrounding the plots of wild flowers. The bench in the garden beckoned her and also delayed her entry into the cottage. The morning sun warmed her arms once she sat. She closed her eyes and thought she could spend the better part of the morning outside, hiking and collecting her thoughts. This appealed to her much more than pacing in the cottage, waiting for any sign of her ghost.

Heather stared at the heads of the yawning tiger lilies in the wildflower patch in front of her. The droopy openings made her think of sex with Steven, which was nice, "great," as he would say. She felt wanted again, a lost sensation, and this in turn made her feel like the gaping lily, all open petals and dusty nectar. Then her mind flipped to worry: what about her feelings for John Timmer? Why couldn't she make herself stop overanalyzing everything? Suddenly, despite her fear of entering her cottage, she had a jittery impulse to log on to her laptop, check email and Facebook in case John had tried to communicate with her. She had forgotten her phone as well, so she'd been completely unreachable for the last twenty-four hours while with Steven. What if John had tried to contact her?

She scooped up her bag and fumbled for the key. The entryway seemed to sigh upon her entry. Her eyes quickly scanned the room, noting that her laptop and stacks of papers – finished passages and notes - on the coffee table were the same. The Hopkins book, that tricky item, had gone with her to Steven's and remained safely tucked in the outer pocket of her overnight bag. She walked briskly to the kitchen, and the coffee mugs sat innocuously on the drying rack. The chairs were tucked neatly beneath the table. No pots and pans were askew. The last place to check before logging on to the outside world: her bedroom.

She took the stairs in twos. Morning light made streaks on the comforter. The clear surface of her nightstand remained the same. Nothing was amiss. She sighed with relief, smoothed the top of her covers, and went back downstairs with her heart pumping quicker than usual; her body readied itself for the dopamine rush that came with logging on.

While her laptop warmed up, she found her phone in the pocket of her work bag. No text messages. She went back to the kitchen table and connected to the Internet, her lifeline to family and friends. Her email account was filled with nothing of interest, a few newsletters, bill alerts, and other junk. She flipped to Facebook. The red message icon made her stomach flip. She had two messages.

The first was from Leann:

Can't wait to hear about the ball and your extra-curricular activities! We're with Brian's family over the Fourth, but call or if your signal is bad write – whenever, could be ANY time of day or night. Hugs, L

The second was from Tessa:

Hi, Mom, Happy Fourth of July (though it's the 5th for you right now)! Guess what, Jackson and I actually cooked out on the 4th. He brought a bunch of green leafy vegetables, etc. from Green Life and made a most excellent salad and these elaborate veggie kabobs to put on the grill. I handled the meat – that marinated chicken recipe you taught me. We had a few friends over (yes, Jackson even pulled a few friends out of the woodwork). Anyway, just checking in about our arrival in Scotland at the end of month. I'm starting to get totally jazzed about the trip, and then – COLLEGE!! Yay. I know your phone signal has been weird, so I thought I would reach out to you for once. Thanks for putting up with my moods. I miss you. xo, Tessa

Whoa! Though Heather was disappointed not to have heard from John, Tessa's message was a breakthrough. Things had been so up and down, so strained since Marc's death last December that Heather wondered if she'd ever find a common, peaceful ground with her daughter again. She knew some mothers and daughters simply were not close in their adult lives, and she hated the thought of this being the case for herself and her daughter. Maybe their trip to Scotland would signal a new beginning.

Ping.

Heather shot out of her chair. Her pulse raced when she saw John Timmer had pinged her on Facebook chat. Had he been lurking there in the chat box, waiting for her little green chat circle to show up, and then PING!? She went to her kitchen window and threw it open, letting in the morning breeze. People had warned her about gloomy, rainy days in Scotland, but so far, the storms had been great purges of rainfall that left her refreshed, and most of her mornings cracked open with sunlight, wisps of white clouds, or ones so puffy they looked like perfect scoops of vanilla ice cream.

She splashed water on her face, got orange juice from the fridge, and sat down to read her message from John.

Good morning, Swan Princess! How are you post-ball? If I didn't say it enough, you looked absolutely beautiful on Friday night. Sorry, I didn't reach out yesterday, work gets in the way, and Scotland doesn't give me any American holiday leave! What are you up to today?

Her heart raced at an unnatural speed. She wanted to be flirty and sexy, witty and charming. Her fingertips rested on her keyboard. What to say?

An image of Steven, naked and sleeping in his bed, popped up like driftwood surfacing at the base of a waterfall. She slammed the vision out of her mind and wrote:

Good morning to you as well. If I'm the Swan Princess, are you Prince Eric? You looked like my prince on Friday.

Definitely flirty, but was it too direct? Too much? Too reliant on story – what if he didn't remember the plot of the ballet? She deleted it and wrote:

Good morning to you as well. That's nice of you to say, John. You looked very handsome yourself. Today, hmmm, I should write, but as you can see,

I'm on social media instead. What are you doing today?

Much better, she thought and hit "reply."

Heather read the words, "John is typing," and her breath caught in her throat. His reply popped up in the chat box:

What am I doing? Taking you out on a date if you'll have me.

Heather almost spit out her orange juice. Hell yes, she'd have him. She'd have him with breakfast, lunch, and dinner. She smiled to herself, but then felt instantly guilty. What about Steven? Her mind flipped again. She and Steven hadn't said they couldn't see other people. There was not a thing wrong with spending some time with John, too. This new dating world, this "playing the field," felt so foreign, so exhilarating, Heather didn't know if she should leap with joy or curl in a fetal ball under her covers. The final, precipitating factor: the ghost. A day with John Timmer meant a day away from her haunted house.

I'm yours. She wrote back and hit "reply" before she changed her mind.

"John is typing" popped up immediately.

You sure are. I'll be there in an hour if that sounds okay with you. Dress for hiking. I have a whole outing planned, and a backpack readied for you. All you need are good shoes and comfy clothes.

Excellent! See you soon. She clicked off. The words "You sure are" made her sigh with pleasure.

***

The comparisons hadn't stopped. But how could they? Steven, too, had orchestrated a date day with Heather, the aggressively-scheduled tromp through Inverness, and today, she was led like a wooly-backed sheep to pasture by John, her hunky friend. So far he had picked her up at her cottage, drove her to the airstrip where he worked, and had one of his pilot friends take them for a "side flight over some kintra." His pilot-friend's accent had been so thick, Heather often felt puzzled by what he was pointing out as they flew over sea from the Isle of Mull to an "airstrip" (open sandy beach on the island of Barra). Heather had let out a yelp – a sound she wasn't sure she had ever made – when Tommy, the pilot, adroitly navigated their little plane into a descent and landed on white sands while he hummed and said to Heather with a wide smile, "the landings here depend on the tides and the puffins," which sounded like "poofeens." John had translated by pointing out the window to a flock of the black and white orange-billed birds perched on a rocky overhang.

After unloading their packs, Tommy gave John a salute and said, "I'll be humming back to fetch ye at 1600 hours, here on this wee patch we call a landing. Nice to meet ye Heather!" Tommy hopped back into the tiny plane and waved through the cockpit.

"Let's hike off and give him as much runway as possible," John said, pointing up the sand bluffs to a grassy-topped wedge of rock and sand.

Heather followed, breathing the salty, clean air and listening to the thrum of the engine mixed with the cries of the circling gulls. The puffins had flown off once they'd landed. John sat down on the grass and stretched his long, muscular legs. A pulse of attraction, where Heather knew her eyes lingered too long on his thighs, rippled through her. She positioned herself a few feet from John on the grass. They watched the plane punch air and lift with shocking speed given the short stretch of beach, and soon the buzz of the plane faded until the only sounds between Heather and John were waves splashing, seabirds calling, and the faint chick-chick clicks of unseen insects.

"So are we going to explore Barra today?" Heather asked, shielding her eyes from the sun and chancing another glimpse of John's legs.

"Nope," he said.

"Okay, if you didn't have my interest at the beach landing, now I'm captivated. What's next?"

"We wait," John said, looking at his watch. "Remember the two brothers we picked strawberries with?"

"Yeah, Mick and Carson, what about them?"

"Their dad is loaded, owns a yacht and other expensive toys. Yesterday, I told Carson and Mick about my plan for today, to get us to this low-populated isle with only one ferry crossing we would have had to drive to – about five hours – and then we would have had to time it with a ferry at Mallaig. And guess what – they asked their dad and offered the family yacht to get us to Canna, our destination."

"I can't believe they offered their yacht to us!"

"I know, crazy, isn't it," he said, scooping sand between his fingers and letting it run out. "You made a good impression on the Graham brothers. They didn't hesitate to help me out if it meant me seeing you."

Heather's pulse knocked at her throat. First, John had talked about his plan with her to the skydiving boys. Second, she was 100 percent positive that this was a real date, one with the possibility of really kissing with John Timmer.

"John," she said. She wanted to ask how he felt about her, but the question stuck in her throat. What if he grew obtuse again? Or what if he said he only wanted to show her another Crofter site to help her research? She couldn't handle those outcomes, not with her dating legs just now walking around, or spreading, for a man. This thought made her laugh to herself. She finished with, "I have to tell you. This means a lot – all these transportation efforts. Would you have come alone if I'd said I couldn't come?"

There, that was an easier route to where she wanted to get to in the conversation.

"No way, I wouldn't have come alone. I planned this with you in mind. If you'd said you had to work, I would have coerced you. If you'd said you had plans with Steven Connolly, I would have rescheduled it." He paused and squinted at the sun, his face unreadable. Then he added, "That's not quite true. If you'd said you had plans with Steve, I would have made you break them." He looked at her, the same sultry, possessive expression he'd had at the ball. His eyes seemed honey-colored in the sun.

Her face got hot; she knew it must be red and blotchy. She looked away from his face, uncomfortable with his direct gaze, so she looked to his hands, which didn't necessarily help because she imagined his fingers touching her inner thighs and working their way into her.

Stop, she thought. She hopped to her feet.

"I think I see a boat," she said and pointed.

John slapped his palms together to shake off the sand. He took a step closer to her, and Heather got an instant tingle through her body, starting at her shoulder because John had rubbed up against her there.

"Yeah, I think that's our ride." He stooped to get their gear. After he handed Heather her backpack, they half jogged, half slid down the dune and waited for the yacht.

Never had Heather experienced such doting from a man, or men, rather; each Scottish pilot, sailor, or driver charmed her with his wiles by making her feel like her every need was anticipated. And John had done that as well. Their time together had already shown this aspect of his personality, where he orchestrated their time together, honing in on her desire to be the one taken care of because she had done so much caretaking in the last few years. With the sea spray kicking up and the wind whipping her hair around her head, she grasped the rail of the Graham yacht and smiled at John who returned it with a grin so engaging, so sexy, Heather wanted to kiss him hard on the mouth. She was definitely getting more of her nerve in the man department, but with John, she really needed him to make the first move.

"Here we be, the Inner Hebrides," the captain, Colin, said, maneuvering into a small dock with four slots for boats. A small brick building with a wooden pavilion next to it came into view once the boat idled in its spot. Vendors with scarves, sweaters, and other goods sat at tables beneath the pavilion. Colin added, "It's the honor system, that is, on Canna. Pay wha' ye can when you buy something. Handmade and crafty stuff, that is." Colin took Heather's hand and helped her off of the yacht. He turned to John, "I'll be back to collect you in four hours. Meet here at the dock, Mr. Timmer. Have a lovely time." John shook his hand and then placed it on Heather's lower back, sending a shiver through her body, but guiding her along the short dock to the vendors.

"Welcome to Canna," a woman at a table with hand-woven change purses and book marks said.

"Hello," John and Heather said at the same time. Heather ran her hand over a set of five bookmarks.

"Do you like them?" John asked, his voice getting the Scottish lilt he sometimes picked up.

"Oh, yes," Heather said.

John paid with a hundred pound note, making the vendor's eyes widen and brighten.

"Thank ye, sir. You do know we work on the honor system here?"

"Yes, certainly, my change goes to the island," he said and handed Heather the bookmarks.

"Thank ye again, and enjoy the island. You're the only visitors so far today, but we don't have any accommodations, either camping or at the inn right now. The Craig family who owns the island, along with the National Scottish Land Trust, is doing restorations to the library and the few rooms they rent out for guests. But many lovely hiking trails are there for the taking. And of course, we have a little tea room and pub." She smiled while the wind off the coast blew her long gray hair out of her face.

"Thank you," Heather said and she and John moved away from the dock toward a path ribboning through a green meadow.

They walked in silence for several minutes. Heather saw a golden eagle circling high above them and pointed. John nodded and stepped behind her when the path narrowed.

"I don't want to lead," she said.

"I know, I get the sense you could use someone leading you for a while," he said from over her shoulder, making her turn and nearly stumble on the path. "Whoa." He grabbed her hand and elbow to steady her. They stood in proximity, his breath on her cheek, and she thought surely this would be the moment he kissed her. But he brushed away some stray hairs that had slipped in front of her eyes from her ponytail.

"Thanks," she mumbled, feeling awkward and far too titillated for so early in the date day.

John released her and took out a map from the side of his pack. "They have quite a few moderate hiking trails, some archaeological sites – the remains of Coroghon Castle, an underground chamber, and an early Christian cross. You know, there have been human settlements on this island for about 9000 years."

"Really? That's a long time. Any of those hikes sound good to me. And you are right about me wanting to be led. I can't tell you how much I appreciate this."

"It's cool. I wanted to do it. Follow me." John walked off in front of her, and Heather hoped this wouldn't be another blister date where the "being led" turned into "being invisible" as another date sought out his own interests at a high speed rate. But John took a few strides and glanced over his shoulder to be sure she was close behind. They still couldn't walk side by side through the meadow. About two hundred yards to her left, the sea churned and Heather spotted more black and white seabirds, ones with black beaks instead of the signature orange ones of the puffin. Razorbills.

Soon the path expanded as it snaked away from the coast and further into the green of the island. Swathes of trees, vibrant patches of leafy bushes, and crags of sandy rocks dotted the landscape. No other humans were in sight; the idea of being one of a handful of people on an island in the Atlantic Ocean thrilled Heather. Then John paused for her to catch up to his side. He handed her a water bottle. She took a swig and smiled.

"I thought maybe you were planning to show me another Crofter house," she said after they resumed walking. She liked having him to her right; once in a while his arm brushed up against hers.

"Hmmm, I did have that thought – just to capture that excitement of when you got the idea for your novel. The island of Hirta in the outer Hebrides has these long blackhouses, which are essentially Crofter houses," he said and adjusted his backpack. His eyes went from her face to her body and up again. "See that's the face you get. I love that joyful look." He smiled and gave Heather a quick one-armed hug as they walked. "The boat ride is long and choppy. It seemed a bit much to ask of the Grahams for the use of their yacht. I also remembered some of our chats on Facebook, you know, when we got on the book kick, talking only about our favorites. Since we're both Harry Potter geeks, I wanted to take you on the train where they filmed the Hogwarts Express – the Jacobite Steam Train that runs from Fort William to Mallaig. There's so much I want to do with you," he said in a low, sensual voice.

John's words hung between them. Heather didn't know what to say. Not only had he planned a date day, he planned several in his head, all based on things Heather loved.

The moment passed. John rubbed his hands together. Was he nervous? "Then of course," he added, "you have to try to see Nessie. I love Loch Ness, never get tired of staring off at the surface."

"I've seen it, it looks like oil at some angles."

"True. When did you get to Loch Ness?" John got some trail mix packages out of his backpack and offered one to Heather.

"A couple of weeks ago," she said and tossed some trail mix in her mouth. She wanted to steer the topic from Inverness because that could lead to Steven. Today was most certainly about John Timmer.

"I loved our book chats. You had some great mystery recommendations, which makes me feel like a bad mystery writer."

"I like your mysteries," he said, finishing his trail mix.

"You've read them?"

"Oh yeah. You know I like thrillers."

"Yeah, I know, but my Monvail mysteries aren't exactly thrillers. They're, well, cozy, as the genre defines it."

"True, they are formulaic, but that's a great way to explore avenues with language, which you really did in your later ones."

Heather couldn't believe he had read her books. Her insides turned from nervousness and excitement. Their book chats had come at a crucial time in her care-taking of Marc; John's recommendations often guided her outside of herself. At that time her body and mind were so drained that leisure activities were only the ones that could happen in her own home, so reading became her life blood. Even if she didn't normally read thrillers, if John told her to read them, she did, and she had liked the books he suggested.

"It means a lot that you read them, let alone have something to say about them. Right now they seem silly, like cookie cutter stories that are vapid."

"Naw, that's the devil in your ear. I hear it all the time when I'm thinking of taking a plunge into something different," he said, drinking a long gulp of water. A trickle went down his neck and Heather studied the line it made over his Adam's Apple; she wanted to trace the flow with her finger.

"What new thing do you want to do, John Timmer?" she asked with a smile.

"I love when you call me by my full name. I feel like a kid."

"Hmmm, well, tell me. You've heard about my new novel, probably more than you care to hear. Give me something on you."

They walked several steps along the trail before he answered.

"I want to stop skydiving and invest in Claire's farm, become a co-owner. I'm at my best there, working with the earth, planning out the schedule and the workers, going to the farmer's markets. I love it."

"Why don't you?" she asked. She imagined him there all the time, and if she bought White Cottage, they'd be neighbors in a sense.

"I get worried about the investment, relying on the weather, tourists, year-to-year shit. I want to do as much as I can for Mia and Graham. It's hard enough that I don't see my kids every day. I want to be sure I'm there for them when I can be, and finances are a big part of that."

"True, but it's also wonderful to be a role model of a father who follows his dreams, ones that are realistic and meaningful, which being a co-owner of the farm certainly is."

"Yeah, maybe," he said. "There, up ahead, it's the old stone Christian Cross. The hill there is near some shade trees and has an excellent view of the island, the sea. Want to eat lunch there?"

"Lunch? You mean you packed a picnic for us?" Heather said.

"Hell yeah, look at me, do you think I could eat trail mix all afternoon? I have to warn you it's nothing special – peanut butter sandwiches with some of Claire's homemade jams, apples, and some crisps."

"It sounds perfect."

They made their way to the cross in silence and looked at the stone engraving before settling down on the hill to eat. John made a production of bringing out their food to make Heather laugh. He beamed back at her, and she told herself that if he didn't make a move, she would. At least she could try to up the flirtation.

They ate in silence. Heather looked off over the island to a rocky cliff covered with perching puffins. Groups flew off, dipping out of sight and surfacing like water bobbers. They'd go off toward the sea while some flocks darted back to the cliffside. Her eyes followed these puffin patterns while she chewed the best peanut butter and jelly sandwich she'd ever eaten.

"The puffins nest here to have their young. Those are groups of adults going off and returning with food for their babies," John said, opening another sandwich and offering a second to Heather.

"Aw, I'd love to see little puffin babies," she said and took the sandwich. "I never eat two sandwiches, but these are so good!"

"Plus, all the hiking and sea air can make you hungry."

"Absolutely," she answered and ate. She tried to think of something flirtatious to say, but she hadn't realized how hungry she was, so all she could think about was her lunch: the oaty bread, the luscious blackberry jam, the crisp apples.

Once they finished, John wiped his mouth with the back of his hand. "Get enough, Heather?"

Before she could think otherwise, she said, "enough what?" in her sexiest voice, which she thought did indeed sound kind of husky.

John's eyebrows arched, and he grinned. "I was talking about lunch, but maybe you had something else in mind?" He licked his lips, a signature gesture Heather had begun to identify as something he did when he wanted to kiss her. At least she hoped so. But now what? She had no follow-up; nothing witty or sexy came to mind. Sweat trickled between her breasts. A surge of wetness went straight to her inner thighs. Who was she? This new sexual being had to be someone else!

"I," she paused and stammered, making a squeaky sound (not sexy). She let out a long breath and rubbed her palms over her face. They tasted like salt. Then a sentence came to her out of nowhere, and without thinking she said, "you're like a salt lick."

John laughed quickly and said, "A what? A salt lick? You mean like for deer?"

"Yeah."

"Where did that come from?"

"From out of nowhere, except the odd meanderings of my brain," she said. She really, really wanted to retreat, to get back to books and other safe topics.

"Hmmm, tell me how your brain meanderings made me into a mineral." His eyes went from hazel to green to brown in seconds. Was it the sunlight filtering through the trees behind them, the ones that made a dappled path on the island floor?

"And dappled," she added, now sounding insane.

"Back up the bus, Finch, you have to speak English for this commoner. I'm a spotty salt lick. Boy, you know how to charm," he said with a laugh.

Heather laughed, too; she knew her face was red hot, but she didn't care. It felt so good to giggle in the open air with the sound of surf crashing beyond them. After several minutes where they would giggle and gain composure, one would catch the other's eye and start up again. Soon Heather's side ached from laughing so hard.

They finally calmed, and Heather reached for her copy of the Hopkins poems. She read "Pied Beauty" aloud to John, who instantly grew somber and listened so intently she thought her blush was sending off rays.

"When I read this, I thought the word 'dappled' fits you because you're kind of this strange combination of things: easygoing and anal retentive, a reader and a bit of an adventurer – not that the two can't go together; you're somewhat of a free spirit, but you're also so responsible. You're dappled."

"I think that's the nicest thing anyone has ever said to me." John smiled at her and said, "Do you always carry poetry with you when you backpack?"

"Well, I had it in my purse and transferred it to the pack when we were at the hanger."

"So you do always carry it with you," he said.

"Not always, it's just that," Heather said and paused. Should she tell him about the ghost? After a few seconds, she added, "I've had weird things happening to me at White Cottage. I heard strange clinking sounds one night, and then I saw a light out near the pond. I passed those off, but the night of the ball this book went from my bedside to the book shelf down in the living room. I have no memory of moving it. I think the cottage is haunted."

John crinkled his brow.

"You think I'm crazy," she said.

"No, I don't. I think it's interesting that your mind immediately goes to the supernatural rather than an earthly explanation."

Heather chuckled. "I know, it seems strange, but another thing is I may have had a visitation. From a ghost, or maybe it was a dream about my main character, Meg." She prattled on, her mind racing: "The dream or visitation was so real. She was right in the bedroom."

Heather didn't mention Steven was in the room, too. "At first I thought I was certain about the book – so sure I had put it on my bedside table and nowhere else after coming up with 'dappled' for you. And after the ball, it was downstairs. On the shelf! Why would I put it on the shelf?"

"So you thought of me before your date with Steve," he said, his voice almost hoarse.

Heather felt a sense of vertigo. Had she ever felt like this? Was this what it felt like to fall in love? She could hardly remember; it had been a lifetime ago.

"Yes," she whispered.

John scooted closer to her and took her hand in his. A thousand jolts of electricity sparked between her palm and her skull.

"That's good to hear," he said in a low voice. "I have a few thoughts and a question."

195

Heather's stomach twisted in anticipation.

"You could have been preoccupied about the ball, and you put it on the shelf to bring some order to chaotic thoughts. I may be projecting my anal-retentive tendencies, but you have a very orderly mind."

Heather nodded. "That is a logical explanation, but sometimes, you know, with spiritual moments in life, there is no logic."

"True," he said, and Heather was very pleased he didn't counter her thoughts. Also pleasing – the way his thumb made circles on the back of her hand.

"What's your question?" she asked.

"How am I a salt lick? You know 'lick' is a very interesting word."

Heather burned inside; surely her cells couldn't take this. She wanted to feel every inch of John's skin on hers. The desire was so great, so palpable, her mental editor checked out, so she said, "Yes, you're the salt lick, and I'm the deer. You have the chemical I need in my body."

John made a sound between a grumble and a groan. He leaned in, and beneath the clear blue sky, under the shade of blossoming trees, on a grassy hill on a nearly uninhabited Scottish island, he leaned in and kissed her. First, his lips brushed hers as softly as feather touches. He pulled back and looked into her eyes and smiled. "Excellent metaphor, Heather, but you can't be the only one who gets to do the licking." Then he kissed her hard, sending a stream of sensations through her whole body. The stars could have been raining down in fire streaks and she wouldn't have moved. Gravity fixed her in this one point on the planet, the one in John's arms.

Live
July 5th, present day

"I'm doing it again, aren't I?" Heather said after taking a sip of her beer at the Lochaline Pub. "I'm talking too much about dull topics related to research for my novel."

John cradled his beer and smiled. "Not at all. I love hearing about kelp and its various attributes."

Heather laughed. "Right. Well, I'll shut up. I can't wait for the food to get here. Though I loved your picnic lunch today, I'm starving and this pint is going straight to my head."

"Excellent!" John said and put his glass up. "Cheers, to spending a beautiful day with my beautiful friend."

They clinked glasses. The cozy pub in the small town of Lochaline, the closest one to Ardorn Estates, started to fill with locals who talked at the bar, having nice "cracks" (a word for "chats" – a new fact she had just learned from John). The dark wood and tucked-away booths and tables gave them a cloak of privacy, where the conversations and laughter made the background hum, but didn't make it hard to talk with John. And, Heather found, it was exceedingly easy to talk with John. She had known this over their on-and-off-again correspondence via chat on Facebook, but now, since their very steamy make-out session on the hill on Canna, Heather felt loosened up and open, pliant like her younger, dancer self.

After Heather drank, she ran her fingertip along the condensation on her mug. "Tell me about skydiving. What it feels like."

"Why don't you come for a jump? I'd take care of you." His tone was playful, on the verge of deepening, and the sound of it made Heather get goosebumps.

"Ah, no, you couldn't pay me to jump out a plane. But I already know my daughter wants to jump. And, it will be hard for me to keep Jackson from your farm."

"I like the sound of that, and so will Claire," he said and paused to finish off his drink. "That's right, I remember you telling me Jackson works at an urban farm in Milwaukee."

"Uh huh, but you're changing the subject. Tell me what it feels like to skydive," she said and drank some more.

"It's exhilarating, but I think I told you, it becomes routine like anything else. I like meeting new people. But really, I think I'm ready to stop."

Their food arrived. John ordered another round of beers, and they dug into their meals for several minutes in silence.

"I was really in the mood for some good pub food. This fish-and-chips is the best I've ever had," Heather said between bites.

"Could it be you're starving?"

"Aye," she said and chuckled. "So that's 'Mince & Tatties'?"

John nodded. "It's so good – beef, veggies, spices, baked in the oven and topped with gravy and a poached egg."

"You sound like an advertisement."

"See, I get excited about food. If I become a co-owner of the farm, Claire and I have talked about expanding the B & B to have a café or pub."

"She's a phenomenal cook," Heather said. She felt less jealousy toward John's earthy Fuck Buddy since she learned Claire leaned more toward women, and since their time on the hill this morning when a flash of John's hands rubbed her body through her clothing. While the touch heated Heather's desire, it cooled the idea of Claire down into the ranks of "friend" or "business partner." She drank more of her fresh beer and slathered her fries in mayonnaise.

"She really is, and so is her girlfriend, Hannah, who comes up with exceptional recipes." John drank again and wiped his hands with his napkin. "Are you happy your kids are coming, or not?"

"Good question. I am excited to see them, and if I buy White Cottage, I definitely want them to see it and get a feel for the place. It's a big adjustment to have their only parent deciding to live abroad, at least for most of the year. After I sell the monstrosity of a suburban house, I could possibly keep a small apartment in Wisconsin, too. Otherwise, they won't have a 'home' to go to on their breaks during college, but then again, they know that already because 'home' is sold. It's a lot to think about, and truthfully, I've been so spooked the last few days with the ghost, I'm starting to rethink buying the cottage."

"Hmmm, I want to get to the bottom of this ghost business. Should I stand guard at the cottage tonight?" John asked. His eyes bore into Heather. She stared back and then let her eyes drop.

"Sure," she answered quietly. Now that the question of where John was staying that night was answered, another question surfaced and escaped her lips before she could think otherwise. "Do you remember sitting next to me one time in catechism class? We would have been in junior high."

John leaned back in his chair; a mysterious smile crossed his face. "Oh yeah, you were such a hottie. Still are."

"Hah, yeah right," she said by way of countering his comment, but secretly eating it up. "Do you remember what you did under the table?"

"Oh, yeah, I was pretty bold back then," he said, drawing closer to her.

"What about now?" Heather nearly whispered. Her heart pounded in her chest. She pushed her empty plate to the side and scooted closer to John.

"Still bold to some degree, but maybe not as bold as then. I recall I put my hand between your thighs, and then asked you if it was all right. Now I'm more of a gentleman. So I'll ask at the same time I do this." John slid even closer and put his hand on Heather's leg. He caught her eye and said, "Is it okay?" in a whisper.

Heather sucked in air and made a quiet groan, hardly able to move for fear she'd break the chemistry of the moment. She nodded and John moved his hand up her thigh and discreetly slid it between her legs. Heather gasped, squirming a little with pleasure. He leaned in and said in her ear, "Let's get the check and go back to White Cottage." He pecked her ear lobe with his lips as she whispered, "Yes."

***

John stood behind Heather at the doorway to White Cottage, kissing her neck and rubbing his hands over her body. She turned the key. She stepped in the entryway, and said, "John, I love kissing you, but I have to look to see if the ghost has been here."

He breathed hard and pulled away from her. "Okay, I'll follow you."

Heather flicked on the light in the living room and scanned the objects of the room. Nothing was amiss.

"Looks good here," she said and moved cautiously to the kitchen. When she turned on the kitchen light, she screamed.

"What is it?" John said.

"Sorry," she answered. "Look." She pointed to the kitchen table where a wine glass sat on the table. There was another one on the counter. "I don't think those were there when I left this morning. But I was nervous. Did I even have wine the other night? I usually have a glass, but I swear I washed the glass. And the one on the counter! Why two? Was I so absentminded I got out one and then another. Am I going insane?"

"No," John said. "The rest of the kitchen is tidy, and there are no other dirty dishes. Let me have a look around the cottage. Do you have a flashlight for when I check outside?"

Heather got one out of the kitchen cabinet. Her heart raced, and her insides felt gelatinous. "John, let me come with you. If you see evidence of the ghost, I want to be there."

"I'm not worried about a ghost. I want to see if someone broke in here to mess with you, or if they're still around."

"Be careful."

"I will. Please, stay here."

Heather sat at the table while John searched. She stared at the empty wine glasses, feeling like the ghost was sending some kind of message to her. Her stomach turned with anxiety. She wanted to flee, leave the cottage for good, but where would she go? She supposed she could ask to stay on as a boarder on Claire's farm, but on a certain level, she felt utterly ridiculous. The bottom line was something strange was happening in her present home. But what? She turned over the idea of someone stalking her, a real person, like John had mentioned, but deep in the fabric of her body, she felt that there was something supernatural happening in the cottage. Had the misty mornings and quiet Scottish hills affected her? Was some spirit, an unsettled soul, trying to communicate something to her? Had Meg, who she believed she had made up, actually been a real person and was now a ghost? As a writer, she figured she would be an open recipient for such a communication.

John returned. "No one is outside or inside the cottage."

"John, I really think it's a ghost."

"I know you do, Heather, but I don't believe in ghosts, but I do believe you believe something weird is happening here." He walked to the stove and put the kettle on. "I'll make you some tea. We'll relax and chat, or do whatever." He smiled. "And if something peculiar happens, there will be two of us to witness it."

"Okay."

John and Heather settled on the couch in the living room with John on one end and Heather on the other. She leaned her back to the armrest, her feet tucked under the cushion. John's back rested on the arm of the other end. His long legs were cramped between the couch and the table.

"Just push the table out some," Heather said.

John stretched and pushed the table farther away. Heather sighed, sipping her tea, her ears alert to any unordinary sounds.

"You hear anything?" John asked.

"No," she said. "Thanks for staying."

"You kidding me? There's no other place I'd rather be." John grinned. "So should we tell ghost stories?"

"No way!" Heather said, giggling. "How about you tell me about the latest book you read, or something I don't know about you?"

John talked, got more tea for both of them, and soon scoured the kitchen for biscuits or cookies for dessert. After hours of talking about everything from books to movies to childhood memories to writing to planting vegetables, they became very comfortable in each other's company, and the energy between them sizzled. No lights flashed outside the cabin; no clinking noises disturbed their conversation; no objects slid through rooms from an unseen hand. Heather's ghost had been quieted with the joyful sounds of laughing and the kind of conversation between two people who simply could not get enough of each other.

Heather rubbed at her feet, and John said, "Here. Stretch out to me." He took her socked feet and started massaging the soreness away.

"Oh no, now I'll surely want to sleep, but the funny thing is, even though it's nearly four in the morning, I feel like I have the energy of someone who just woke for the day." She sighed and watched John whose arm muscles flexed. His hands, strong and sinewy, worked her toes, and she got goose bumps up her legs and arms. They had spent so much time talking, joking now and again about watching for the cottage phantom, that Heather had noticed, but did not act on, the charges of attraction between them. This was the first they had touched since the pub in Lochaline, which felt like days ago rather than hours.

So many things passed through her mind. Steven surfaced, and she shoved the thoughts down. She didn't want to feel like a two-timer; even though no boundaries had been drawn, since she had been a person who had been cheated on, the idea of sleeping with two men in one weekend made her queasy. The flip side: her skin and organs pulsated with John so near, and her body craved his touch, his presence, his laugh – every inch of him needed to be examined, known, and then, she hated to admit, owned by herself. Who was this person who used to be the nearly-celibate Heather?

"Do you want to watch the sun rise?" he asked.

Heather sat up from her slouch. "Oh, yes."

"Come on," he said, placing her feet gently on the ground and running his palm up her leg.

"John," she whispered, barely able to speak.

"I know, I want you, too. But for now, let's go see a new day start. It's calling us. How else do we end such a perfect day?"

They sat hip to hip on the couch. Heather smiled and brushed his lips with hers. When she stood, she took his hand and led him to the orange and yellow light breaking through the mist.

Remember
April, last year

"Is this where you want the raised vegetable bed?" Leann asked, arm on the shovel.

"I don't know," Heather answered. "You're the gardener. What do you think?"

"I like the spot. You have full sun right now, and probably get some shade from the dwarf dogwood in the late afternoon. It's good," Leann said.

"Okay, let's do it," Heather said.

Late April brought crisp air, warm sunshine, and a cool breeze. Heather had wanted to do something industrious this weekend; she'd been tiring of the same routine: drives along the lake and shopping trips to far-out stores for something to do. One Sunday, she drove forty-five minutes to a far-off Home Depot to purchase low-energy light bulbs. Just for something to do on her own and for herself, leaving Jackson and Tessa with Marc. Though that outing left her with a terrible sense of guilt for sticking the kids with caretaking duties.

Now, Heather glanced to check on Marc, who sat in a plastic chair at the table on the deck. The umbrella obscured his face, but moments ago he had been staring off with a blank expression, thinking of the past, or lost in thoughts completely unique to his brain. After the horrible holidays full of mood swings and violent outbursts, Heather started the year with a doctor's visit for Marc's changes. The doctor put Marc on a medication that had leveled his moods, curtailing the violent swings and physical urges. Sometimes Heather felt badly, like she was turning him into a zombie, but she couldn't live with him any longer as he had been. It was the medication or a nursing home. The last few months had gone more smoothly than the ones in the fall and early winter, with the days piling on one after the other, a blend of being busy and utterly bored.

Heather grabbed the other shovel from the shed and joined Leann in digging the ground for the raised bed. The sun toasted the top of Heather's head, heating her scalp and easing the tension in her shoulders. Though she tried to cure herself of clenching her teeth and tightening her shoulders when caring for Marc, she found herself clenching and tightening when he called her name or made any sudden movement. These bodily reactions, along with chattering teeth when he needed her in the middle of the night, were results of the time he hit her in November. As if reading her thoughts, Leann stepped back from her turned-up dirt and studied Heather, long enough to make Heather pause.

"How have you been sleeping, Finchy?"

"All right. About the same. Most nights I have to take something, otherwise I'm up listening for Marc."

"But you have the baby monitor on, right?" Leann asked, her brown eyes worried, her sandy blonde ponytail brushing her shoulders.

"Oh, yeah. That's another thing I tend to do if I don't take a sleep aid – check the monitor repeatedly throughout the night to be sure it's working. Believe me, it's better I'm upstairs in our old bedroom again, but I get nervous that Marc is the only one on the bottom floor sometimes. That's when I end up on the couch."

"Oh, sweetie. I wish I could make things easier for you. But you did the right thing moving rooms. You'd never sleep again in the same room with him, not since last fall and winter. Brutal."

"Yes, it was," Heather said and resumed digging.

She and Leann worked in silence until she heard Marc flick on the radio and turn from station to station. He stopped on static, so Heather called up to him, saying, "Honey, please turn to some music instead of the static."

"Okay," he said. Moments later he said, "I think I'll get my guitar and play a while."

Heather stood and leaned on her shovel. Sweat trickled between her breasts; her shoulders ached a little, and these physical reminders of being in the world, not just a spectator, gave Heather a feeling of satisfaction.

"Marc, honey, you haven't played the guitar in some time."

"Yes I have," he said. His fingers played with the dial some more.

Leann whispered, "Does he even have a guitar anymore?"

Heather shook her head.

"Heather!" he called. "Please get my guitar."

She and Leann exchanged helpless looks. Heather leaned in to her friend and said, "Give it a few minutes. He'll probably forget about the guitar."

Leann nodded and went back to digging. Heather got on her knees and started pulling up weeds and clearing dead leaves and rocks from the area that would be a new vegetable bed. This new plot could bring some joy to her dull days. Maybe she'd learn to can food. She had always wanted to be someone who canned and pickled foods. If a natural disaster struck, she would be the woman with a basement packed with stored goods.

Crack. Slam.

Heather dropped the shovel and ran to Marc who lay in a crumpled heap on the floor of the deck.

"Jesus!" Leann yelled and followed.

"I tried to go get my guitar," he said. "I'm sorry."

"Don't apologize," Heather said, assessing his eyes. He must have cracked his head on the table or deck because a goose egg formed, purple and blue on the side of his temple.

Leann leaned in. "Should I call 9-11?"

"Let's wait a minute," Heather said. "Marc, does anything hurt?"

"No," he answered. "Yes, my head. I think I hit my head."

"There's a bruise forming," Heather said. "Leann, help me get him into the chair. I'll call the triage nurse on duty. My guess is that if he didn't black out, there isn't a concussion."

Leann righted the tumbled chair, and the two helped Marc back to the seat. Heather got an ice pack, wrapped it in a towel, and gave it to Marc to hold on his head. Then she called triage. After a series of questions she had grown accustomed to (Marc's medical history, medications, and symptoms), the nurse advised Heather to monitor his behavior for the next twenty-four hours, and if he didn't vomit, grow listless, or pass out, it wasn't a concussion, and the bruise would heal.

Leann brought out lemonade for all three of them. She scooted her chair beneath the table and started telling Marc about her garden. From trumpet vines to clematis, Leann talked on and sipped her drink. Heather held the ice pack on Marc's head, checking every few minutes to see if his pupils were different sizes. After twenty minutes, Marc put his hand over Heather's and said, "It's getting cold."

"Okay, I'll put it in the freezer for later."

Heather chucked the pack away and opened the fridge. A six pack of Spotted Cow, her favorite Wisconsin beer, waited for her. Her drinking had increased again over the holidays, but with the turn of the year, the ability to get outside, and Marc's medication, she had gained more control. This would be her one drink of the day. She brought out one for Leann as well.

"I play cover songs mainly," Marc said to Leann, the bump on his scalp drawing Heather's eyes like blood in an open wound.

Leann spotted the beer and nodded, mouthing, "Hell yeah."

The snap and exhaustive hiss of the opened beers brought on more relief than Heather cared to admit. The afternoon sun fell over the dug-up ground, Heather's raised bed. She tried to conjure the joy of moments ago, when earth and sunshine and the spring breeze brought renewal, but the feeling had faded. She gulped her beer and checked Marc's bump one more time. Why did she feel a shadow falling over the scene? What new curtain of worry or fear waited to drop on top of her home?

How would she make it through another new turn?

Live

July 8th, present day

Heather walked the cobblestone streets of Old Town Edinburgh along the path she had learned the last few days. The meandering "wynds" or lanes and the narrow "closes" or alleyways had confused her at first, and instead of trying to rely on the spotty GPS on her phone, she learned the way to her hotel, the Rutgard, by navigating the city with a laminated map. She turned onto Victoria Street, noting Ye Old Town Bookshop, where she had spent her first day in the city among the shelves, and then pausing to enjoy the view of brightly painted storefronts: turquoise, fuschia, almond, lining the street and contrasting the brilliant and clear blue sky. Even though hours of sunlight remained until the evening, Heather wanted to retreat to her hotel room, pull out her laptop, and finish the day with writing. Okay, if she was honest with herself, she also wanted to chat with John on Facebook.

She wove along Victoria, recounting how she had come upon this unplanned trip to Scotland's capital. Two words gave it away: the ghost. She adjusted her purse and tucked the map away because two more turns would put her on the street of her hotel, an easy location because it kept the Edinburgh Castle in its view. Edinburgh Castle, a pewter-colored fortress, rested on the crags and slopes of a dormant volcano, a fact Heather marveled at. This last turn, another tight corner with one long row of brownstones and stores that meandered like Diagon Alley in the Harry Potter books, led Heather to the small Rutgard Hotel, a peaceful, tucked-away place that didn't have the neighborly intrusions of a Bed and Breakfast, but it was just as cozy. And, as Heather had noted to John when they'd researched places for her to stay, a more modern hotel had less of a chance of being haunted.

Heather walked through the entryway of the hotel. The lobby had leather chairs and oak tables and desks. Two computers were available for use, but Heather had her laptop, and that itch to get connected to people, namely John, propelled her to take the stairs rather than wait for the elevator. Heather rushed up the stairs and into her hotel room. She loved the squat bed with the hotel's signature white wood headboards and bright pastel fabrics for the bedspread, throw pillows, and curtains. The room smelled like starched sheets and vanilla candles, comforting. She also loved how if she sat on the bed propped up on pillows she had a view of the entire room, even the black and white tiled bathroom. Rutgard felt safe, homey, and not haunted.

Heather washed her face and changed into her pajamas while her laptop warmed up. She jumped when she heard her cell phone ring. While scrambling through her purse with one hand, she toweled her face with the other.

Leann!

"Hello," Heather said.

"Heather! I've been dying to reach you. Sorry for the phone tag. How are you?"

"Fine, good. But how are you? How was the Fourth with Brian's family?"

Leann sighed. "The usual. His mother annoyed the bejesus out of me. It's the little things. I either work too much in the summer months or not enough. I have the same conversations about how being a realtor causes an ebbing and flowing in my life – anyway, the description fell on deaf ears because then she made her little comments about my weight. Ew, I get annoyed thinking about it again. Anyway, how about you? Your message said you're in, oh I forgot which Scottish city – I didn't even know you had a trip planned now? I feel out of it! You didn't drive, on the wrong side of the road, did you?"

"First, don't feel out of it, and no, I'm scared to drive here. John drove me to Fort William, and then I took the train to Edinburgh," Heather said, flopping onto the cushy bed and leaning back into the pile of pillows.

"So John drove you and not Steven, do tell," Leann said. "I'm going to the den and closing the fucking door. My family can leave me be for a while."

Heather hadn't talked to her best friend since before the ball, which felt like weeks ago when in reality only five days had passed. She recounted the pissing contest between John and Steven at the ball, her blossoming attraction to John while on a date with Steven, and having sex with Steven. Then she detailed her date day on Canna with John. When she got to the ghost moving her book and the wine glasses, and how that prompted her to go to Steven's place for a day with more sex and to stay up all night talking with John, Leann said, "Holy shit, this is a gothic romance, girl! But wait, didn't you tell me you wanted to buy White Cottage. Are you going to, you know, with the haunting?"

Heather loved this response on two levels: first, Leann didn't even question the ghost's existence, and second, it indicated that she agreed the said ghost could be a deal breaker. Though John had supported her by staying up and talking her through the scary night after the wine glass incident, he had admitted he didn't believe in ghosts. Leann got right down to it, and always, no matter what, met Heather where she was. Right now she did indeed feel like a character in a gothic ghost story.

"Leann, I'm not sure. I really want to live here – at least part of the year – and I love the cottage, the location. It's been so good for my spirit, my writing."

"And you're dating, actually dating, two different men. But this seals the deal. I'm coming to live with you for a while each year. I can't be so far from you."

"I know," Heather said, tearing up. She hadn't faced this fact yet, but more so than missing her children, only because they were starting their own lives on their own, she would be somewhat lost without weekly contact with Leann. Then her mind flipped to both Steven and John. Both men lived in Scotland. No matter where Heather decided to live, she would end up longing for someone. "Leann, I don't know what to do. I feel really lost these days. Actually, lost may not be the most accurate word. I feel dizzy with all the changes. Each day feels like ten because so much happens. I can't keep up. If not for my inspired writing, I would be all twisted up."

"And hooray for that, Heather. You've been trapped in your life for so long. Let's face it, and as we've discussed before on our walks, this was going on before Marc's stroke. You haven't been happy. At all. You patched up and moved on, tried, really tried, to pretend you were happy, but you weren't. Take it from your BFF who has known you forever. I've seen you happy, and you haven't been for a long time."

Tears rolled down Heather's cheeks. Was this happiness, this dizzy and out-of-time feeling?

"You're right. I'll make a decision about the cottage soon. But it's not a good sign if I'm scared to be there," Heather said, letting out a chuckle and swiping away the tears.

"Good point. You know I have to ask you this because I always want the grit. Why didn't you go stay with Steven again? To avoid the cottage."

Heather considered and said, "Not comfortable. He's great, nice, attentive, but he gave me this patronizing look when I mentioned the clinking sounds and the light being something more, like a ghost. I haven't mentioned the other spooky things because I didn't want him to think I'm certifiable. And then there's John Timmer."

"Ah, yes, hunky John Timmer with the planes, trains, and yachts, all to get you to an isolated island to neck. I'm digging John. And he stayed up with you to keep watch for the ghost," Leann said.

"Exactly, but he said he doesn't believe in ghosts. He took me seriously though."

"Oh yeah. The way I see it you have two men taking you seriously." Leann laughed at herself. "Why didn't you stay down on the farm with John?"

"He mentioned it for when a room opens up, but they just got a family who took up the available rooms. Plus there's John, the skydiving brothers, and though Claire's girlfriend Hannah shares a room with Claire when she's in from Fort William, they occupy two rooms because one is an office. No room at the inn."

"I bet John would have shared with you," Leann said and giggled.

"I know. But that's too fast. Even as I say the words I feel like the world's biggest hypocrite. I jumped into bed with Steven, so he's my sex mate as of late, but I feel more emotionally connected to John. And, you should read our Facebook messages to each other the last couple of days!"

"Really? Goodness, you've been busy, girl!"

"I know, right? Who the hell am I, Leann? See, like I told you, I feel dizzy."

"Okay, give me some information about the messages. I know you're modest, or at least you used to be! But please, are you sexting?"

"I have no idea," Heather said with a laugh. "I've never understood the nuances of sexting."

"Oh, who cares, Finchy, give me something here."

"The conversations have grown more intimate, more intense. In truth, it's the most open I've ever been in terms of answering questions about sex."

"Good for you! Keep at it. I hate to cut you off, but I looked at the time, and I have to get to a meeting with a client. Too much work in the summer, so says my mother-in-law. I say you hop on Facebook right now and get a little 'chat' rush."

Heather laughed. "Okay, friend. Take care."

Heather opened her Word document to work on her next chapter, but after about two hundred words, she logged on to Facebook, scrolled through posts, hit "like" several times, and stayed logged on while she jotted notes on her outline and tried to work a scene where her main character Meg met up with her new lover. The scene wasn't working, and Heather doubted everything she had written so far in the chapter. Then, *PING*. John has sent her a message on Facebook.

How's Edinburgh today, Heather?

Lovely, she answered. *I did the modern art museum and walked all through New Town. I'm back at the hotel and in my pajamas at a very early time.*

Hmmm. Hotel. Pajamas. I'd love to be there with you. Believe me, I would be if I didn't have 'tattie' week on the farm where Claire's working me in the potato fields like an indentured servant. I've cut back on my jumps, and conversations with you have spurred me to talk to a financial planner about investing in the farm.

Good for you! I think you should, Heather typed. She wanted to steer the chat back to how he wished he were with her in the hotel, but she wasn't sure what to say. Then she saw the words, "John is typing," and she waited.

If you've been walking, I bet your feet are sore. Would you like a virtual foot massage? I'm the best in this department, or so I've been told on this side of the Atlantic.

Sure, I'd love one.

John wrote, *First I'll put one warm towel on your back and rub your tired feet with another wet and warm towel, stroke each one of your toes. Then I'd apply some oil. I stroke each toe with my fingers and gently massage the back of your legs, slowly moving up to your back, gliding my fingers underneath the towel, just stroking gently. I'll allow my fingers to go deeper but only if you give me the sign, if you spread your legs just a bit and invite my fingers to continue.*

John! She answered. *What am I supposed to do with this? You need to be here.*

How about some cosmic self-pleasuring?

Once again, their conversations moved in this direction, where Heather talked freely about sex, and even masturbation, a taboo topic she never really discussed with anyone. Maybe it was her Catholic upbringing, or maybe it was her modest, quiet nature. Even if she did masturbate from time to time, she certainly didn't tell anyone she did. Now she had fully admitted to John that even this self-pleasuring had decreased over the last few years; was it because of her caretaking role, or was she afraid to have any sexual feelings because she no longer had a partner in Marc? With John it was so easy to be open, free, alive!

Heather thought about an earlier note from John: *I only like girls who masturbate and talk about it. Long theory breaks down to this: "look here, this is what my body likes! Can you do that with your mouth, penis, or toe?"*

She smiled and answered, *Okay.*

A little while later and after few hurried messages, Heather realized how it seemed ridiculous that she holed herself up in a hotel in Edinburgh to flee a ghost in her cottage. She should go back and face her fears, and then she could be with John for real. In the flesh. But what about Steven? The queasy-doing-something-wrong feeling came back.

As if on cue, *PING!* Another name popped up in her Facebook chat: Steven.

Heather, how are you? I've missed you these last few days! How's Edinburgh? Since I can't be there with you because of work, I bought you dinner at the finest restaurant in the city. I know the owner, and it's all set up for tomorrow evening at 7:30. What do you think?

"John is typing," showed up in the parallel chat box. Heather's stomach turned.

John wrote, *I understand your need to get away from your cottage ghost, but the timing is wrong. I want you so much, Heather. When you come back I'll keep watch at the cottage and take care of you in the corporeal sense.*

First, Heather wrote back to Steven: *Yes, dinner sounds great. Give me the information, and I'll be there. I, too, wish you could join me.* She did mean it; Steven was so nice, attentive, caring. And, he was the first man she had dated since Marc; she felt bound to him somehow, and like she was cheating on him with her burgeoning relationship with John. She had no idea how to balance all of this. Going back to her safe lack of social life seemed comfortable now. She could simply sign off with each of them and call it a night. No, she owed them both some truth.

To John she wrote, *Yes, that sounds like a plan, but John, I need to work some things out first.*

John answered, *Hmmm. Let me guess. Steven Conolley?*

"Steven is typing," and then seconds later came, *PING.*

Heather jolted in her bed.

Steven's note had the name and address of the restaurant, and then he wrote, *If I were with you, I'd take you to this fine restaurant with candle light and wine. Then we'd go back to your hotel and I would make love to you all night.*

Jesus! What was she to do with all of this?

To John she wrote: *Yes, I need to figure things out about Steven. And you. I'm not good at playing the field, John.*

To Steven she wrote, *That sounds lovely. But since you can't be here, don't go into too much detail. It will make me long too much for you.* Not completely a lie, but a generous exaggeration. Who did she long for? John.

But then John wrote back, *Got it, let me know. Nothing has to be set in stone here, Heather. Have fun! Life is too short.*

Then John logged off, the green chat dot disappearing in an instant.

Heather felt immediately lonesome for him. Did John have numerous Fuck Buddies he chatted with, leading to a virtual love of mutual masturbation? Was she simply a notch in his belt, or more accurately, another green chat dot of flirtation? Did her relationship with John mean anything in reality if he was so quick to turn off?

"Steven is typing."

Steven wrote, *I understand. I'll log off now, but do tell me how you like your evening tomorrow. I will live vicariously through you. Kisses, Steven.*

Steven logged off. Heather did the same, clamping her laptop shut and trying to close her mind to both men. This wasn't happiness; it was a new virtual torture device! She vowed to stop with both of them. She wasn't meant to "have fun" – life wasn't about fun only! It was about duty, loyalty, and love, but what did that mean really? A farce. No, no more of this. She decided to throw herself into writing, reading, and enjoying this new place. No more "chats" or flirtatious messages with either man.

Heather clicked off the light and popped in a sleeping pill. She waited for the cotton haze to envelop her, allowing her to sleep.

Remember
July, last year

Heather, Tessa, and Jackson entered the Sunny Oak Nursing Home. Heather did her usual breath-holding technique, not with puffed-out cheeks, rather like sinking under water, until they reached Marc's room where she let out her breath into her shirt sleeve and acclimated to the urine-slash-bleach-slash-masked-poo odor.

Marc's broken leg stuck out in front of his body while he sat in his wheelchair. Though he wore different clothes than the day before, stubble dotted his cheeks. Heather leaned in and kissed Marc on the forehead, taking in the scent of unwashed hair and sour breath.

"Hi, honey," Heather said.

She stood over him, flanked by Tessa and Jackson, and waited for an answer as Marc's eyes focused, which took longer these days. Finally, he said, "Hello." He put his arms out for a hug from Tessa, who dove in and held onto her dad.

"I have the newspaper for you, Daddy," Tessa said and placed it on his lap. Marc touched the news print gently and slid his finger through the sections, an ingrained motion, pre-stroke. Some papers slid to the floor, so Jackson bent to pick them up.

"I'll help you sort through these," Jackson said. "Then how about I push you through the grounds? It's a nice day."

Heather stepped away from her family and into Marc's bathroom where she could examine things. She counted the adult diapers and gathered his dirty laundry in a basket except for the one plastic bag of soiled clothes. He must have soaked through some again, either from increased incontinence or not enough prompts to use the toilet. Heather gritted her teeth. She had hated putting Marc in a nursing home, but after another fall and a broken leg, care at home had become too difficult, a fact she discovered after trying to transfer him into bed one night when he nearly fell again because of a lack of balance and the awkwardness of the cast. He required two people at all times to help him with most transfers and personal care needs.

Heather stared at Marc's toothpaste and toothbrush. Growing livid, she let out a huff. Tessa sidled up to Heather in Marc's bathroom.

"What's up, Mom?"

Heather scrunched her face and said, "Your dad's toothbrush is dry, and his toothpaste hasn't moved since yesterday. They aren't prompting him to do his teeth, so he forgets."

Tessa cocked her head to the side and glanced from the brush to Heather's face. She smirked, slightly, but suppressed her grin. "Mom, you set a toothpaste trap for the staff here?"

Heather squinted, not sure if she wanted to laugh or cry. How did she get here: a forty-something woman who visits a nursing home daily and touches toothbrushes for evidence of use.

"Yes, I put his brush in one cup and the paste in another. They haven't moved. That means he hasn't brushed his teeth since yesterday morning when I was here." Cry, she definitely felt like crying, not laughing.

"Okay, okay," Tessa said, touching Heather's shoulder with one hand and grabbing the toiletries with the other. "I got this today, all right? You just try to relax."

Heather's shoulders sank; her heart pumped and pumped, making her pulse throb in her neck like a drumbeat. Being alive – there was no choice in the matter. She wanted to go somewhere else and never return. She yearned to slip away, disappear, and become mist.

"Thank you," Heather answered. "While you do that, I'll try to bring this up with the staff. Delicately."

"Sounds like a plan," Tessa said to Heather. Walking out of the bathroom, she said, "Hey Dad, before we go for a stroll, let's get you gussied up."

Marc smiled. "Okay."

Heather walked to the nurses' station, doing her breath-holding thing, and nodding to people in wheelchairs who sat outside their rooms, waiting for the next thing to happen – maybe a meal or a game of bingo. Once at the station, she waited and watched the call light blink on and off for room 120. Finally, she had to take a breath, relieved that no new food smell had infiltrated the entryway yet. She found the beef stew day unbearable; the dark meat and overly-cooked vegetables spread like slop on the cafeteria's plastic plates.

A woman in scrubs, probably Heather's age, bustled behind the desk, putting up a hand for Heather to wait. "Give me a minute, sweetheart." The woman's name tag said, "Gladys," and below the name read, "Floor Manager." Heather thought luck had come her way to meet with the manager rather than an attendant.

Heather waited, watching the call light go on and off, and then it stopped.

"How can I help you, m'am?"

"I'm Marc Barrington's wife. He's in room 111."

"Yes, I've seen you here," she said, her bright eyes scanning the hall and landing on Heather again. "Do you need some help with something?"

"I don't want to complain, but I don't think he's been brushing his teeth as he should, and I wondered if he'd have fewer accidents if he was prompted to go to the toilet more often. That's the key, he needs to be told, or he forgets." The air conditioning unit blared on above them, causing Heather's skin to get instant goose pimples.

220

"I understand, Mrs. Barrington," Gladys said. "We're in a state of flux here lately. I have lots of staff turnover, people in and out of all kinds of shifts and time blocks. With that said, as much as I'm trying to schedule the same attendants with the same patients, it's been hard this month. We're hiring, but it will take some time to get people trained and into a routine to give patients – your husband – the consistent care he needs. I ask for your patience."

"Of course," Heather said, not wanting to push things, but realizing no solution had been given on how to get his teeth brushed every day. Heather swallowed, not wanting to confront Gladys, who obviously worked hard and had far too much on her plate. Nonetheless, Heather said, "I recognize the trials here. I wondered what I should do to make his personal care improve while he's here without having to do it myself. Not that I mind, I took care of Marc at home. I don't mind doing it; it's just that while he's here. Well –"

"Well, honey," Gladys cut in, "it's our job here." Her large, doll eyes blinked and connected with Heather's. "Truthfully, the people I do have could use a push some days – some cut corners as all get out. I'll bring it up in a staff meeting, but the way you get the wheel oiled is to be coming in here every day, like you're doing, and keeping the attendants on their jobs. Write a sign." Gladys stooped behind the desk and handed Heather a black marker, paper, and tape. "Write a note about the routine to the staff and post it in your husband's bathroom. Then they know family is watching. I'll say something, too, and hopefully, things will improve."

Heather took the supplies, thanked Gladys, and headed back to Marc's room. Heather couldn't place how she felt: overwhelmed, sad, or completely despondent? Even here, in a place where meals came on trays and every mundane action was carried out by employees 24/7 – even here, she had to orchestrate life for Marc, the man who had been so strong, so capable. A foreigner lived in his body now. Had he not had the stroke, Heather would have divorced him, and he'd be going to some island vacation with his new, young wife Erin. Instead, Heather wrote out the sign about toothbrushing, shaving, and prompting Marc to piss and shit. She taped it up, thinking she'd call Erin and get her in to see Marc, to help out. The thought almost made her laugh. She wouldn't do that, nor would she divorce him now. Her rut in the road snaked endlessly to the future, where the days blurred and faded. Heather wished she would fade along with them.

Live
July 12th, present day

Heather picked up the room service menu at the Rutgard Hotel in Edinburgh. Her day exploring Edinburgh Castle and doing the walking tour of the "Royal Mile" near the castle left her exhausted and famished. Her new vow to check Facebook and email only one time per day had been very hard at first; she had grown itchy while going through the city, wanting to log on to the Internet at various cafes, or check for Wifi on her phone while walking, but she refrained. Soon she felt freer, more open to getting a feel for Edinburgh, and she scribbled notes about her novel constantly. The break had been exactly what she needed, even though she hadn't heard from John for almost four whole days. Four very long days.

Her cell phone, which sat next to the hotel phone, vibrated, and Heather jumped to it, her heart kicking up to a faster rate.

The screen said, "Steven."

"Hi, Steven," Heather answered, trying to mask any disappointment. Steven had checked in daily with her. Even though John had planned to pick up Heather at the Fort William train station upon her return trip tomorrow, she hadn't heard from him, so when Steven offered to do it, she'd said yes.

"Would you like to go to another fancy Edinburgh restaurant for dinner tonight?" he asked.

Her posh meal the other night, a gift from Steven, had been luxurious. Heather hadn't minded dining alone that evening because the staff kept her company and well-fed the entire night.

Despite this experience, Heather only wanted to remain in her hotel room, eat a room service meal, and go to bed.

"Steven, that won't be necessary. You're spoiling me by buying me dinner even when you're not here."

"But I am," he said.

Heather scanned the room and felt instantly silly.

"What do you mean?"

"I'm in your hotel lobby," he said. "Put on your nicest outfit, and come downstairs. We're going out."

"Really?" Her fatigue washed away; excitement bubbled up in her chest. Maybe she did like Steven more than John. And he was here, in her lobby, ready to take her on a date.

"Aye," he said.

"I'll be down soon," she said, growing nervous. Should she invite him to the room? They had slept together after all. "If that's all right with you."

"Aye, I'll answer some emails while I wait. The WiFi is excellent in the lobby."

"Okay."

Half an hour later and wearing the only skirt and blouse she'd packed, Heather met Steven in the lobby. He hadn't noticed her at first, his neck bent over his IPhone, typing as quickly as one can on the small device. When she stood to the right of his shoulder, he glanced up and gave her a wide grin.

"You look great!" He stood and pecked her on the lips. "Give me one minute to finish this text. Then we go to Woodford Restaurant."

"Is it far?"

"No, we can nip over to Victoria Street. Ye getting to know the way about here, are ye?"

"Yes, that's not far, so we can walk. I'll wait over here for you to finish," Heather said. Steven's "minute" turned into ten, and Heather pulled out her phone, dying to log to Facebook because as Steven had said, the WiFi was excellent in the lobby. Instead, she made sure it was on vibrate and nestled in her purse. She hated to admit it about herself, but if she happened to get a call, she wanted to know about it, even if she chose to ignore a call from John Timmer.

After fifteen minutes, Steven approached Heather and took her hand. "I'm so sorry, love, let's go. You're going to love this restaurant."

"Thanks for coming, Steven, it's nice to see a friendly face," she said and really meant it.

Steven took her hand and led her to Victoria Street; the dusky pink and yellow sky glowed around them, casting dull rays and smoky shadows on the line of brownstones and store fronts. She breathed in the scent of car exhaust mixed with the crisp air of evening. She smiled at Steven, taking in his clean, fresh face and bright eyes. He looked much more rested and vibrant than after the ball and her overnight at his place. They walked, hand-in-hand, to Victoria Street and into Woodford Restaurant, a tucked-away place nestled between a bakery and a whiskey shop.

Tables with linen cloths and thick, wooden chairs dotted the main dining room. The hostess greeted Steven and led them to a table set off from the main room and overlooking the cobblestone street with its pastel shops. As soon as they sat down, a waiter came with champagne, uncorking it and pouring glasses for the two of them. Steven raised his glass and said, "To Heather, my American girl."

Heather chuckled and blushed. She wasn't sure what to say back, so she drank a healthy swig of the bubbly drink, grateful for the burn it left in her throat and chest. Steven spoke to the waiter at length about where and when they got their halibut and lobster. He asked Heather if he could order for the two of them, and she said, "Yes!"

She felt warm and cozy and friendly toward Steven. He had come a long way to see her, and maybe they'd sleep together again. Of course, they would. He hadn't mentioned getting his own room. The idea of being with him again made her both queasy and excited. Forget John Timmer. Steven decided on a shellfish sampler platter for an appetizer and entrees of the braised duck for both of them.

Halfway through the shellfish platter, Heather's purse buzzed at her feet – her cell phone! As much as she wished she could ignore it, she knew she couldn't.

"I'm going to find the ladies' room," she said.

"It's across there," Steven said, pointing and standing when she did.

Heather pushed through the door to the bathroom, her hand ready to grab her phone. Two cushy, red couches lined the walls of a lounge area outside another room that had the bathroom stalls. Cranberry candles burned, giving off soft flickers of light on the ceiling. Baskets with towels, tampons, and hand wipes sat on two squat tables. Heather suppressed an urge to stock her purse with tampons and hand wipes. She sank into one of the plush couches and listened to a voicemail message – from John.

"Hey, Heather, it's John. I'm checking in about tomorrow and what time I should get you at the Fort William train station. I hope you're doing well. Give me a call," he said, his voice far more casual than Heather could ever muster on a voicemail to him. She pressed his number to return the call, her heart pounding in her chest.

"Hi, Heather," John answered. "Got my message."

"Yes, I just listened to it," she said. Now she felt like some kind of attack was coming on; she felt dizzy and queasy, and her heart raced so much she had to steady her pulse by pressing two fingers against her wrist. What should she say? So elated to have had a message from John, she didn't even think about what to say to him.

"So how are you feeling about returning?" he asked.

"Um," she stammered. "Well, I feel okay. I'm ready to leave the city, though I've loved Edinburgh, it's just I'm ready to be home." She liked the sound of "home" associated with White Cottage. The ghost there felt far away, leaving only the desire to be in her cozy bed in her lofted bedroom or to sit at her kitchen table and look out on the pond.

"You aren't spooked to go back?"

"I am, but I'm ready to face it." Not at all true – she felt like a big chicken.

"What time should I get you at the Fort William train station?"

"Well, I hadn't heard from you, and Steven called and offered. So…"

"So you have a ride," John said. "That's cool."

"It is?" she asked.

"Whatever. You told me you had to work things out with him. So work it out." John's voice cracked. What to say? A flood of thoughts filled Heather's head, but nothing came out.

"Look, John, I'm new at this, this dating thing, and our messages at the beginning of my stay here were amazing. I'm having a hard time processing everything."

"I get it, Heather, it really is okay."

She didn't want it to be okay. She wanted John to fight for her, to drive to Edinburgh and say she should be having dinner with him and not Steven.

"It's okay with you?" she asked, her voice low, shaky.

"It has to be."

"So you don't care if I date him?"

"Of course I care. I want you, I've told you that."

Something stirred in Heather, a buried, churning thing, deep in her womb. But a veil came to cloak the feeling just as quickly. What if she was just one of many for John?

"You may have all kinds of girls you want," she blurted. She didn't think about what she thought she should say; she spoke: "For all I know you send those kinds of erotic messages to women all over the world. You have all kinds of young women who jump with you out of airplanes. Don't deny it. I've seen the pictures on Facebook. Instead of a girl in every port, you have one at every drop zone, but with technology as it is, you don't have to see them face to face, simply text them and get them to do your will, right?"

"Heather, look, yeah, sometimes I see a couple of people at once, but it has been a long time since I did that."

"See!" She said, almost a yell, but she didn't see anything at all. What did he mean by "see" – did he sleep with more than one woman at once? Did he mean sexy chat? Her head spun. She wished she could see the future, or at least be able to divine the real parameters of this new dating world of her forties.

"I'm not seeing anyone else right now. You're the one dating Steven." John said Steven's name harshly; the tone spoke layers of irony.

"What do you have against Steven?"

"He's a bit much. You have to admit that. Bit of a blowhard."

"No, he's not. He's kind and attentive. And here!" She hadn't wanted to tell this to John, or did she?

"You mean now?"

"Yes, he came to see me in Edinburgh. He's driving me back to White Cottage tomorrow."

"Christ, he doesn't mess around."

"Maybe you should go and chat with some other girl. Pick her up and take her to some isolated island."

"Heather, I called because I told you I'd get you at the station."

"That's the only reason, then. Well, I get it," she said, but she didn't get any of this. Mainly, she couldn't understand the nonsense that was coming out of her mouth.

"You think what you think, Heather. You need to get back to Steven, and I better go. See you," John said.

What the hell was that supposed to mean?

"Right. Bye," she said and ended the call.

Though she worried about being away from the table for so long, she had to call Leann.

"Hey, Heather, what's wrong?" Leann sounded comatose, and then Heather realized it was 3 a.m. in Wisconsin.

"Nothing, I'm sorry to wake you."

"It's all right. What's up?"

"I'm on a date with Steven in Edinburgh. He came to see me, a surprise, and we're out to dinner, and then John called. So I went to the bathroom and called him back."

"So you're calling me from the crapper after you called John from the crapper?" Leann giggled, waking. "Love it. Girl, your life is getting so fucking interesting I can hardly stand it! Let me get out of bed. Give me a minute." A shuffling sound came, and then Leann said, "So did you start erotic messaging John from the bathroom while on a date with Steven?" Leann giggled again, sounding like she did in middle school.

"No," Heather said. She chuckled, imagining her friend in her pajamas, hair tousled.

"Hey, I just read in a magazine that Martha Stewart has admitted that she's done some sexting."

"I have no idea how to process that information," Heather said. "Listen, give me some advice. I shouldn't be away from the table much longer. Steven will think I'm sick on the shellfish. I can't do this playing-the-field thing. I've never done it, and now I'm so out of practice, so out of my league with these handsome, professional, seasoned men. I always thought I'd be the woman who had a husband until I died. I wanted to grow old with Marc, at least I did when I was younger. And then our marriage got distant and stifled and our baby died, and something died in me, and I got cold toward him. Did I make him have an affair?" Heather started crying in loud sobs.

"Oh, honey, it's okay. You're thinking too much. Catch your breath and stop this crazy talk. You didn't make him have an affair! Nonsense! Now, listen to me, you can do this. You are not out of your league! Give me a break. You're a novelist, a grant winner, and a hottie. Get back on that date, get your ride back to your haunted house, and then you can sort this out. It'll be okay. I know it's hard for you to live in the moment, especially with motherhood and all the caretaking you did for Marc, but, try, really try to do it. Enjoy your shellfish and the attentions from Steven. It'll be okay."

Once again, her best friend had saved her. Heather said, "I'll try," wiped her face with one of the complimentary hand wipes, put on more lipstick, and went back to the table. When she returned to the table, Steven stood, looking concerned, but too polite to say anything.

"Sorry for taking so long," Heather said. "Wow, this braised duck looks delicious!" She meant it, and she dug in, savoring every juicy bite.

Remember
Early December, last year

"Mrs. Barrington," Dr. Marshall said, "Your husband could still have quality of life after we operate. Otherwise, the increased bleeding on his brain will most likely bring on a vegetative state."

Being accustomed to words, Heather fixated on the word "could," a modal auxiliary in the sentence that indicates a possibility that may or may not happen in the future. Thus, after another brain surgery, Marc may have quality of life, or he may not. What kind of quality? He definitely wouldn't be getting better. The other phrase, "vegetative state," made a clear picture. Heather glanced over at her children. All color had drained from Tessa's face; she twisted her hands and took long breaths. Jackson ran his hands through his hair, nodding to the doctor, crinkling his brow in deep thought.

This surgeon, Dr. Marshall, was new on the scene. Heather instantly missed Dr. Ghani's penetrating brown eyes, his pragmatic, yet optimistic, way of putting things. Dr. Ghani had also been involved in saving Marc's life; his surgical hands had done the job, relieving the bleeding on the brain, coaxing Marc back to the side of the living, and yet, many months, years, and thousands of hours had passed since Marc's stroke. In that time, Heather and her family had altered, becoming a unit of need and giving. How much more should they give to save Marc? What would Marc want if he were clear-minded? This new surgeon hadn't walked the many slow miles behind Marc; he saw a young stroke victim, an intriguing case study.

231

"May I speak with my children alone, doctor?" Heather asked.

Dr. Marshall nodded. "Of course, I'll be back in a few minutes."

A few minutes – would that be enough time to determine Marc's fate?

The doctor's office closed in around Heather. Winter sunlight showed dust on the fake potted plants. The plaster wall with generic prints swarmed and swooped toward her. Her head light, her body tense, she knew she had to speak to Jackson and Tessa. Both children looked as sick as she felt.

"Kids, I'm so sorry this is happening. Let's discuss this."

Tessa turned to Heather. "What is there to discuss? He needs the operation to live."

Jackson's blue eyes got watery and connected with Heather's. She knew he shared her thoughts: what kind of life? How could they endure seeing Marc even more incapacitated? Heather wanted to say the words out loud, but Tessa, so young and innocent, stared at her. She had no questions about whether or not to operate because her father's life was an absolute yes, and no other option stood before her. Without seeing the future the same way as a middle-aged woman raising and protecting children, the answer materialized as if no question had been posed. Tessa wanted her daddy to live.

"Tessie," Jackson said. "We don't know how Dad will be after surgery."

Could, could, could. He could have quality of life. But he could easily be worse.

Could she handle worse?

NO!

Tessa's eyes filled. She wiped them away with the back of her hand. "I know, but we can't just let him die. You heard the doctor."

"He's new," Jackson said and then bit his lip. They had all aged so much since Marc's stroke, and though her children were budding youths, they each had their own beaten-down quality that manifested in their bodies. For Jackson, his cheek twitched nervously just like Marc's used to, and his hands were ashy and dry from so much washing. Increased care-taking meant increased hand-washing. For Tessa, dark circles were beneath tired eyes.

"Dr. Marshall is older than Mom," Tessa said. She glanced at Heather. "No offense."

"None taken, sweetheart," Heather said. Her turn to chime in; she knew what Jackson had meant. It had nothing to do with age. "I think Jackson means that we've been through many doctors, therapists, nurses, and Dr. Marshall has just been introduced to your father's case. Your dad is young and healthy in many ways, like his heart, so the doctor really wants to save him."

Tessa stood up, her hair carouseling outward in a feathery blonde whoosh. "I want to save him. He's our dad," she said, crying, looking to Jackson who crunched over and stared at the floor. Tessa turned to Heather, "And your husband! We can't let him die. We can't!" Tessa sobbed, making Heather run to her side and grab her in a big hug. Heather's sweater got soaked at the shoulder from Tessa's tears.

Jackson wiped tears silently, but said nothing.

She had to say something to help her daughter. But what? Her only thoughts were the antithesis of comfort, something to the effect of, "Honey, he may become completely incapacitated even if we operate." That wouldn't help. How could she live with herself if, in this moment, she denied Tessa this chance? Could she be the hand that strikes Marc down, slowly, with an interminable push to the grave? Could, could, could. The modal auxiliary popped up again like a deranged clown jack-in-the-box, saying, "Here we go round the mulberry bush…" Again.

"Okay, okay," Heather said.

Jackson looked up to Heather, his eyes full of emotion; she wasn't sure what emotion, but she knew she had to be the one to say it. They were the children after all; there was no one else above Heather to make the decision or cast the net into future waters of the unknown.

"When Dr. Marshall comes back, I'll tell him we'll do the surgery," Heather said. In her back pocket, she knew Marc's living will said he didn't want extreme measures to keep him alive. She may have to face those measures later, and maybe the surgery would precipitate his death. She cried into Tessa's shoulder then, her guilty thoughts sprouting like prolific ferns in her brain. He could die on the operating table. He could need extreme measures to keep him alive. He could die sooner rather than later. The thoughts were reasonable, and helped pull the guilt-fern from its roots. Heather couldn't deny Tessa on this. It was sound reasoning, and with each salty tear down her cheek, Heather felt a little freer.

Live
July 13th, present day

Steven stood on the red step in front of White Cottage with Heather's suitcase. She paused with her hand on the door knob, afraid to enter in case the ghost had been there. What would be out of place? In bed last night and after mediocre sex, Heather had finally mentioned to Steven her real concerns about the haunting. Steven was not a bad lover; he seemed distracted, as was Heather who couldn't get John out of her head even while naked with Steven. Not good. Steven had listened to her points briefly and said he'd talk to the cleaning staff about misplacing things. This had made Heather shut up. She knew the cleaning schedule, and things had been misplaced on days no one had come to clean. Had she forgotten she'd moved them, or had it been Meg, the bleeding, pleading woman from her dream?

Steven shifted from foot to foot. "Are you having trouble finding your key, Heather?" – a polite way to get her to move along. Steven had taken some hands-free work calls on the drive back from Edinburgh. Heather knew he was anxious to get on with his life. Perhaps that was the point: Steven fit Heather in; he juggled so much with running the estate. She, too, had simply become one more thing, and she even felt this phenomenon in bed. His mind on the next work thing, he moved through sex as if through a check list. The result was not exactly orgasmic for Heather.

"Found it," Heather said, holding up the single key attached to a block of wood. She slid it in the lock and turned. A cool whoosh of air blew her hair out of her face. The ghost? No. Just an evening breeze off of the pond, where golden eagles circled above. Owls and other nocturnal creatures twitched in the nearby woods, gearing up for night. The oncoming darkness, a cloak that would soon fall over the cottage and the entire estate, hung as a pregnant curtain in the sky. Things would certainly get scarier at night.

Steven carried in her bag, setting it near the door and shifting on his feet. "Well," he said.

Heather wanted to think of something to get him to stay; if more attraction pulled them together, she could attempt to seduce him and lure him upstairs, but the act, these physical episodes that had been gone from her life for so long, didn't appeal to her. She wished she wanted him more. She wished John stood in the doorway.

"Thank you, Steven, for everything," she said and pecked him on the lips.

He smiled and took her hand. Giving it a squeeze, he said, "I'll be very busy with negotiations on the forestry plan in the next several days, but I will be thinking about you, my fair lass." He came in for another kiss, a good one in the Steven-Heather match up.

With her heart and mind so distracted by John Timmer, should she simply break up with Steven? But break what – they hadn't talked about any terms to their relationship.

"I'll ring you soon, love," he said, pulling away, inching out the door.

"Bye." She waved to him and watched him drive away, his car fading, and her last connection to a corporeal being went with him. Now she was alone. Alone with her ghost.

A scent of rain hung in the air, and the dusky evening cast a murky glow on the pond. Before long, the sun would dip lower. A chill ran up her arms. She went back inside and locked the door. In a rush, Heather moved through the cottage, taking in every object, making sure things were not misplaced. Her skin prickled with each fast foot step; her eyes scanned every corner and nook. Nothing strange, nothing amiss. She sighed and headed to the kitchen to make tea. She would love to call Leann, but it was 1 a.m. in Wisconsin, and when tested, the cell phone connection blipped and died. Hopefully, she had Internet. Even though she didn't want to admit it, she longed for contact with John.

After making tea, she nestled on the couch, a position that made her think of her all-night chat with John, when they drank tea and talked, watching for the ghost. Guilt washed over her: how could she sleep with Steven and have such strong feelings for John? The dating Heather of twenty years ago was a one-man kind of girl, and she believed that was the right thing to do, to be with one man for her whole life. Now, the mid-life Heather shook off the old self, like molted skin, resolving that the easy answers of her twenties were no more. The forties brought complexity, layers upon layers of possibilities and options on how to live. The question of how to live appeared in multiplicity, a fireworks' burst in the night sky, showering the ground with light and sparks.

She sipped her tea and glanced at the mallet from John's farm. As a joke, or maybe not a joke, he had brought it for her the day he drove her to the train station to leave for Edinburgh. He'd said, "Here, now you can club the ghost if you get scared."

She'd felt silly taking it, but didn't refuse. Somehow, she knew she needed a weapon. A weapon against what – she wasn't sure.

Still light out, but growing darker at close to 9 p.m. Grateful for the late sundown in Scotland, she charged up her laptop, unable to stay away from social media and email much longer. Her stomach twisted, her groin pulsed: she had a message from John. She clicked on the red flag and read.

Heather, I wonder if you're back from Edinburgh. Are you all right in White Cottage, or should I assume Steven is staying over with you? Just wanted to make sure you're okay.

Heather sat forward on the couch. He wrote her! John worried about her safety! Forget their last conversation. Forget if he sent erotic messages to other women; it didn't matter. Okay, maybe it did, but right now, all she wanted was to talk to her friend, her longtime friend who had emerged and become such an attraction with a gravitational pull yanking her to his point on the planet.

Heather clicked on John's name to open the chat box.

Hi John, Yes, I'm back in White Cottage. I'm okay. Steven is not with me.

What else should she say? She wanted to know what was between them. Was it more than friendship, more than flirtation, whether online or in person? Heather waited. A light rain started to pitter-pat on the roof and windows, making her think of chattering teeth. She rose and looked out to the front of the cottage. The garden bench became a slumbering animal in the semi-darkness. In the breeze, the high wildflowers and native grasses swayed like puppets with invisible strings.

Long minutes went by before Heather heard, *ping*. She ran back to her laptop to see a message from John. Her heart raced.

I'm glad to hear you're back. How was Edinburgh?

Oh, goodness, were they back to the casual chat of two years ago? Heather didn't think she could stand it. She decided to do the exact opposite of what she usually did because this new Heather was bolder, wiser, and more direct. Weary of always skirting around other people's needs, she wrote without overanalyzing:

John, tell me. Do you have other women you're writing to? I know you said you aren't seeing anyone here in Scotland right now, but you can be rather vague and dodgy. I've never had such open discussions with anyone, especially about sex and desire, and if you do that with other women … I don't like it.

Heather hit "send" and waited. Afraid she wouldn't see the words, "John is typing," she slapped the laptop screen into the folded position and paced the wood floor of the living room. Dark clouds obscured the low-hanging sun, making the cabin take on a shadowy blue hue. Heather clicked on the floor lamp. She jumped and slid in her socked feet when her computer pinged, signaling a Facebook message.

Okay. Honesty time? John wrote.

Then he followed with: *From both of us, right?*

She answered: *Yes.*

Minutes went by where Heather stared at the screen watching the words, "John is typing." Finally his message appeared.

Yes, I've had some online correspondence with women similar to the nature I've had with you, but none right now. I told you I'm not dating anyone seriously. You, Heather, seem to be pretty hot and heavy with Steve. True?

Heather's throat burned. She felt like nothing more than a chat box rub off. How in the world did she get here? She resented John for roping her in, making her believe she was something special, the first woman he had opened up to about sex, relationships, desire. Now she only felt like a scrolling roll on a long Facebook friend list. She didn't think much about what to say, she wrote with fast, hot tears starting from her eyes:

I knew it! I knew, always felt, that your avoidance or vagueness meant something. Now I know, I'm one of many women, nothing special. Just so you know, I've never, NEVER, talked (yes, even though it was through the filter of chatting on Facebook) with a man so openly about desire. And it happened in a matter of days! And the date on the island! I should simply back off now, John. I'm too vulnerable. I can't play any games. I should focus on my work and healing and stay away from you.

Send. Wait.

Nothing. No response, and yet she saw the maddening little check mark near the message, indicating that he had seen it and at what time (moments ago).

Finally, a message appeared.

Are you sleeping with Steve?

What could she say? She said yes to honesty, so she answered.

Yes.

Nothing. Minutes ticked by, and the rain picked up, making furious ticks on the window pane. She should add that it didn't mean much – she liked Steven, and he had been attentive, up to a certain point, and comfortable in the mundane feel of marriage. But there was no spark, no burn. And now the entire thing felt muddled with her immature need to make John jealous, and the uncertainty of how to end it, especially with the looming possibility of her purchase of the cottage.

This hurts, Heather. John wrote.

Now her heart flipped. As instantly as she had wanted to hurt him, when it happened she wanted to soothe the pain, have him close to her, tell him she wanted to strip off his clothes and twist their long bodies together.

Then he followed with: *Is your phone working? Can I call you?*

She checked her phone. No signal. Her breath caught with the thought of hearing his voice.

My cell phone has no signal. Can we keep chatting?

Sure. You scared tonight?

A little. She lied. Now that the sky rolled out into darkness because of the rain and the darkening hours of approaching night, her skin prickled. The lights in the cottage flickered on and off. Heather jumped to her feet and ran to the kitchen, grabbing her flashlight and the stowed candles and matches in case the lights went out for good. Though the evening air had a chill, Heather started sweating; the wetness cooled her skin in an instant. She grabbed a fleece blanket and wrapped it around her shoulders.

Electricity on. No ghostly sounds or lights.

She thought she would handle everything just fine. She had to get through at least one night in her cottage on her own if she planned to purchase it. She couldn't avoid it forever, as tempting as it was to ask John to spend the night. No, she had to sort this out, get to the bottom of what they meant to each other. So he had had other online "girls," whatever that meant. He wasn't chatting with them now, and if he was, she was the one sleeping with someone else.

Could she become a woman who had more than one man? The idea – so foreign, yet somewhat alluring – seemed impossible, but that was the married woman thinking. Not only was she new to the dating world with real-life men, this virtual world constructed an ether of possibility and torture, creating multiple ways to get rejected or to feel like another notch in a man's belt, another message in his inbox.

But he was hurt by her relationship with Steven. She went back to her laptop, which she had to reboot because of the flickering of electricity. She tried to log back on to Facebook to continue her chat with John, but then a notice popped up telling her how to troubleshoot her Internet connection problems. She went through the painstakingly long steps, but after several attempts she had to accept her lack of Internet, lack of phone, her disconnect. She hoped John wouldn't see this as a blow off. What if he did? What if whatever that was starting between them would die before it really began?

A crack of thunder sent a jolt through her body. She tugged at the blanket and searched the cottage again, for any sign, any movement of her belongings. Upstairs in her room, the air itself felt electric and powerful; cool bursts sent her bedroom curtains flying. She clamped the window shut, but changed her mind and cracked it a half inch to circulate air. The moonlight and sharp flashes of lightning illuminated the lofted room, making Heather chill with anxiety. The night had just begun and she had no idea how she'd get through it.

Resolved, she went back downstairs, grabbed a generous glass of wine, and swallowed an over-the-counter sleeping pill. She stripped off her socks, slipped into pajama pants and a light hoodie from her suitcase, and settled on the couch under the blanket, her laptop perched on her stretched-out legs. Without Internet, she opted to put in a DVD from one of the bookshelves, something on the history of the Highlands. Every few minutes she clicked on the Internet icon and tried to connect. After an hour of this torment, her eyes grew heavy and she fell asleep.

Heather opened her eyes to a darkened cottage. The outlines of the furniture came into view after she sat up and surveyed her surroundings. Heart pounding and ears ringing a high-pitched din, Heather dropped her feet to the floor, glancing a moment at her toes. When she looked up, Meg – blurred and bloody – hovered in the doorway of the kitchen.

"Let go," Meg said. "Go!" Meg gave Heather a blazing, fierce look instead of the scared, horror-struck expression from the last visitation, or was it a dream? Once again Heather appeared awake, but things seemed off, and her zip-up sweatshirt was unzipped, showing her breasts.

Pulling her sweatshirt closed, Heather steeled herself, even though she shook with fear.

"What? Let go of what?" Heather asked, but in a blink of her eyes, Meg vanished.

Heather sprang awake. She felt for the zipper of her sweatshirt; her pulse thundered in her neck.

Clink, clink.

The lights were still on in the cottage. Under the lamp light, the darkness that had filled the cottage during the dream/visitation felt like a far-off, magical cave. The introductory song replayed on the Highland movie that had finished on her laptop. This was it. Meg, her ghost, was back. Was she now outside the cottage? Or had the sound come from inside?

Clink, clink.

Heather was sure Meg would not hurt her. But what if it wasn't Meg who was outside the cottage? What if someone had come to hurt her? Maybe Meg's words served as a warning; what if someone had been stalking Heather, and now he came to kill her?

Heather shook off the blanket and grabbed for John's mallet as she stood. The storm had diminished while she slept: no thunder or lightning – only the ticking of rain drops on the windows. Shaking, she moved forward, grabbing her cell phone, but seeing she had no signal. Hand still on the weapon and eyes scanning the sitting room, Heather tried to log onto the Internet, but a message popped up saying she had no connection.

No car. No connection. What in the world should she do? Face her would-be attacker? Creeping softly, Heather walked with the mallet in hand. The floorboards of the cottage creaked under Heather's bare feet. A full moon blinked at her through the window from behind a haze of clouds. Though the mallet from the farm felt powerful in her clenched hand, her body shook, and her mind thought of Tessa and Jackson, her children who would be orphaned if whoever was outside murdered her. Her legs, now leaner and stronger from her days of hiking rocky Scottish islands, stretched and her toes pressed against the wood floor with each tip toe.

Heather took a long, calming breath. Ballerina toes, she thought. She could be as swift and silent as the Swan Princess.

Tomorrow, would someone find her bleeding and near death? No, she told herself, there had to be a logical explanation for the things she had been hearing during the night. But right now, logic failed her: each nerve in her body, alert and fearful, sparked with life. Ready to spring, she moved through the cottage, cataloging the things as she went: furniture, quilts, pots and pans, candles, books, paper, her items from home. Would she see an apparition in the cottage or out the window? Would Meg be guiding her to safety? Sweat beaded on her forehead and a drip slipped between her breasts.

Another clink sounded from outside. Then the same fleeting wind-chime whispers she had heard before. Heather's head felt as if a hot-air balloon were lifting it into the sky; the ringing in her ears kept on and on.

The wildflowers she had picked sent a waft of fresh blooms to her nostrils. The smell calmed her quickened pulse. Deep breath, another step – she had to get to the bottom of this, even if something happened to her. She was done being afraid. She was done living as if life always dangled like a delicate ornament, like the glass ballerina Marc had given her fifteen years ago.

No more. Let the glass dancer fall and shatter; let her catch air, spin, and plummet, even if it's the poor soul's last and only flight.

She just might bounce and roll.

She just might escape death.

She just might survive.

She just might live.

She stood in the doorway of the kitchen, right where Meg had been. Wind cut in the open kitchen window, sending a wine glass from the table tumbling.

Crash!

Glass shattered; the sound reverberated. The sound held onto Heather's ears, filling them with a simultaneous crashing and ringing. Was someone there, outside of the cottage, obscured behind the curtain?

Heather screamed and dropped the mallet. She turned away from the kitchen, away from the shattering sound, which seemed to get louder, closer, or was it in her ears? Heather couldn't think of anything to do but slip on her shoes near the front door and bolt outside.

Another crashing sound came from the opposite side of the cottage. Heather's last bit of courage abandoned her, and she struck out into the woods, away from the haunted cottage.

Live
July 13th-14th, present day

The woods, Heather's refuge, engulfed her. She ran on a faint path, her feet twisting on gnarly roots, but she didn't fall. She kept running, deeper into the clammy cool of damp leaves and wet branches, the spindles like shadowy arms, taking her in.

Just go, go, she thought. Meg had told her to go, and she did. Get as far from the cottage as she could.

A harsh breeze whooshed through the leaves, sending a spray of water over Heather. She swiped the drops from her eyes and sprinted. Jumping a cluster of overturned branches, she grabbed at air and slammed the other side hard with her feet. After a moment's pause she breathed and started off again. Misty glimpses of shadows and moonlight dotted her path, which twisted and disappeared, then reappeared.

After a few more minutes of running, a thought forced her to ask: where? Where am I going? She pumped her legs, felt each footfall stomp earth.

Don't stop, just go.

A dark form flew past her from above; she crouched and listened, breathing like she'd run a marathon.

Hoo, hoo. An owl sounded above her. Other animals skittered in the underbrush. She was headed toward the hotel and restaurant, or so she thought. Why hadn't she struck out on the gravel road? Even when it became a rutty dirt path, it followed the hedgerow right to the center of the estate. Something cracked in the distance, causing Heather to spring up. A fallen branch or something else? Something supernatural or something human behind her? What if the broken glass signified a rapist or murderer breaking in through the cottage window?

After another crackle, Heather shot off again, terrified and spurred on by an unseen force. All she wanted was to run – run away; keep moving.

Snaggy thorns tore at her pajama pants and slashed the thin sweatshirt covering her upper arms.

"Shit," she whispered, but instead of stopping, she picked up speed. The path had virtually disappeared, only a slender ribbon of worn dirt weaved in front of her. She pushed on.

Go, go. Get away. Run.

Then her foot caught on a rock. Her body flew forward; her arms pin-wheeled, trying to guide her hands to latch onto a branch, something to break her fall. Nothing. Heather's inertia took her aloft and into a leap, a motion she had done on stage many times in a dance, but this time it was without direction or control. She flailed, contorted, and slammed down, her head cracking against the exposed root of a tree.

The night sky and the rustling leaves quivered with spots. Heather rolled, her head spun in dizzying revolutions. She tried to move but couldn't will her body to respond. She lifted her palm to her forehead, the point of blossoming pain, and felt blood, warm, distorting.

This can't be, she thought. A head wound? No...no. A far-off conversation about concussions whispered from behind her thoughts, but she couldn't place it before she blacked out.

Remember
Early December, last year

Heather pressed the "start" button on the automated coffee machine in the hospital waiting room. Over the course of the last week, she'd grown addicted to the synthetic sweetness of the vanilla cappuccino. The machine's offerings weren't frothed to coffee-shop stiffness, but the consistent warmth and burst of caffeine and sugar calmed her, nonetheless. Or maybe the routine of visiting this one isolated waiting area in the Elmline Hospital (top in the neurosurgery field) provided the necessary solace in her long days of being by Marc's side post-surgery.

Right after the surgery, he had woken up, eyes glossy and vacant, and glanced at Heather, Jackson, and Tessa with an inscrutable expression. He stared at Tessa and then, clear as a tuning fork chime, said, "Hi, Tessa."

Tessa had hugged him and talked and talked until he'd gone to sleep again. He'd slept for nearly a week, which could have been the start of an indefinite coma, but finally he'd emerged from the cottony, post-surgery haze and blinked his eyes. Awake, but unable to talk or take in food, the doctors had asked Heather if they could put in a temporary feeding tube in his nose. For two days now, liquid food went in through Marc's nostrils, and he barely woke to notice it.

Yes, a few moments away from Marc's feeding time to drink a premix coffee drink was a fine idea.

She sat on the foam green sofa and stared out the darkened glass of the window. Her reflection, a trick of light and shadow, gazed back at her. She had given up working while at the hospital, pushing deadlines and shifting projects to other freelancers, so the time away from her kids or Marc's hospital room brought on emptiness, not a bad empty, but a pouring out, an unfolding of all muscular and neurological effort. She made herself blank.

Jackson and Tessa appeared behind her. She hadn't heard them approach, but there they stood, watery images in the waiting-room window.

"Hi, Mom," Jackson said. "Can we talk to you about something?"

She drank a long sip and nodded, patting the sofa next to her, making room, though not feeling like talking.

Both kids plopped beside her, Jackson perched on the edge to Heather's immediate left, and Tessa was half obscured on the other side of her brother. They glanced at each other, a secret conversation shared and ping-ponging between their miniscule eye motions.

"Mom," Jackson said. "We don't think Dad would want the nose tube."

Heather wanted to pipe in right away with a sharp voice saying, "Of course he wouldn't! But we operated, and this is what they do to people they save: they feed them!"

Instead, Heather said, "I know."

"Why did you let them put it in?" Tessa asked. Her voice wasn't accusatory; it whispered, like a smaller child talking to her dolls.

"Well, it's procedure after a surgery like this. Sometimes. Dr. Marshall hopes your dad will show more responses in the next couple of days." Heather wasn't so sure, but what now?

"You have power-of-attorney or something like that for Dad, right?" Jackson asked.

Was this going where Heather thought it was? Were they going to ask her to pull the feeding tube?

"I do," she said. She thought it best to keep her responses short.

The three sat in silence for long seconds. Heather sipped her now tepid drink. She didn't know what to think. She should say something. But what?

"Mom," Tessa said. "Do you think Dad will get better?"

What a question!

"Well, I can't know for sure. Do you mean get back to where he was before the surgery, or better than that, which do you mean?"

"I guess I mean to where he was, like, about six months after his stroke, something like that," she said in a hushed voice.

The poor baby, Heather thought. She couldn't lie to either of them even with her desire to protect them.

"No, I don't. I think with the various falls there has been more brain damage. So I don't know what to expect, but I'm fairly certain he won't get to that level of functionality again."

Jackson nodded. "I thought the same thing."

Tessa's arm, covered in goose pimples, caught Heather's eyes. She needed a sweater; it was winter in Wisconsin. Why hadn't the child grabbed one before they'd left for the hospital?

Jackson looked at Tessa, again the nonverbal communication passed between them.

"If you can do it as Dad's power of attorney for health stuff, we think you should ask the doctors to take out the feeding tube," Jackson said, face drained of any color.

Heather leaned forward on her knees so she could look both in their beautiful faces. Too much! They carried too much burden!

"Do you both understand that your dad is not at a level where he can re-learn how to swallow again?"

The cherubs nodded, eyes wide, faces expectant.

"Without swallowing," Heather said, "he won't eat or drink, and then he will die."

$X + Y = Z$

249

How could she possibly sound so matter-of-fact, so clinical at this moment?

"After this we won't be in hospitals anymore; they'll send him to a different facility. It's called hospice. It's where people are taken care of until they die. Are you asking me to prevent that from happening? Should we let your father…" she swallowed choking on the word, "go?"

Jackson and Tessa were crying now, but nodded, "yes."

Heather hugged both of them and said, "Okay. I agree with you. Your dad wouldn't want to live like this. We're making the right decision for him."

As the three walked back toward Marc's room, thoughts flipped through Heather's brain: she would have to face Dr. Marshall and tell him that after saving Marc they now planned to let him slip away, slowly. She would need to stick to this plan, the plan of death that was best for Marc. It was what Marc wanted. Wasn't it?

Secretly had she wanted him dead for so long that now she motored through decisions, pretending they were for Marc, but maybe her heart had willed this future to come forth. She shook off the guilt. She had the power to pull the plug, and with her children, in the midst of coming of age, she had to be the one to set them free, and if she flew along with them, so be it.

Live
July 14th, present day

Rain again. Bright lights, strong hands.

Her body wrapped in a blanket. She opened her eyes momentarily and saw him.

"John," Heather whispered. She couldn't hear her voice. This was it. She hit her head after falling in the woods, and now she had a traumatic brain injury. Could she feel her toes? The drizzle pitter-pattered on her face. She lay on the forest floor, eyes flickering open to the shadowy canopy. John pointed while talking to the paramedics. Was that Steven's voice in the background, sounding like a cartoon character?

No one noticed she had opened her eyes. Everyone talked and talked. Droning, it sounded like some kind of machine. She couldn't handle keeping her eyes open one moment more. They felt as heavy as lead. She closed them and slipped into blessed sleep.

***

"I'm staying." John's voice cut through the murk. Heather, very accustomed to hospital rooms, realized right away by the feel of the sheet and the blipping sound of the machine to her right, that she was lying in a hospital bed.

"I don't think I feel comfortable with that." Steven's voice had an on-the-verge of anger tone, but softened with the Scottish lilt.

"Are you going to stay then?" John asked, confrontational and direct, like an animal fighting for territory.

Heather kept her eyes locked shut, but her ears homed in on their voices, which came from the edge of the room, possibly near the doorway.

A rustling sound, maybe a nurse skirting past the two men, and then the familiar tinging Steven's phone made when he had a text. Heather could feel his distraction even without seeing him.

"I cannae, I told ye that," Steven said. "The new forestry plan goes before the local courts today. I have to speak there, or we will not get the land commissions we need for the –"

"Save it, Steve," John interrupted. "I don't need a forest preservation lecture. Not now. I'm staying. Go do your thing."

"I'm dating, Heather, you're not. I dinnae like you here. I've seen how you look at her. I'll get someone from the inn to come and watch over her today."

"Absolutely not," John said. "Stop acting like the two of you have been exclusive for months or something. Maybe in your domineering mind you have been – did you pay any attention to how Heather looked at me, say, the night of the ball? Of course, you saw it, that's why you don't want me here. Try and move me, prick, and we'll take this outside. She's had a shock, a concussion. They're going to release her, but someone needs to watch out for her, make sure symptoms don't get worse. I'm doing it."

"Timmer, I've had it with yer cocksure ways, like ye own the bloody bill on women."

"Gentlemen," the nurse said. "Is there a problem with ye two blokes?"

"No, m'am," John said.

A slight mutter from Steven, probably a "no."

"Good then," she said. "Whoever is staying, take yer post, and whoever is leaving, go on with ye. I don't need any more disturbances here, and neither does Ms. Finch."

Was this a dream? John was staying. The thought lifted Heather above the contours of the rooms, drifting on a breeze. As soon as Heather heard Steven and the nurse leave, she opened her eyes. John stood at the window.

"John." Her voice croaked and cracked.

He rushed over to the bedside.

"Heather, how're you feeling?"

How did she feel? Shall she say, as light as a hollow-boned bird on air because you're here? No, they had had a bit of a chat spat the last she spoke with him. But he was here, at her side.

She opted for an assessment of her physical state, "Groggy. My head hurts." She touched the right side of her forehead, which had a large adhesive bandage on it.

"I'll call the nurse. She said she could give you some pain medication when you woke for good. You've been really out of it, in and out of consciousness."

Heather worried she had said something in her semi-consciousness, but this was John before her, a man she had been the most honest with in her entire life, and that included her husband. "Did I say anything inappropriate?"

John smiled, his hazel eyes looking more like milk chocolate today. "The paramedics said you kept saying my name in the ambulance. I followed in my car, so I didn't hear you. Since you've been here, I've only heard you moan." He locked eyes with her. She cleared her throat, embarrassed that the word "moan" from John's mouth gave her a surge of pleasure. He unlocked the sexy stare and trotted off for the nurse.

After relief came from the pain medication kicking in, which also brought on drowsiness impossible to avoid, Heather forced herself to talk with John before she fell into a deep slumber.

"How did you find me? Why did you come?" She asked, her head already feeling better, lighter.

"When you didn't write back, at first I thought you'd blown me off, but that didn't seem like you, so I tried your phone constantly. I also kept sending texts, chat messages, and emails. When I didn't hear anything, I got worried because I know how scared you are right now to be in the cottage alone. I thought I'd forget about crossing bounds and head over to the cottage. The door was wide open, and you were gone. There was a broken wine glass in the kitchen. I searched on my own around the cottage, and then into the woods a bit, but I couldn't find you. I called the estate to get Steve and some people to help me. One of the garden guys found you in the woods, not too far out, but you were out cold. We didn't want to move you, so we called the paramedics."

"The ghost," Heather muttered. A thick veil closed over her. She couldn't keep her eyes open.

"I know, my sweetheart," John said. "Don't worry about that now. Get some rest. I'll be here when you wake up."

Remember
Mid-December, last year

"It's not easy to stop feeding someone," Heather said over another cup of vanilla cappuccino. She had been grateful that the hospice facility had the same generic machine spewing out the same sugary, caffeinated drink.

"Oh, sweetie, I'm so sorry," Leann said and patted Heather's hand. The hospice had a nice kitchenette area just off the front lobby. A refrigerator held stored leftovers and drinks for people staying with the patients, family and friends who drifted in and out of the death rooms wearing the same tired and numb expressions, as if they hadn't slept a full night's sleep in weeks, which in some cases may have been true.

"It's okay," Heather said, even though it really wasn't okay. It wasn't okay that Marc was dying in room #5 down the hallway, and that Heather had set his imminent death clock by ordering the nose tube to be removed. Then a series of decisions, each hacking away at the minutes Marc had left on the planet: "Do you want to treat his pneumonia with antibiotics, Mrs. Barrington?" "Do we allow sips of water, Mrs. Barrington?" "Do you want a swallow test, Mrs. Barrington?"

"So, do you have any idea about, you know, when?" Leann asked. She looked so beautiful, her friend, with light make-up and liquid brown eyes.

"We've been here five days. When we were first admitted, the intake nurse said it could take over a week or more. Every patient is different."

"So when Marc drinks a sip of water or something, will that, what's the right way to put this, extend things?" Leann asked. Her fingertips traced the top of her paper cup.

"It's called 'recreational eating,' an amorphous word that caused me great distress in the hospital when I had to sign off on it. Once I got here, though, the nurses helped me to understand that it is simply for Marc's comfort. If he wakes and asks for something like water, or ice cream, anything soft or liquidy, we can give him a few sips or bites. It will not be enough to 'sustain life,' as the nurse put it." Her matter-of-fact recitation of this end-of-life eating shocked Heather.

Tears welled in Leann's eyes. She wiped them away as quickly as they had started. "You want to go home for a while, take a nap? I can stay this afternoon."

"Maybe," Heather answered. After a few seconds, she added, "I know it sounds silly, but I've started watching reruns of that old show, 'Big Valley.' It's on at 2 p.m."

"Isn't that with Barbara Stanwyck?"

"Yeah, that's the one. She's this widow running a family ranch in California. The Bionic Man is in it, too," Heather said.

"Lee Majors."

"Uh-huh, and Linda Evans from Dynasty – it's quite a cast."

Heather and Leann sat and sipped their coffees, staring off. Leann got up and threw her cup away and sat back down. The wall clock ticked on. The coffee machine hummed. The ice in the soda machine rattled.

"The hardest part when we first got here was Marc's agitation. He looked scared to death," Heather said. "Well, not 'to death,' not quite yet." A nervous giggle followed at her dark humor that broke into a hearty laugh. Leann caught on and laughed along with her friend. Heather's shoulder shook. Blessed relief came with the release of giggles, like they were two school girls at lunch rather than two forty-somethings in a hospice facility.

"It's almost 2 p.m. I better get back for 'Big Valley,'" Heather said.

This brought on another fit of laughter until both women had to wipe their eyes with paper napkins.

"Yeah, that's great, an old ass show about a widow. That's just what you need, Finchy."

"Hah! You're right. Isn't that great, just great!" Heather laughed harder. Only when another family member of a hospice patient passed through did they get control of their laughter.

Heather wiped her face with a paper towel and headed back to Marc.

Live

July 15th, present day

Heather lay on the couch at White Cottage while John made lunch, canned tomato soup and grilled cheese. She had been released from the hospital two hours before with papers about concussions and when to come back to the doctor if certain symptoms showed up. Apparently, memory loss or other problems didn't occur right after the injury. This made Heather nervous even though the doctor believed she'd have no further troubles.

John came in with a lap tray holding steaming soup, the sandwich, and a cup of hot tea. The day was cool for mid-July, cloudy with a misty rain and a light breeze that wafted in through the window behind Heather, bringing in the scent of the wildflower mix and the nearby pond weeds.

"Here you go," John said, positioning the tray on Heather's lap and scrutinizing her bandage.

She touched her head. "Is it bleeding?"

"I don't think so," he said. "I think I need to check the stitches and change the bandage after lunch."

"This looks delicious. Thank you."

"Dig in. I'll get mine and be back."

By the time John returned with his food, Heather had plowed through half of hers.

"I didn't realize how hungry I was," she said.

"It's good. You need your strength."

They ate in silence. Heather didn't allow her eyes to rest too long on the roses Steven had sent. She knew they irked John by his reaction, which had been a scoffing sound while he muttered, "blowhard," under his breath. The group at the Solace Art Fund had sent a bouquet as well, along with a delivery of groceries from Lochaline, an action John noted as both practical and thoughtful while gesturing to Steven's flowers and making a humpf sound, as if to say, "not like the blowhard's gesture."

After lunch, John pulled out a Scrabble game from his duffle bag, and they played for over an hour. Heather stared at her letters and strained to keep her eyes open.

"Hey, Heather, let me help you upstairs. You can stretch out in your own bed," John said.

Ting. Heather had a text; while at the hospital and now at White Cottage, messages had been coming through from Tessa, Jackson, and Leann, all concerned about how she was faring. At first she had tried to keep up, but then John took over the communications from his phone and kept them all updated. He had even worked out the details of Tessa and Jackson's arrival in two days' time. He had cleared things with Claire, so both her kids could stay at the farm and work, or they could be gophers at the drop zone until Heather felt well enough for sightseeing.

"It's my phone," she said. "I'll check it and then go rest."

She read the text from Steven.

Hi Heather, I'm glad to hear you're now safely deposited in White Cottage. I'm sorry I can't come round to see you today. Maybe tomorrow. This forestry business and other things have gotten out of hand in my days away. Much love & take care. S

Had he been away from work? It seemed, even in Edinburgh, that the work kept happening.

Heather started to answer, but stopped. She could hardly keep her eyes open, the pain pill completely taking effect and making her body feel gelatinous. John had gone to the kitchen while she checked her phone. Heather hadn't done much moving around, but she thought she could handle getting up and climbing the stairs. She stood and the room spun for a couple of seconds, but she oriented herself and flopped back to the couch just as John returned.

"Whoa there, Finch. I'll help you." They sat hip to hip on the couch, and despite the wooziness, tingles coursed up her arm and through her entire body because of the proximity to John. He hooked his arm in hers, all business and concern, and helped her stand. They shuffled together to the stairs. Because of the narrow turns on the staircase, John walked right behind Heather, his palm steady on the small of her back. The tingles turned to throbs, and when they reached the top stair, Heather considered pretending to faint so she could fall into his hunky arms.

But John seemed focused on getting her to bed for her to rest and not to make love. Had she blown her chance with John? Maybe he thought they were simply old friends now, but no, he had practically said otherwise to Steven. She simply did not know how to navigate this, and for right now, as she eased into the soft cotton sheets, and John pulled the light quilt over her body, she wanted only to fall asleep.

When Heather woke, the clock next to her bed said 4:11. Disoriented and wondering if day or night, Heather went gingerly to the window and pulled back the shade. The sun, half hidden behind puffy bruised-colored clouds, shone high in the sky. Afternoon. Afraid to brave the stairs, but desperate to pee, she called down to John who practically leapt up to meet her.

"You're awake! I've missed you! No spooks have shown up," he said, grinning widely. His full mouth curved into a delicious smile; his white teeth shown like the ivory of piano keys.

"I thought I'd get up and go to the bathroom, but I'm afraid the stairs could bring on major vertigo."

"Here, take my arm," he said.

Heather touched his round bicep and ran her hand down his forearm. Then she laced it through the crook of his arm. All the while, John watched her fingers. He glanced up at her and puffed out his cheeks, his face unreadable, but turning crimson. Were her light touches that much of an arousal for him? The thought made her warm and wet between her legs.

He guided her down the stairs and to the bathroom. She went ahead and brushed her teeth, combed her hair, and dotted some lip gloss on her lips. Her bandaged forehead garnered most of the attention, and her pale face looked drawn out and thin. She pinched her cheeks to get more color.

John lingered nervously near the bathroom door. "Oh, I sent messages to Jackson and Tessa about how I worked it out for the Graham brothers to pick them up at the airport and take them to the farm to stow their stuff. If you're up for it, we'll meet them over there. I know you're weak, but it's a short drive, and I knew you'd want to see them."

"Yes," Heather said in a breathy voice. He had taken so much care, given her so much attention. Had she ever been treated like this? No. Marc never fussed over her, not even during pregnancy, childbirth, or after Gerard's death. John had a surprising capacity for care-taking, one not mired in a checks-and-balance system; his easy nature went along doing what needed to be done, and being aware of her needs, her desires. This thought alone made her want to reach out and kiss him. Could she? Would he reject her?

"Thank you, John," she said, moving forward. "I, well, I was wondering if I could kiss you."

He made a sound deep from his throat and nodded. They stepped toward each other. Nervous, but tantalized, she reached for his shoulders, his chest, and then she chanced a small peck on the lips. He pulled back and said, "You feel okay. You won't pass out or anything, right?"

"No, I won't," she said and moved in for more. Slowly their lips connected, and their hands explored the outside of their clothing. John moved his mouth down to the side of her neck, cradling her head with one hand, and touching her cheek with the other.

They paused. "Do you want to go upstairs?" he asked.

"Yes," she said.

Their ascent was charged with the pull between them, as if gravity had centered itself between their two bodies, pulling them like a taut string, connecting them in an even push and pull. Once upstairs, he guided her to the bed, eased her to her back, and lay beside her, gently rubbing her breasts, making her groan with pleasure.

"Do you like that, Heather?" he asked.

She opened her eyes. Had a man ever asked her that in bed? She couldn't remember. Such a simple question, a simple yes or no answer would suffice, but the results could bring her to a cataclysmic point.

"Yes." She breathed slowly, trying to stay in this one moment with John on her bed, stroking her, making her wet and longing for him.

He kissed her lightly on the mouth, all the while his one hand worked down her body, touching points as if his fingertips were feathers. "I'm a little scared I may hurt you," he said.

"You won't," she said. He could do anything to her in that moment and she wouldn't resist; there was no possible way she could not succumb; her singular thought was to open herself fully to him.

"Hmmm, how about I work my way over you, and you tell me if your head hurts. Tell me what you like. How it feels," he said.

"I don't know," she said, feeling nervous and incapable of honesty all of the sudden.

"Sure you can. You're a writer. Write me a story about how this feels. I love your voice. I love your skin. How about this," he said, opening her pants, sliding them off. "Is this okay?"

"Yes," she said.

He rested beside her and helped her take off her shirt, her bra. Soon she was completely naked beside him. He stared at her, but she didn't feel self-conscious.

"Jesus, you are so beautiful," he said, voice hoarse.

"No," she said and instinctively, her hand went to the small bump of her stomach, the curve there.

"You are," he said. "You should feel it about yourself. Feel how special you are." He guided her hand.

He watched, and she did feel beautiful, adored, even cherished with his eyes on her.

"I want you, Heather. All the time. Every day," he said. He kissed her lips, down her neck, and stopped at her breasts. "What about here," he said, taking her nipple in his mouth. "Does this feel good?"

"Yes," she whispered, and then her body, which had been ignored or overlooked or taken for granted for so long, awoke.

Remember

Mid-to-late December, last year

Heather had been staring at the white wall in Marc's hospice room for an indeterminate amount of time. Last night had been so hard. The nurses had said he didn't have long, so Heather and the kids decided to stay overnight. Jackson had taken the reclining chair, and Tessa and Heather had slept on slender fold-out cots. Two times they had believed Marc had breathed his last struggling breath, but he'd revived himself, gasping and resuming his belabored breathing, which matched the same rhythm that Heather found herself tapping her finger to, taaaap, ta-tap, taaaap, ta-tap, and it seemed to infiltrate her moments of no-thought. Blankness.

Now, at mid-morning, there were no more alerts from the nursing staff; the day trudged on with glaring reflections off the fallen snow outside, the shuffle of women in scrubs, and the usual start and stop routine of the room's heater. Soon it would be lunchtime, another chance for one or two of them to pop out for a sandwich or soup, and then "Big Valley" would come on at 2 p.m., of course.

Jackson entered the room and squatted next to the chair. Even though Marc hadn't been conscious for days, they had decided not to eat in front of him. Some may have thought this was out of respect or empathy, which to some degree it was, but if Heather dug deeply, she had to admit that she didn't want to encourage any more recreational eating if he came to again. Eating and drinking, no matter how minuscule, prolonged urine output, a sign of living. Bowel movements had completely ceased, making Heather's thoughts drift inanely to try to attach a precise time and date for the final time she had wiped his ass.

"Mom," Jackson said. "Go get some coffee or something. Take a break."

It took Heather a moment to register the words. Her eyes went from Marc, chest heaving and eyes locked shut, to her son, young, alive, and moving beautifully about on both of his legs. He took her hands in his without faltering. He helped her stand and put one arm around her, leading her from the room of the dying husband. Husband. How long had it been since she'd felt she had one?

"Come on, Mom," Jackson said. "I'll get you one of those coffee drinks you like."

They passed Tessa in the hallway. She waved, pointed to Marc's room, and said flatly, "I'll be in there."

Where else was there to go? Strangely, these last days of Marc's life were similar to the last days before giving birth. An unreality took root for Heather during those times. So uncomfortable and pained, she had a warped sense overtake her where a part of her believed she would stay pregnant forever. And now, part of her believed she would stay in this limbo with Marc and visit him near death endlessly.

Jackson led her to a table. She sat and stared at the print on the opposite wall – a landscape of mountains and a tranquil lake. The vanilla cappuccino materialized in front of her. She knew to wait a few minutes before she drank; the coffees were scalding out of the machine. A hunched elderly woman Heather had seen every morning entered through the front automatic door. She clutched her knitting bag and turned down the hall to her husband's room. Heather thought taking up knitting was a great idea.

Her random thoughts broke when Tessa charged from the hall. Her face seemed illuminated in light, or was the shiny glow the sheen of tears?

Tessa spoke and gestured frantically, but at first Heather couldn't make out any words. Tessa's voice and the sounds around her were muffled, distorted. Jackson pulled at Heather's arm, yanking her from the chair and jarring her to life.

"Mom!" Jackson said. "He's gone. Tessa said he died."

"What?" Heather asked. For a second she almost added, who? Who died?

Then it hit her: Marc.

Her husband had died.

Live
July 17th, present day

For two days Heather had stepped out of time. Her new life routine ebbed and flowed around life with John Timmer. He fussed over her head wound; he made love to her, and for the first time in her life, sex meant love to her: why else did it feel like thousands of birds were bursting through her abdomen and taking flight? Sometimes the twittering bird-wing feeling came from her groin or toes, a slingshot orgasm of flight – high, flapping congregations of sensations that were hers alone.

Heather felt contentment and joy: pure, uncomplicated joy.

She lay on her bed, staring at the billowing curtain, content to be in the space between John's shoulder and chest. He dozed, but held onto her, and once in a while he roused to rub her stomach or breasts, her legs or back. And then, he'd grow hard next to her thigh, and they'd start again. Again and again.

There had been no ghostly happenings since she returned to White Cottage. Did John somehow keep the ghost at bay? Maybe it was her fearful and embarrassing act of running away that had ended the haunting. Or perhaps her return to face the supernatural showed enough strength to show she would not be scared off again. The idea of someone stalking her felt far-off and unreal, yet the thought nagged at her. Why had Meg told her to go? To let go?

John stirred and played with her hair. "I love your smell," he whispered. "Even when you sweat, I love it."

Heather smiled. She knew exactly what he meant. She could sniff at his hair or the curve of his neck and collar bone without rest.

"I feel the same," she said. "John."

"What's up?" he asked, dozy.

"We'll go see my kids at the farm later today. The ghost hasn't shown up, but it could. I need to break with Steven. And then there is the question of someone stalking me while I'm alone in the cottage, or maybe it's another ghost, one that makes the clinking sound. I mean, the police said there was absolutely no evidence of any human tracks in the area around the cottage."

"Whoa." He hugged her closer to his body. "That's going through your mind. And here the only thing I'm thinking about is how I love your smell, and your hair and skin, it's so soft."

Heather smiled. "It's flooding in. Reality. And I haven't written a word in days."

"Back up the bus, Heather Finch." He rested on his elbow. "First off, I agree with the police, no human has been stalking you. As for the ghost…" John trailed off and cleared his throat before continuing. "You did mention having a sleeping pill, drinking wine, and hearing a loud ringing in your ears."

Heather opened her mouth to protest, but John put his hand up.

"Please, I do believe you dreamt about your character, Meg, and maybe she visited you in your dreams. I know what that's like. After my dad's death, I've had visitations from him in my dreams at key points in my life, where he guides me."

"But your dad was real," she said in a quiet voice. "I made up Meg in my mind."

"I'm going to quote Dumbledore on this one, when he talks to Harry at King's Cross station, you know, in the last book."

"Yes." Heather was such a Harry Potter fan that she knew exactly what line John planned to quote.

"Remember how Harry asks Dumbledore 'Is this real? Or has this been happening inside my head?'"

Heather nodded. She knew how Dumbledore responds, but she could tell it was important to John to tell her.

"Dumbledore says back, 'Of course it is happening inside your head, Harry, but why on earth should that mean that it is not real?' You see, it's like that for you with Meg. You created her. You made her up inside your head. Of course, that is where she'll visit you – in your mind while sleeping. She's a part of you."

"So this part of me was telling me to let go, and another part freaked out and bolted from the cottage. Sounds just like me." Heather laughed. Somewhat satisfied, she sighed and said, "There's still all that other stuff I need to face."

"Baby, you aren't the only one making life changes or thinking about them. I've taken as much time off in a row as I can from jumping. I'm using this hiatus and running with it. Today, I plan to give notice, ease off my client list, and make a leap to buy a share of the farm."

Heather rolled to her side. The sheet felt cool against her naked body, but John's hand on her hip made a crackling hot spot. She tried to focus: "That's great, John! I think you're doing the right thing." She pecked him on the lips and ran her hand through his thick hair.

"Hmmm," he said, pulling her to him and kissing her hard; his tongue moved in tantalizing revolutions in her mouth. She ran her hands to his groin and he shuddered. She pushed him to his back and straddled his body. "Reality can wait for a while longer." Then she went down.

***

"I just got a text. Jackson and Tessa made it to the farm. Claire is cooking. We're invited to dinner," John said. Fresh out of the shower, he smelled like soap, and yet his every day woodsy smell broke through.

Heather had spent a longer than usual amount of time on her appearance. She didn't want to appear frail and head-wounded in front of her kids.

"You look pretty," John said, running his hands up and down her bare arms.

Heather glanced down at the purple sundress and toyed with her hair.

"And you've downsized the bandage," he added

Her hand went to her forehead and touched it gingerly. "Yeah, does it cover everything?"

"Yep," he said, stepping away and gathering his keys. "Let's head out."

Heather followed, but paused on the red step after she locked the front door. John turned to her, and the sunlight behind him caused a halo-effect, like he was swimming in a haze of yellow.

"What's wrong, Heath?"

"It's broken, our time here. It's been this heavenly thing, just with you, and now - I love my children - but others will be infiltrating."

John cocked his head to the side, his face half obscured because of the sun rays hitting Heather in the eyes.

"I know." He stepped closer, took her hand, and led her to the car.

Remember
Mid-to-late December, last year

"No!" Tessa shouted and stomped aimlessly around the hospice parking lot; caged within an internal space. The black body bag had done it: the zipping in – Marc's form sliced from view; he was sealed like packaged meat. Heather understood her daughter's screams, so much so that she didn't react at first. Her feet crunched on the salted ice. She re-wound her scarf. Jackson went for Tessa and held her from following the funeral home's car out of the parking lot. Heather stood stock-still for several seconds – too long in the mother-response world – because she wanted to cheer Tessa on, to say, "Yes, chase it down, unzip your dad, a resurrected and maimed Jesus, but still, someone to love!"

Tick. Tock.

Finally, Heather joined Jackson and held Tessa, too, murmuring *shh, shh,* like a mom. Her eyes flickered, focusing on Jackson's light-weight jacket. His arms struggled against Tessa's thrashing frame, but with Heather's effort they kept her back, until Tessa quieted, crying softly into Heather's shoulder.

"We killed him," she muttered. "We killed Daddy."

This roused Heather; some slumbering, buried guilt stirred in her belly like a rising animal.

"No, now, honey," she said. "No."

Jackson cried and wiped his tears away with a fist. He shook his head; his breath made white puffs in the cold air.

Tessa bore her blue eyes, bright as crystals, on Heather. "Why? Why

271

didn't you step in? You should have kept the feeding tube in. You had power of attorney. Dad would have wanted to be here. He would have wanted to see Jack and me grow up, go to college. You know, other things, too, like walking me down the aisle when I get married. Shit like that!" Her voice cracked, and fresh tears streamed from her eyes.

Heather knew this was coming. She'd seen the furtive, accusatory glances Tessa had thrown her way as Marc struggled to breathe in his final days. She had tried to prepare herself for this moment, but she had been so numb – so vacant – nothing came to mind.

Jackson shook his head, gasping, and through gritted teeth said, "Tessie, drop it. Don't blame Mom. We all made the decision."

But why not, Heather thought; she had been blamed for everything else: Marc's affair and even, if she searched, she could be responsible for Gerard's death, Marc's stroke, his falls – all a precursor to death. Blame his death on me.

Tessa sobbed and ripped from their arms. "I can't stand this! I can't fucking stand this! I want a normal family with normal problems! Not this. This!" She motioned to the frozen ground, the charcoal-colored dirty slush near where the cars in the lot parked, and the gray sky ready to unfurl more snow. "We have to follow him! We have to get him out of that bag!" Tessa's eyes danced from Heather to Jackson.

This shook Heather from her daze. She connected with Jackson's eyes, which blinked and dropped tears. Snot ran from his nose that he didn't bother wiping away.

Heather had a feeling what would come next and she readied herself.

"No," Heather said in a low voice. "He's gone, Tessa. We can't get him back."

"NO!" Tessa screamed and started to bolt. Both Jackson and Heather darted after her, but Tessa broke free. Jackson was too fast for her; he tackled her in a snowy pile near the hospice sign. Heather stood dumbfounded, watching her two teenage children cradle each other and weep.

Live
July 17th, present day

Heather hadn't expected to break down when she saw her kids, but she did. Seeing Jackson, tanned and smiling while he helped Claire in the kitchen, and Tessa who chatted with the Graham brothers and snapped fresh beans into a silver dish, made her heart crack open, as if she had birthed them again, fully grown into new, free humans – without the burden of caring for their father.

"Mom!" Jackson saw her first and rushed over; he grabbed her in a tourniquet-tight hug, pulled back, and surveyed her head. "You okay? Any sign of trauma?"

The poor boy.

"Nope. I'm fit as a fiddle," she said smiling and crying.

"Don't cry," Jackson said, and Tessa was there. The three folded into a hug; something they hadn't done for a long time.

John moved off and stepped in to help Claire. The Graham brothers abandoned the beans to fetch something Claire had asked them for in her quick, almost inaudible manner.

Heather held her kids and smelled their familiar tangy scents, the mix of their shampoos or lotions and their skin, a deep-seated odor woven in their cells, a smell Heather could identify blind-folded.

"I'm so happy you two are here," she said, wiping away her glad-to-see-you tears. "We have so much to catch up on."

Carson Graham poured whiskey into squat glasses John had grabbed from a high shelf. Claire bustled in and out of the screened-in porch with bowls of food. Heather glimpsed a heap of mixed greens, a fish dish, and boiled potatoes with fresh herbs.

A knock at the door brought Finlay and Jackie. "Thank God you're all right!" Jackie grabbed Heather in a big hug. After more hugs and introductions, Finlay and Jackie were given their whiskey glasses.

"Take the tatties out there, ye beggar," Claire said to Mick, the shorter, younger brother. "Then we'll toast our guests."

Mick lumbered off with the potato platter, and John passed out the glasses. When Mick returned, John raised his glass. "To our resident writer and ghostbuster, Heather Finch."

"Amen to that," Claire added, drinking before anyone clinked. "And to my new business partner, John Timmer, may ye never regret working with the likes of me." Claire drank again, making everyone else say a hurried, "cheers," followed by swigs from their own glasses.

The amber liquid burned Heather's throat. Since it was toast time, she lifted her glass and said, "To my kids for coming to Scotland, to Claire for having us for a meal that is making me salivate, to the Graham brothers…" Heather was at a loss, but she wanted to say something nice.

"Nay, Ms. Finch," Mick said. "Dinnae worry about including us in your toast."

"I can cheer them for putting up with me nagging," Claire said and drank.

Jackson seemed amused, but unable to keep up with Claire's drinking. Tessa smiled into her whiskey glass, but didn't drink much.

Heather added, "Thanks to Finlay and Jackie, and the grant that brought me here."

"Cheers," everyone said and drank.

Heather, looking into John's eyes, said, "And to my longtime friend, John Timmer, thank you for coming to get me in the forest, for taking care of me, for…" She wanted to add, "making love to me," but that seemed too much for the eclectic gathering.

John blushed, his slightly freckled skin more pink than tanned, and finished his whiskey.

"The food's on the porch," Claire said. "Let's dig in."

Everyone sat around the large table Claire had set up on the screened-in porch where B&B guests enjoyed the view of the farm while eating their meals or sipping tea. Heather pictured John working here as a co-owner, fussing over guests, analyzing numbers, putting his anal retentiveness to farm plans rather than the "gear maintenance" of skydiving.

"Wow," Jackson said, "the food is amazing, Claire. Thank you!"

"Absolutely," Tessa added, smiling. "We've been cooking for ourselves, which has been hit or miss." Tessa gave Heather a sheepish look. Heather interpreted that as a way to say she was missed.

"Cheers," Claire said, breaking a crusty loaf of bread and passing the basket.

John engaged Carson and Mick in conversation about slowly passing his client list to them, and both listened and nodded, especially Mick who shoveled in his food and drank camel gulps of water. Heather was so grateful to be with her kids and John on one of those summer nights that embedded itself in the memory with a painted impression of senses – the quiet green of the farm hills, the clink of silverware on plates, the taste of spices on her tongue, the smell of hay and cut grass.

Soon John chatted with Finlay and Jackie about some of the approaching summer festivals. Jackie and John started drinking a lot of water, but Finlay filled his whiskey glass a second time.

Claire and Jackson had broken off into an organic farming conversation that held Heather's attention for a while, but soon she leaned over to Tessa and whispered, "Are you getting excited for college?"

Tessa beamed. "Oh, yeah, I've been slowly buying the things you said, you know, on the list you left me." Again, there came that miniscule, thankful face, and Heather decided in that moment that the best move she could make would be to move away from these two for a while, let them stretch their own muscles, establish their lives without worrying that she wouldn't have a life of her own outside of them. Tessa listed the goods she and Jackson had been collecting from thrift and discount stores. She talked about her full load, forensic science already a declared major.

"Are you sure you want to declare it so soon? You may get there and want to pursue a different path," Heather said, thinking of her own start as a dancer and ending up a writer, but then again, that course came by way of unplanned pregnancy.

"Oh, I'm sure, plus if I go the science route from the jump, I have another way to get more scholarship money," Tessa said, forking a boiled potato into her mouth.

A lull hit all the simultaneous conversations at the same time. Claire broke the silence by saying, "Heather, I'm relieved to hear you're on the mend. That was a fright, you getting the concussion."

Heather swallowed her bite and said, "Now it feels like something out of a dream or a book."

"Any more ghost movements since you returned?" Tessa said this in a joking tone. She had scoffed at the idea when Heather had brought it up in one phone call, saying, "Mom, that's idiocy, there's no physical evidence for such a thing."

"No, not since I got back from the hospital," she said. "I wondered if it was because John was there with me."

"You think this ghost only wants to haunt you?" Jackson asked; as a poet, he opened to more imaginative, magical allowances in daily life.

"Maybe," Heather said. "I need to decide what to do."

"How you mean?" Claire asked, hopping up and lighting a metal lantern that hung from a post. A small glow fell over the table.

"Whether I should buy the cottage or not – talk it over with the kids, and there had been another buyer. And I need to be able to sleep there alone." Heather blushed suddenly because an image of John, naked and sprawled on her bed, flashed in her mind. "But I'm confident I can be there alone. John made me think about how visions can come in dreams, the idea that the dead come to speak to us there, in a dream landscape and show us the path in front of us. I don't feel as scared. In fact, I plan to sleep there alone tonight, since you graciously offered rooms to Jackson and Tessa. Whatever has haunted me is something I want to face. If Meg – she's my new main character – appears to me, I won't be afraid. I'll listen."

"I know something about this," Jackie added. "My grandfather has come to me in dreams a couple of times since he died when I was a child. They have been at pivotal points in my life, one of which was moving to the Highlands."

"Do you think Meg was real, I mean," Jackson spluttered, his face red from the whiskey, his eyes bright: "Do you think you're channeling a past life and fictionalizing her real story?"

"I don't know," Heather said, feeling warm and loved by this gathering of people.

"I need to step in before this gets really new agey. Mom," Tessa said. "Did you ever see something move, like the wine glasses you mentioned – did they slide across a table?"

"No," Heather said, "but –"

"And the clanking sounds," Tessa said.

"Glass shattering," Heather said. "The night I ran I heard glass shatter."

"Which you said was a wine glass falling off a table that is located near an open window," Tessa said. "And there is a psychological reason why you heard things."

"There is?" Jackson asked, his face now beet red from the whiskey.

"Yeah," Tessa said. "When people are grieving, like we have for Dad, and you add a lack of sleep, or strange dreams, and Mom probably heard the sounds, or they reverberated, in her head."

Heather bit her tongue. After these mending moments, she didn't want to start a fight with Tessa. After years of a troubled marriage she hadn't recognized at the time, and after the stroke, affair, and caretaking, Heather didn't feel much like a mourner. Again, she sealed her mouth about her lack of feeling of grief about Marc.

She said, "Tessa, I did not make this up."

"I'm not saying that, Mom, what I'm saying is that there is a perfectly good Scooby-Doo explanation for your 'ghost.'" Tessa smiled at her metaphor; John and Jackson cracked up. Most of the Scottish people, except the Graham brothers, appeared nonplussed.

Heather announced: "Have you seen the cartoon? There's always a ghost –"

"We know it," Carson cut in, laughing.

"I dinnae know it," Claire said, "but I tend to live under a rock here on the farm, no teli, rarely on the Internet, except for business."

"It comes to this," Tessa said. "There is no ghost, no visitation from a supernatural force. You have no facts except for slips of memory on where you left things, or the effects of being isolated on a stormy night in a new country."

"If you want a real Scooby-Doo ending, let's say Mick and I haunted you," Carson said, "because our dad is Niles Graham, the other bidder on the cottage. We made the connection the day we picked strawberries." Carson chuckled and drank more. "He's out of the running, though, Heather, so the cottage is all yours." He lifted his glass and toasted the air.

"Dad was at first interested in buying the cottage for the two of us. It's close to the drop zone," Carson said. "And I'd be on the estates, which I've always wanted to get my hand in, in the business sense, so I'd be that much closer to Steven Connolly."

Steven's name dislodged a buried guilt that blossomed and retreated. She still had to address that one.

"See, they would have gotten away with the haunting if it hadn't been for us meddling kids," Tessa said, laughing. Jackson cracked up like it was the best joke in the world.

"It's yours," Mick said. "There are other places to live, but it seems like you belong there, especially if you're charging willy-nilly into the woods at night." Everyone roared with laughter, even Heather, who had long gotten over feeling foolish about these types of things.

Heather blinked and processed everything. Thoughts swam in her head, making her slightly dizzy; one thought floated to the top of the information; something she felt in her bones and sinew:

She could buy White Cottage and not be haunted.

A little while later, and before John drove her back to White Cottage, back to her ghost, back to Meg, Heather, Jackson, and Tessa stretched on their backs on a hill near the farm house, full from the meal and tipsy from the whiskey.

"Mom," Jackson said, staring up at the sky, wide and waning into evening. "I'm going to miss you if you move here. I may have to start angling for summer work on the farm, just to be closer to you."

"Hah!" Tessa said, plucking a long piece of grass and biting it between her lips. "You are such a mama's boy."

"Yes, m'am, and proud of it," Jackson said.

Heather laughed and maneuvered herself behind her children to slip her arms around and under each child's neck. If they were jumping out a plane, there would be a natural tandem link between them – a harness like John had told her about, only invisible and stronger. "I think that's a great idea, and you can come here, too, Tessa, in the summer, if you want."

"Well, if you two are here, duh, of course, I'm coming. Unless I have some hot science job." Tess paused and then said, her voice lower, more serious, "I also think Jack and I should find a big enough apartment for you to come home on holidays, or for longer stretches if you want.

You've always said that the beauty of being a writer is that you can do it anywhere. Why not in an apartment with us?"

Heather's heart swelled. She looked sideways at Tessa who appeared golden and youthful in the dusky light. "I would love that, but you don't have to make a special room for me."

"We already talked about it," Jackson said. "We'll turn the third bedroom into a study room with books, desks, and a spare bed for you when you come stay."

"Yeah, we figured – you, books, desk – what more do you need, right?" Tessa tried to have a joking tone, but Heather could tell she was expectant, like a child waiting for permission.

"Yes, thank you," Heather said, hugging them closer. "I'd love that. And I have to be near Leann at least part of the year."

"Exactly," Tessa agreed. "Then we have a plan."

***

Heather tucked the sheet up to her chin and watched the moonlight claw through the upstairs window.

Come on, Meg, she thought, waiting for sleep that didn't come.

When John had dropped her at the door of White Cottage, Heather had kissed him goodnight, her heart jackhammering in her chest from the thrill of his full lips and how they meshed with hers and from the anticipation of being alone in the cottage.

"Are you sure you don't want me to stay over tonight?" John had asked.

"I'm sure."

"I'll make it worth your while," he'd said with a smile.

"Oh, I'm sure you would."

Heather lay there reliving the final touches, his palms sliding down her arms, and sighed. Before long, with the thought of John kissing her, she slept.

"I'm here," a voice said in her dream. Heather sat up and looked down to see herself, not bare-breasted as in other visions, but in her same night shirt, and the crisp sheet crumpled over her lap.

"I can't see you," Heather said, her eyes searching to make out shapes in the darkness of her room.

"But you hear me," Meg said.

Heather recognized her ghost's voice, and this time, instead of sending shock waves of fear throughout her body, she felt content.

"I do." Heather strained her eyes more and caught a wisp of a peasant dress, maybe earth-tone colored and without a pattern. Soon she made out an apron, and then her eyes went up to see Meg, full-faced, not bloodied, but clean-scrubbed and glowing.

"You made it back here," Meg said.

"Yes," Heather answered, straightening up and gaining confidence, "and so did you." She paused, collecting her feelings. "I'm happy you're here, Meg. Thank you for helping me."

"Oh, yes," Meg answered, her form starting to fade so soon, her voice growing thinner, more echo than cadence. "Sometimes all one woman needs is another woman to walk around in her house for a while. Someone did that for me long ago, and it helped me."

Heather put her hand in the air to beckon her to stay, but it became clear as Meg's image faded that it was a wave goodbye. She wanted to thrust it back and forth vigorously to show her thanks again and again, but Meg was gone.

And almost instantly, a peaceful sleep swept over Heather.

Remember
January, earlier this year

It was only 7 p.m. on a weekday, so Heather wondered if it was too early to go to bed. She slipped into her coziest pajamas and emerged from the bathroom. She passed Tessa, who was hunched over homework, in the kitchen.

Tessa glanced up and said, "You're not going to bed this early, are you?"

"Of course not," Heather said. She didn't know what to do now. She wanted to step into what had become a daily ritual of drinking a glass of wine, taking a sleeping pill, and drifting into a dreamless sleep without nightmares; no dreams of letting Marc fall from buildings or down stairs, no dreams of him hitting or raping her, and no dreams where he'd become a disembodied voice from a body bag. The habit beckoned her. But no, Tessa demanded the straight and narrow, that Heather toe the line of the living. Heather opted for a handful of Oreos, a tall glass of milk, and social media.

Heather fired up her laptop and dug into her cookies. Against her own judgement, intentions, and wishes, she went straight to Facebook and scrolled through the feed, though not thinking about much, her mind taking in images and snippets of posts, and her taste buds relishing in the mushy chocolate and cream-filling of a dunked cookie.

The chat circles to the right of the feed went on and off. Heather's eyes landed on John Timmer's green circle. Her mind quickly calculated that it was 1 a.m. in Scotland.

"What are you doing up so late, John Timmer?" Heather said aloud and gulped some milk.

Ping.

Heather slid in her seat, dribbling milk down her chin. She had a message from John. Her heart raced.

Hey, Heather Finch, I know you've been having some hard days since Marc passed. I've been thinking about you. Wanna chat?

Heather felt a fluttering in her chest and stomach. She rested her fingertips on the keys for a fraction of a second before typing the word, "yes."

Running Wild Press publishes stories that cross genres with great stories and writing. RIZE publishes great genre stories written by people of color and by authors who identify with other marginalized groups. Our team consists of:

Lisa Diane Kastner, Founder and Executive Editor
Andrea Johnson, Acquisitions Editor, RIZE
Rebecca Dimyan, Editor
Andrew DiPrinzio, Editor
Cecilia Kennedy, Editor
Barbara Lockwood, Editor
Chris Major, Editor
Cody Sisco, Editor
Chih Wang, Editor
Benjamin White, Editor
Peter A. Wright, Editor
Lisa Montagne, Director of Education
Pulp Art Studios, Cover Design
Standout Books, Interior Design
Polgarus Studio, Interior Design
Nicole Tiskus, Product Manager Intern
Alex Riklin, Product Manager Intern

Learn more about us and our stories at www.runningwildpress.com

Loved this story and want more? Follow us at www.runningwildpress.com, www.facebook/runningwildpress, on Twitter @lisadkastner @RunWildBooks

RUNNING
Wild
PRESS